The Russian

JAMES PATTERSON
& JAMES O. BORN

CENTURY

1 3 5 7 9 10 8 6 4 2

Century
20 Vauxhall Bridge Road
London SW1V 2SA

Century is part of the Penguin Random House group of companies
whose addresses can be found at global.penguinrandomhouse.com

Penguin
Random House
UK

First published in Great Britain by Century in 2021

www.penguin.co.uk

A CIP catalogue record for this book is available from the British Library

ISBN 9781780899466
ISBN 9781780899473 (trade paperback edition)

Printed and bound in Great Britain by Clays Ltd, Elcograf S.p.A.

The authorised representative in the EEA is Penguin Random House Ireland,
Morrison Chambers, 32 Nassau Street, Dublin D02 YH68

Penguin Random House is committed to a sustainable future for
our business, our readers and our planet. This book is made from
Forest Stewardship Council® certified paper

The
Russian

Why everyone loves James Patterson and Detective Michael Bennett

'Its breakneck pace leaves you gasping for breath. Packed with typical Patterson panache . . . **it won't disappoint**.'
Daily Mail

It's no mystery why James Patterson is the world's most popular thriller writer. Simply put: **Nobody does it better**.'
Jeffery Deaver

'No one gets this big without **amazing natural storytelling** talent – which is what Jim has, in spades.'
Lee Child

'James Patterson is the **gold standard** by which all others are judged.'
Steve Berry

'Patterson boils a scene down to the single, telling detail, the element that **defines a character** or moves a plot along. It's what fires off the movie projector in the reader's mind.'
Michael Connelly

'James Patterson is **The Boss**. End of.'
Ian Rankin

THE CITY OF NEW YORK

POLICE DEPARTMENT
One Police Plaza
New York, NY 10038

PERSONNEL FILE

Req #: 2014-P1-10945
File #:

Detective
MICHAEL BENNETT

☑

6 FOOT 3 INCHES (191CM)   200 POUNDS (91KG)
IRISH AMERICAN

EMPLOYMENT

Bennett joined the police force to uncover the truth
at all costs. He started his career in the Bronx's
49th Precinct. He then transferred to the NYPD's
Major Case Squad and remained there until he moved
to the Manhattan North Homicide Squad.

EDUCATION

Bennett graduated from Regis High School and studied
philosophy at Manhattan College.

FAMILY HISTORY

Bennett was previously married to Maeve, who worked as a
nurse on the trauma ward at Jacobi Hospital in the Bronx.
However, Maeve died tragically young after losing a battle
with cancer in December 2007, leaving Bennett to raise
their ten adopted children: Chrissy, Shawna, Trent, Eddie,
twins Fiona and Bridget, Ricky, Brian, Jane and Juliana.

Following Maeve's death, over time Bennett grew closer to
the children's nanny, Mary Catherine. After years of on-
off romance, Bennett and Mary Catherine decided to commit
to one another, and now happily raise the family together.
Also in the Bennett household is his Irish grandfather,
Seamus, who is a Catholic priest.

PROFILE:

☐ AMENDED REPORT

BENNETT IS AN EXPERT IN HOSTAGE NEGOTIATION,
TERRORISM, HOMICIDE AND ORGANIZED CRIME. HE WILL STOP
AT NOTHING TO GET THE JOB DONE AND PROTECT THE CITY
AND THE PEOPLE HE LOVES, EVEN IF THIS MEANS DISOBEYING
ORDERS AND IGNORING PROTOCOL. DESPITE THESE UNORTHODOX
METHODS, HE IS A RELENTLESS, DETERMINED AND IN MANY
WAYS INCOMPARABLE DETECTIVE.

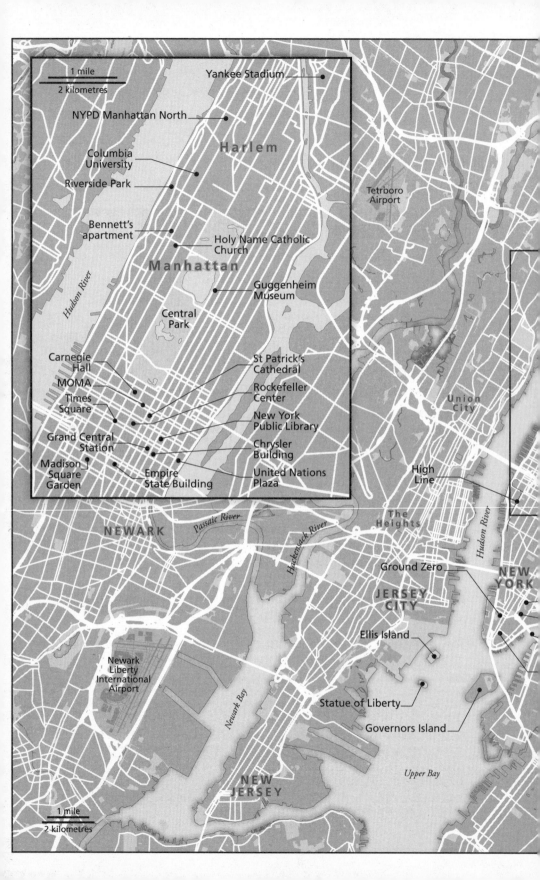

1 mile
2 kilometres

Yankee Stadium

NYPD Manhattan North

Harlem

Columbia University

Riverside Park

Tetrboro Airport

Bennett's apartment

Holy Name Catholic Church

Manhattan

Guggenheim Museum

Central Park

Carnegie Hall

St Patrick's Cathedral

MOMA

Rockefeller Center

Times Square

New York Public Library

Grand Central Station

Chrysler Building

Madison Square Garden

Empire State Building

United Nations Plaza

Union City

High Line

Passaic River

The Heights

Hudson River

NEWARK

Ground Zero

NEW YORK

JERSEY CITY

Newark Liberty International Airport

Ellis Island

Hackensack River

Newark Bay

Statue of Liberty

Governors Island

Upper Bay

NEW JERSEY

1 mile
2 kilometres

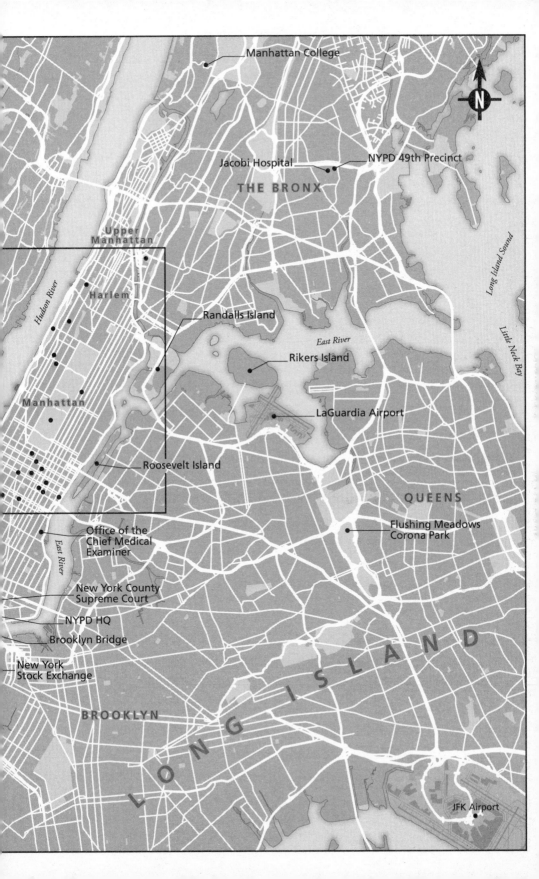

Manhattan College

NYPD 49th Precinct

Jacobi Hospital

THE BRONX

Upper
Manhattan

Harlem

Randalls Island

East River

Rikers Island

Manhattan

LaGuardia Airport

Roosevelt Island

QUEENS

Office of the
Chief Medical
Examiner

Flushing Meadows
Corona Park

New York County
Supreme Court

NYPD HQ

Brooklyn Bridge

New York
Stock Exchange

BROOKLYN

LONG ISLAND

Long Island Sound

Little Neck Bay

Hudson River

East River

N

JFK Airport

A list of titles by James Patterson appears at
the back of this book

The
Russian

CHAPTER 1

I CHECKED THE street in both directions in front of an upscale coffee house called Flat Bread and Butter on Amsterdam Avenue near 140th Street. The street was about as quiet as New York City gets.

There's never a good time to be breaking in a new detective on the squad, but this moment was one of the worst. The new detective's name was Brett Hollis. He was a sharp up-and-comer. He may not have been experienced, but he looked good. Full suit and tie. Not a hair out of place. He almost looked like he could be one of my kids dressed for church.

Occasionally I have a hard time trusting a well-put-together cop. I figure cops who take the job seriously have a permanent disheveled look. Like mine.

Hollis was also young. Maybe too young.

My lieutenant, Harry Grissom, hadn't used the word *babysit,* but he'd said to make sure this kid didn't get into any trouble. Sort of what a babysitter does. Normally I wouldn't mind, but we were in the middle of a major murder investigation.

Chloe Tumber, a first-year student at Columbia Law, had been found stabbed to death with some kind of sharp tool. One Police Plaza was keeping recent developments quiet, but Chloe was the third victim—after one in the Bronx and another in Brooklyn—to die by similar means. The stab wounds had been made by blades with slightly different markers. We suspected the killer had a toolbox full of sharp implements.

I turned to the rookie and said, "Remember, this guy Van Fleet is a person of interest. Not necessarily a suspect. Follow my lead."

Hollis nodded his head nervously, saying, "We need to call in our location."

"Why?"

"Policy says we have to check in on the radio for safety reasons."

I smiled at the young detective. "I appreciate your knowledge of the NYPD policy manual, but in real life, if we called in every location we stopped at, we'd do nothing but use the radio all day." I stepped into the coffee house without another word, trusting Hollis would follow.

The coffee house was narrow, with about ten tables and a bar with ten stools. A good-looking young man wearing the name tag JESSE stood behind the counter and welcomed us.

I said, "Is Billy around?"

"You guys cops?"

Hollis stepped forward and said, "What about it?"

Jesse shrugged. "You got the look. Listen, Billy doesn't steal from me and he shows up for his shifts—that's all I care about."

Jesse set down his rag and jerked his thumb toward the rear of the narrow coffee house. "He's in the back."

I followed Hollis through the constricted hallway, boxes of paper towels and toilet paper stacked along the walls. Hollis walked past the bathrooms and storage room into the kitchen. That's where we found Billy Van Fleet. The tall, slim, pale twenty-eight-year-old was busy washing dishes. He looked up and smiled, clearly making us for police officers. Guess we did have the look.

I saw Hollis take a step forward, and I placed a gentle hand on his shoulder, saying, "Be cool."

"What can I do for you, Officers?" the dishwasher asked, drying his hands and straightening his shirt.

I held up my shield. "Billy Van Fleet?"

He nodded.

"When was the last time you saw Chloe Tumber?"

"Why?"

Hollis's demeanor changed in an instant. "We're asking the questions," he snarled.

Van Fleet held up his hands and said, "Okay, okay, just asking."

Hollis kept going. "How about you tell us where you were last night between 8 and 11 p.m."

Van Fleet kept his eyes on Hollis, which I figured I'd use to my advantage. Maybe I'd let my new partner lead the interview. That way I could watch Van Fleet and see what made him nervous.

Right now he seemed very calm. Until suddenly he wasn't. Without warning, he spun and sprinted away from the sink, blasting through the rear exit. He was fast.

Hollis broke into a run, calling over his shoulder almost cheerfully, "He's our man!" just as Van Fleet hit the safety bar on the door, letting sunshine flood into the dark kitchen.

CHAPTER 2

I COULD'VE BROKEN into a run with Brett Hollis. But that would've been counterproductive. Hollis was trying to keep the suspect in sight. I was sure he'd give this guy a good run for his money. But veteran cops don't engage in foot chases. Experience is supposed to teach you something. It taught me to either find a car or use my head.

I knew this neighborhood. Every block of it. Traffic had picked up on Amsterdam Avenue, and no one runs toward a busy street. This guy had a plan. I figured he'd take the alley a block down and move away from any pedestrian traffic. If I were him, I'd head toward St. Nicholas Park. It wasn't that far away.

I broke into a light jog. We needed this guy—make no mistake. Van Fleet was the first lead we'd had in Chloe Tumber's homicide. Which, despite the different blades used, looked to be connected to those two other cases. All three victims were young women who'd suffered gruesome injuries moments before their deaths. And the three crime scenes looked similar. *Messy.* Though I couldn't shake the feeling that the mess was deliberate, almost designed for effect. We were still developing a theory as to why.

I found the garbage alley I was looking for between two buildings, with its gates, as usual, left wide open. Then I saw an abandoned dog leash. A long one. Maybe twelve feet, and already hooked to a pole behind a pizza place. I took the leash in my hand and stepped to the other side of the alley.

Ten seconds later, as if on cue, Van Fleet slid around the corner, ducked a drainage pipe that stuck out into the alley, and picked up the pace again. He never even saw me. As he neared the dog leash, I jerked the line. His feet tangled and he tumbled down onto the alley's nasty asphalt, slipping in some pizza grease congealed in the middle of the alley and knocking over an empty forty-ounce beer bottle like it was the last bowling pin in the lane.

Before I could even reach Van Fleet, Hollis barreled around the corner. He didn't notice the drainage pipe, and ran full speed into it, headfirst. The impact made the pipe reverberate like a gong and knocked him completely off his feet. I could only imagine what the collision sounded like inside his brain.

I cuffed the suspect, then looked over at Hollis. His nose was flattened, blood spraying from it like a busted sprinkler attached to his face. "You okay, Brett?"

He mumbled, "I'm good," as he struggled to his feet. Blood poured onto his clean white shirt and made dark stains on his power tie.

With Van Fleet's hands cuffed behind his back, I helped him

up and started to lead him back to the coffee house. I didn't want to embarrass Hollis, so I walked slowly as he tried to keep up.

Hollis's wound was so spectacular, a corner bodega owner abandoned the outdoor displays she was stocking and rushed inside for a handful of crumpled paper towels. She forced them on Hollis, who held them to his nose.

Hollis wasn't complaining. I had to admit, I liked his toughness.

CHAPTER 3

AS SOON AS we got back to Flat Bread and Butter, we slipped in the same back door we'd all burst out of. I don't think Jesse even realized we'd left the building.

I sat Van Fleet down on a stool next to an oven. "Why'd you run when we asked you about Chloe, jerk-off?"

"She's always complaining that I'm too clingy, that she's too busy with law school and her part-time job to have time for me. She said if I didn't give her some space, she'd call the cops on me." He sighed.

"What'd you do when she said that?"

"Nothing. I haven't called her in a week." He paused and cut his eyes to Hollis and me. "Okay, maybe I *tried* to call her a couple of times."

Hollis plopped down on a chair next to a metal desk built into the wall. He didn't look good. I said, "Why don't you go get that checked out, Brett?"

"I'm fine." He'd added some paper towels from the kitchen to the ones from the bodega. It was a giant ball of paper, slowly turning dark red.

I turned back to Billy Van Fleet. "Three days ago Chloe Tumber made an official complaint against you, said that you'd been stalking her. I don't suppose you can tell me where you were last night, can you?"

"Here." He shrugged. "I was here from 6 p.m. until one o'clock. Never left. Jesse was here with me the whole time."

I shot a quick look at Hollis, who jumped off his chair and headed to the front of the restaurant to talk to Van Fleet's boss. A minute later, he came back and nodded. "It checks out."

"Someone slipped into Chloe's apartment last night and murdered her. Your history of harassment, plus the running, makes you look like a good suspect. Convince us otherwise."

For his part, Van Fleet looked legitimately stunned. "Chloe's dead?"

I quickly filled him in, leaving out the details of the bloody scene at her apartment.

It had been gruesome. I could tell Hollis had been trying hard to hold it together back at Chloe Tumber's apartment. He'd choked up. "He stabbed her in the eye?" he'd said, his voice breaking.

He'd picked right up on the most distinct detail, the kind that could never be revealed to the media for fear of giving ideas to budding criminal minds.

I'd held his arm for a moment and said, "Everyone gets a little shaky in the aftermath of a violent murder, Brett. This is bad. Really bad. I wanted you to see how bad things can get."

All cops are human. Any one of us who tells you crime scenes don't affect them is lying. Yes, we're professionals. Yes, we've seen it before. It's especially hard for those of us with children. Every time I view a messy crime scene, it's hard not to think of the victim as someone's kid, and I always say a silent prayer for them and their families.

But Billy Van Fleet was taking the news remarkably well.

"If you didn't kill her, who did?" I asked.

Total silence from Van Fleet.

I looked at him and said, "We need to find out what happened to Chloe, if there was anyone who wanted to hurt her. I don't understand why you wouldn't talk to us."

"Never talk to the cops. Never snitch. It's bad for the reputation," he said, like it was a mantra.

"What reputation? Aside from a lot of petty arrests, you live with your parents and work at a coffee house that makes Starbucks look like a hellhole," Hollis scoffed.

The skinny white guy had a smile on his face as he said, "I'm a gangsta—that's what we do. I learned a long time ago that nothing happens to me if I run from the cops. I figured it out on my second arrest. I'm up to sixteen arrests and haven't been proven wrong. I've never gotten one extra day in jail for running from the cops. I even have a blog about it."

Gangsta? Give me a break. Van Fleet had none of my young partner's toughness. And I was less than impressed at how quickly he seemed to have already moved on from the news we'd just delivered—that the woman he'd been obsessed with had been murdered. Then I made a connection. "Has this got something to do with your half-ass acting persona?"

"There's nothing half-assed about staying in character. It will serve me well when my one-act play opens Off-Broadway next month. I'm playing a convicted felon who doesn't put up with any shit."

I said, "Well, I'm playing a cop who's tired of putting up with shit."

I was pissed off. And we were no closer to finding Chloe Tumber's killer.

CHAPTER 4

DANIEL OTT, TECH consultant, gazed at the New York *Daily News* sitting on his desk in the Manhattan Family Insurance office. He smiled. The headline, in bold letters, said, THREE'S NO CHARM IN BIG APPLE MURDERS.

Numbers were logical. People were not. Besides, he loved the thought that all of New York City was reading about the murders he had committed.

When Ott looked up, he noticed the heavyset office administrator, Warren Talbout, heading his way. Ott quickly resumed his work, installing the desktop computer software his company had created to facilitate communications integration between phones and computers.

Talbout, who wore a graying walrus mustache, stopped by and said, "How's the upgrade going, David?"

Ott looked up. "It's Daniel. And the upgrades are coming along fine. I should be finished later today."

The office administrator nodded and waddled away. Ott wasn't upset the man had gotten his name wrong. Few people in any of the offices where he worked bothered to learn his name. He was only ever anywhere for about two weeks at a time. Just a reasonably friendly, totally nondescript guy who made it easier for them to move data between their phones and their computers.

In fact, he liked to think that no matter where he went no one ever noticed him, like a forgettable piece of furniture. He was about five foot ten and one hundred sixty-five pounds, slim for adult males in the US. With no distinctive features whatsoever.

Young Ott had been taunted for being thin and sickly. But as he learned and grew, he found he could do things no one else could. He understood math and numbers like most people did language, though he was also good with languages. He'd easily landed this job with Computelex. He made plenty of money and got to fly across the entire country—business class.

Mostly, Ott blended in and traveled with hardly anyone even speaking to him. He was happy he'd found uses for his super-power. Now he was the one doing the taunting.

Ott read some of the article. No comment from the NYPD spokeswoman about details connecting the murders. Ott knew TV news wasn't as careful as print. News shows would play up an angle to increase ratings; before too long, they'd create special graphics and theme music for these murders.

He didn't want to be too obvious, but he couldn't keep his eyes off the page. He'd stop every couple of seconds to look up and nod hello to someone walking past. Everyone who worked at the insurance company stayed busy and avoided idle chitchat. That focus gave him room to indulge himself in this big comfortable office, with its north-facing view of the park and abundant takeout options—all the trappings of a secure, safe haven.

His cell phone chimed with a short, low, professional tone. He smiled and snatched the phone from his belt. Technically it was his lunchtime. His mouth stretched into a wide grin as he said, "Hello, sweetheart."

He was surprised by giggles and his two daughters singsonging together, "Hello, Papa!"

"Hello, my little dumplings. I thought it was your mother calling."

"She's right here. We wanted to surprise you."

"And what a great surprise it is." Ott's three-year-old, Tatyana, and five-year-old, Lilly, were his absolute prizes. He worked hard so that they would never know hard times. And he was raising them to be polite and respectful. Thankfully their mother, Lena, had few of the arrogant habits most American women did.

Lena was Polish and had proven to be a good wife and a great mother. She was simple and sweet, very meek. They'd met online, and Ott quickly knew she was the woman for him. He even spoke a fair amount of Polish. They used it as a code to talk privately around the girls.

He chatted with his daughters, who told him about their homeschool lessons, the books they were reading (or pretending to read), and how they'd raced their mother and won.

Ott never would've imagined he could feel as much love as he did for these girls. He wondered if either of his parents had felt anything for him approaching the love he had for his daughters.

He doubted it—his father had barely acknowledged him, except to make mean jokes, and his mother had just seemed exhausted all the time. When she died, Ott had felt relief for her, that she could finally rest. Since then, he'd probably spoken no more than thirty words total to his father.

Lena got on the line, and his mood shifted. His wife tended to bring up less enjoyable topics, problems that needed solutions. She said, "We need to enroll the girls in a dance class. And the dog has a cough again."

Ott hid a groan as he hurried his wife off the phone. "I'm sorry, dear, I have to get back to work."

She said she understood and told him she couldn't wait to see him. He smiled after hanging up, thinking about his two separate—and very different—lives. Over the past year, it had become clear that he needed both to survive, though it was a daily challenge to keep them from crashing into each other.

Ott loved his wife and girls, but he couldn't deny himself the pleasure he got from killing. The feeling could make his head spin, and he had an increasingly difficult time containing his urges. He felt the sensation in his entire body, like wave after wave of excitement. A release. A renewal. He wouldn't describe it as sexual in nature—it was more primal and satisfying.

Usually the victims were obvious to him. It had to do with their attitudes. That was his catalyst, his reason to act: he could not abide women with insolent, demeaning attitudes. He no longer put up with arrogance and ridicule from women. Nor could he understand why American women thought they were smarter, prettier, and more important than anyone else in the world. There was something about their egotistical speech patterns that shocked his nervous system.

His work dictated the pace he kept in his avocation. Since he only took victims outside his home area, occasionally choosing his next victim from an office where he had done contract work, the length of his business trips determined how patient he could be.

He did his best to be patient, let some time lapse. Usually. But sometimes the urge hit him so strongly that he couldn't wait.

He'd been in New York for only about a month now and had already succumbed to the temptation of three perfect victims. It was more than he usually allowed himself, but then again, in a city as big as New York, he was almost surprised the media had even connected them. Not that he was concerned. At each crime scene, he'd been careful not to leave any evidence that could be linked to him, and careful about security cameras.

Today would be his last day in this office. He'd figured out a way to reroute the company's computer network to integrate more easily with the software he was installing. He never bothered to explain his work to the clients, just to his boss back at Computelex headquarters in Omaha. HQ was the only one he needed to impress.

Ott moved from his desk to work at a control box in a tiny room at one end of the floor. He had been in there before and realized that from that vantage, he could hear everything in the manager's office, the copy room, and the break room, which all surrounded the control box.

As he worked, he overheard two women talking. It took him a moment to realize they were standing in the break room. He recognized one of the voices as belonging to an intern, a smart girl from somewhere north of the city.

He was about to go back to his desk when he heard the

intern say, "How much longer is that telephone tech going to be here?"

The other woman said, "I think he's supposed to finish up today."

"I'm so glad I'm studying communications in college. I'd hate to do such lonely, anonymous work. It doesn't suit me."

Ott stood still for a moment. Silent. Furious. *Who the hell is this arrogant bitch to think she is better than me?* In fact, he was widely recognized in the industry as one of only six or seven techs in the whole country who could do what he did. And he got paid well for it too. More than this bitch intern would ever make in communications or whatever useless degree she was getting.

His hand started to tremble with anger. Then he smiled with a new sense of purpose.

He always felt energized the moment he found a new victim.

CHAPTER 5

IT WASN'T QUITE nightfall by the time I got home to my family. I've spent my career trying to keep my family life as separate from my work life as possible. If I'm thinking about some gruesome crime I'm investigating, I'm not focusing on the kids the way I need to be, and it's important to focus exclusively on the children for a fair amount of time each day.

But today was one of those days that wore me down. The unidentified killer who'd violently murdered these women had gotten into my head. It was hard to stop thinking about the case, even as I was welcomed home by three beautiful, happy young girls.

Though frankly I'd expected more than 30 percent of my kids to greet me at the door.

That's right, I have ten children. Six girls and four boys. All adopted. Each with his or her own unique personality and challenges. And I wouldn't trade a single one of them for any-thing in the world, though as anyone with a lot of kids will tell you, it takes an enormous amount of energy.

My twins, Bridget and Fiona, were always good for a double hug, and my youngest, Chrissy, still insisted on a giant hug and a quick lift and whirl around the room. It's possible she didn't insist as much as she used to. But I still did it anyway, every day.

I wandered farther into the apartment and found my fiancée, Mary Catherine, sitting at a small writing desk in our bedroom, working on some wedding details. We were getting married in a matter of weeks, and the quick look she gave me revealed that she was feeling rather overwhelmed.

"I need some fresh air," Mary Catherine said. "Get changed, real quick. You promised we'd ride our new bikes at least three times a week. Let's go."

I knew not to argue. Also, it's bad policy to ignore com-mitments. And I never break a promise. It took me only a minute to slip out of my work clothes and into sweatpants and a Manhattan College T-shirt. Underneath the school's logo it said, PHILOSOPHY, IT'S SO MUCH MORE THAN A MAJOR. The kids had gotten me the shirt as a joke gift for my birthday since that had been my major in college. I loved it. The joke was on them. Philosophy *was* a lot more than just a major.

As we slipped out the front door, Mary Catherine called over her shoulder, "Ricky, finish up dinner. Your great-grandfather will be here in a few minutes. He can get everyone organized. We'll be back in thirty to forty minutes. Less if I have to call an ambulance for your father."

Mary Catherine's lilting Irish accent didn't make these sound like a series of orders she expected to be carried out precisely.

But both the kids and I knew that when she used that tone of voice, she was on a mission. In this case, it was our newest hobby: riding mountain bikes.

You might ask, *Who buys mountain bikes when they live in Manhattan?* The answer is, anyone who wants to work up a sweat without going forty miles an hour on a racing bike.

We collected our bikes from the basement and took off. Within twenty seconds of riding behind Mary Catherine, I knew we were headed to her favorite bike trail, which runs along the river next to the Henry Hudson Greenway. It was an easy trail to get to from our building, and if she wanted to work out hard—which she obviously did—this was the spot. When Mary Catherine got like this, it was all I could do to keep up as she pedaled with wild abandon. And God help any poor tourist who happened to step in front of her.

I was huffing and puffing a little bit as I pushed my Fuji off-road mountain bike to catch up to Mary Catherine. Between gasps for air, I managed to eke out, "Something you need to talk about? This isn't just blowing off steam on the bike path. This is running your engine so hard you could blow a rod."

That made her smile and slow her pace considerably. There really weren't many people around. This was also where she liked to talk about sensitive subjects. It was about the only way we could be sure the kids weren't listening in somehow.

Mary Catherine said, "Everything just seems to be happening at once. The wedding, the kids getting all sorts of new interests and making new friends, and Brian's readjustment to life after prison. It's a lot to take on."

"No doubt. And you've done a phenomenal job."

"I didn't drag you out here for compliments. We both need

the exercise. I'm going to fit into that wedding dress if I have to have my spleen removed." Mary Catherine paused, then said in a serious tone, "I'd really like to talk about Brian."

Even a smart-ass like me knew not to joke. "What's up?"

Mary Catherine said, "He disappears during most of the day. Just slips out sometime in the morning and sort of reappears in the afternoon."

I said, "I've been careful not to question him too closely. It's important we show that we trust him."

"Yes, but I feel like we've been walking on eggshells, maybe giving him too much leeway. He's got to understand the rules we laid down when we allowed him to return home, the rules about making good use of his time. And I worry that he's *not* making good use of his time. I worry that he's breaking our trust."

"I get it. But he hasn't been out that long. He's still re-adjusting. Let's give it just a little time. At least a few more days. Then we'll sit down with Brian and see what's going on. How's that sound?"

She looked over her shoulder and said, "Like we're going to have to ride really hard for that to be okay with me." She started pumping the pedals faster than I thought possible. If nothing else, this new hobby was going to shore up my aerobic ability. Not that I was planning to engage in any foot chases.

CHAPTER 6

WE RODE FOR about half an hour more, then returned home. It didn't take long for us to store the bikes in the basement. We chained them in the storage area and gazed in amazement at the ten other bikes of various sizes locked up next to them.

I'd read that New York was in the top ten of US cities for biking. Certainly the dozen members of my immediate family helped contribute to that statistic.

I planned to stay in my sweaty clothes for dinner until Mary Catherine gave me a look.

"Oh, c'mon," I said. "It won't kill the kids to smell their dad once in a while."

"I wouldn't have a problem with it usually," she replied, "but we're having a guest for dinner."

"If you start calling Seamus a guest, we're never going to have a comfortable dinner again."

"It's not your grandfather. Jane has a friend coming over."

"That's nice. What's her name?"

"It's a boy." She hesitated, then added, "A boyfriend."

"You mean a friend who happens to be a boy, right?"

"You wish."

I thought about it for a moment. "I'm not sure I'm ready for Jane to have a boyfriend."

"Fathers never are. Yet the fact remains. We both need to clean up because the boy will be here shortly."

"Is he from Holy Name?"

Mary Catherine nodded. "Allan Martin III."

"Is his dad the hedge fund guy?"

"He is."

I wasn't sure how to respond. This was a lot for me to take in. Jane was my third-oldest child, after Juliana and Brian. I'd come to terms with Juliana dating, and I thought I was prepared to deal with the other girls doing so too. Apparently I was wrong. I still had four even younger daughters. I hated to think what my future held.

Mary Catherine got cleaned up first, then I took a quick shower. When I wandered back into the kitchen, I was impressed to see how efficiently Ricky, my second-oldest son, had managed to pull together a spectacular spaghetti dinner and get everyone involved. I saw the table was already set, and my grandfather, Seamus, sat at the far end, sipping a glass of red wine, looking well dressed in his clerical collar.

"Comfortable, Seamus?" I asked as I strolled into the dining room.

"Aside from the sarcastic questioning, everything is great. How about you, my boy?"

"Peachy."

Then the doorbell rang and I heard my normally reserved, incredibly smart daughter Jane squeal. An honest-to-God squeal.

What is happening?

Young Allan Martin III turned out to be a nice-looking man who showed good manners as well. He shook my hand and looked me in the eye. He looked a little like his father. Tall, with blond hair and brown eyes.

Jane stood next to him like they were attached by some invisible, and extremely short, cord.

I noticed, though, that when Brian walked past Allan, he bumped the young man. It looked a little like an accident, but I wondered if there was more to it.

Then Mary Catherine and Ricky called out in unison, "Dinner is on the table!"

CHAPTER 7

EVEN IF YOU'RE used to dinner at our apartment, the sight of all thirteen of us could be overwhelming, though Allan seemed to take it in stride. And, of course, he sat right next to Jane.

I watched Brian, who quietly observed everything around him without showing much interest or emotion. He sat three spots from the end, hunched over his plate of pasta. It was a habit he'd gotten into during his months in prison, and correcting it wasn't on my list of priorities at the moment.

My youngest, Chrissy, had taken to sitting right next to Brian at dinner, as well as at any other time. It was as if she was afraid her big brother might be taken away again. For his part, Brian seemed to appreciate the attention. Never said a word when she scooted her chair a little too close. He always took her hand when she slipped it into his. But tonight he seemed focused on Jane's new boyfriend.

Mary Catherine broke the tension by asking Allan how he liked going to Holy Name.

Allan smiled and said, "My mother thought about sending me to Regis for the superior academics, but my dad wanted me to have a real-world experience. He says attending Holy Name helped him mix with all kinds of people as he was building his career."

I mumbled, "You don't get much better at 'all kinds of people' than this family."

Seamus laughed at that.

Then Brian focused his laser-beam eyes on the young man. "Who do you hang out with at Holy Name?"

Allan hesitated, as if he wasn't sure he was supposed to answer questions from the gallery. He threw out a few names, then shrugged and added, "I also hang out with John Chad and Tim and Terry Jones."

Brian didn't hesitate to say, "The Jones brothers are bad news. I'd recommend you stay away from them, especially if you're going out with Jane."

Jane gave her brother a look. "Chill out, Brian. Those boys are in all of our classes," she explained.

Mary Catherine was about to follow up, but I placed a subtle hand on her leg under the table. I wanted to see where this was going. I also, selfishly, wondered if Brian would ask questions I might shy away from.

Trent, my youngest son, said, "You're on the basketball team at Holy Name, right?"

"Yes, I'm a guard on the varsity team."

"That's not saying a whole lot. I was the captain of a basketball team once. It didn't mean I could play," Brian retorted.

As Jane's sisters Bridget and Fiona erupted in nervous laughter, I realized Brian was talking about the team he played on in prison. I looked over at my grandfather, who was eating quietly but keeping an eye on Brian. The two of them had always had a special connection. I wondered why he was staying so silent.

Brian said, "I heard you play lacrosse too. Holy Name's got a pretty good lacrosse team. How do you think they'll do in the city tournament?"

Allan brightened at the question. "I think we'll take home the trophy this year."

"What makes you so sure?" I asked.

He smiled and said, "Because I'm captain of the team."

Brian subtly rolled his eyes, but I liked Allan's confidence.

Mary Catherine started to engage the young man in a much friendlier and warmer tone. "Have you given any thought to where you might go to college?"

"My parents are insisting on an Ivy League school."

Mary Catherine beamed and said, "You could even stay in the New York area. Columbia is a great school. Even Cornell is at least in the state."

Allan winced and said, "My dad calls Cornell the community college of the Ivy League. He's been pushing me toward Harvard, but I'm worried they're a little stale. From what I know of the place, they're mired in too much tradition. It's a new century, and I want to be on the cutting edge."

I revised my opinion—Allan wasn't confident; he was a cocky little shit. I silently began to hope that Jane would quickly get tired of this entitled ass.

But the way she was looking at him didn't give me much hope.

CHAPTER 8

IT WAS LATE in the evening and I thought everyone was asleep in my little hostel on the Upper West Side. Lying in bed, I used a penlight to read reports from a dozen different detectives about persons of interest who'd been interviewed regarding the recent homicides. I reread a couple of Brett Hollis's reports. One of them had a few speckles of blood on it. Like tears on a sad letter. I didn't know if this made him a tough guy or a biohazard.

I needed some sleep. All the sentences were starting to run together, and it was becoming difficult for me to pick out the useful information in the interviews.

Detectives Terri Hernandez from the Bronx and Javier Tunez from Brooklyn were both leads on homicides similar to my Chloe Tumber case. I knew I could rely on the accuracy of their reports. They were both too sharp to make careless mistakes.

I was startled when Mary Catherine turned in bed and squinted at my weak light.

"I'm sorry. Am I keeping you awake?"

"Are you kidding? I have so many thoughts swirling in my head I'm surprised I even lay down."

"Need more help with the wedding planning?"

"Nah, I've got a handle on the wedding plans. Seamus has been great. He has a good sense of what's important, and he's really come through on a couple of details at the church I needed him to handle. It's like having me mam's help, without all the criticism."

"Don't worry, the criticism will come. Just give it time."

We both giggled. I waited a moment, then said, "Are you getting cold feet? I'd understand. I wouldn't like it, but I get it."

"It's nothing to do with that. Though it is just a bit…overwhelming to think I'll be stepmother to ten children. I love them all to pieces, but it's loads of responsibility, isn't it?"

I marveled at my incredible luck. I had found not only a beautiful woman but one who loved me *and* my kids too.

"I worry about them all," Mary Catherine continued. "I already told you my concerns about Brian, and now I'm a little bothered by Jane's new boyfriend. Does it ever end?"

"Not really, no," I told her truthfully.

Mary Catherine gave me a smile, which reassured me. Then she kissed me and I felt even better. She brushed the papers off my stomach and took the penlight out of my hand. Her soft lips caressed my neck and she nibbled at my ear.

Then Mary Catherine wrapped her delicate hands around my face and pulled me toward her as she stretched out on the bed.

I mumbled, "What's going on?"

"Really? The city's best detective can't figure it out? I worry for the fate of our citizens."

The more she kissed me, the less I worried about anything else. It was exactly what I needed.

CHAPTER 9

I WAS ON edge the next afternoon as I stepped through the front door of One Police Plaza. My lieutenant, NYPD veteran Harry Grissom, and I had been called in for a meeting, and I'd brought Brett Hollis along as comic relief. The swath of white bandages across his face would distract anyone. To his credit, Hollis had not complained once about breaking his own nose while chasing Van Fleet through Harlem.

The conference rooms in this public face of headquarters, where the NYPD often hosted other agencies, journalists, or politicians, tended to be more plush and technologically up-to-date than the cheap furniture and threadbare carpet in the precincts. These rooms looked like government offices are supposed to.

As soon as we stepped into the second-floor conference room, which overlooked the parking area for the highest-ranking

NYPD administrators, I froze. I turned to Harry and said in a very low voice, "I didn't know the FBI would be here."

"Neither did I," he said, stroking his long gunslinger mustache.

In the room were four FBI agents, all of whom seemed to be in a staring contest with us lowly NYPD detectives.

That was the real problem: law-enforcement agencies working together. Even though the national rate of unsolved murders was just under 60 percent, no one really thought the solution was to trust people from other agencies. Not only because they were worried other agencies might steal their cases but, even worse, other agencies might screw up any cases they were brought in on. It was petty and stupid, and I was as guilty as anyone.

It was pretty clear what this meeting was about, even before I saw detectives Terri Hernandez from the Bronx and Javier Tunez from Brooklyn already at the table.

Hernandez smiled and said, "This must be important if they're bringing in big guns like you."

"Nah, can't be that important. The FBI is here."

That comment made Tunez bark out a laugh. Ever since an overzealous FBI agent had tried to charge him with workers' compensation fraud, accusing him of overstating his injury claims from a car accident, Tunez had no use for the federal agency. He'd won his case easily, but he still suffered from the stress, as well as speculation in the press—the media never seemed to believe the FBI could be fallible and screw things up more often than local police.

NYPD inspector Lisa Udell was running the meeting. With her professional demeanor and terrifying reputation, I knew she'd make sure things didn't get out of hand. She was known for chopping your nuts off if you did something stupid. I could get behind that kind of administrator. If you act stupid, you should face the consequences. The flip side of the equation was that if you were in the right, Udell always backed you up. Every time.

Inspector Udell said, "We all know why we're here. We have three murder cases in Manhattan, the Bronx, and Brooklyn. The FBI has graciously offered their help to investigate the similarities in the crime scenes. I thought it would be best if we all sat down and talked about where we are in our investigations."

The door to the conference room opened and two more FBI agents rushed in. One of them looked at me and smiled. I couldn't help but smile back. Emily Parker had helped me out a dozen times over my career. And we'd once come within a moment of having a romantic relationship. That was before Mary Catherine and I had gotten serious. Now I just counted Emily as a good friend who happened to be a damn good cop. No matter who she worked for.

The other FBI agent who'd entered along with Emily was a sharply dressed, forty-something black man. He cleared his throat and said, "My name is Robert Lincoln. I'm the assistant special agent in charge of our New York office. The FBI is prepared to bring in resources and personnel to move this case along."

Every veteran detective in every big city in the US has heard this song and dance before. And in my experience, the assistance flowed only one way: away from us. The FBI seemed to count the NYPD as a resource only to inflate their numbers. They rarely added to a case.

ASAC Lincoln said, "Let's not waste any more time. If you tell us what you've got, maybe we can help."

Harry Grissom said, "We've got three murders and a ton of work to do. What we don't have is time to waste on pointless meetings. I'm sure you've seen our reports. All three known victims were young, white females. They all died from wounds from a sharp implement. But not the same one. Additionally, they each sustained a wound to the left eye. Assuming we're dealing with the same killer in all three circumstances, I think we can safely note that as his signature. Also, each of the crime scenes was excessively, intentionally bloody. The killer's clearly doing that on purpose. And his mutilation of their left eyes is a detail so distinctive that it must be kept from the media. You got some magical database that can point us in the right direction, that's great. But if you're just looking to make sure you're at the podium during a press conference, we need to get back to work."

I couldn't keep my eyes from shifting over to Inspector Udell. I respected an administrator who would remain silent while someone expressed themselves so clearly and disrespectfully to the FBI.

Lincoln didn't seem flustered by the pushback. He calmly straightened his tie and looked directly at Harry Grissom. "Look, Lieutenant, we know you're overworked and understaffed. We think we can help. All we need to do is set up what we're calling Task Force Halo. My people can report to me, and your people can report to you. It's as simple as that."

It hadn't gone unobserved that the sharp ASAC had somehow used *Lieutenant* as if it was some kind of insult.

Grissom took a moment to gather his thoughts, then said, "I appreciate your interest in assisting the NYPD to be more efficient. But in my long experience, task forces tend to slow things down. We're still running and gunning on this case. None of us has time for the extra administration and politics a task force would create. That doesn't mean we can't work together. But it *does* mean that this will be the last official meeting that takes time away from our actual investigations." Harry stroked his mustache once, then looked at everyone around the table. "Am I clearly understood?"

Sometimes I just wanted to kiss my boss.

CHAPTER 10

LIKE ANY MEETING attended by too many law-enforcement officials, this one didn't end as quickly as I would've liked. I still didn't mind taking a moment to chat with Emily.

"Are you in New York permanently?"

She nodded and said, "As permanently as any assignment with the federal government. I like working here and in Virginia. I don't mind if they ship me between the two."

"Tough on the social life."

"It can be a challenge, sure. But we can't all fall in love with someone we pay to watch our kids." Before I could rise to my own defense, Emily said, "That came out a lot cattier than I meant. I'm probably just a little jealous of a beautiful girl with an Irish accent."

"Well, to show you it wasn't a fluke, Mary Catherine and I are getting married in a few weeks."

"The kids must be over the moon." She cut her eyes to the ASAC, who was now talking animatedly with Grissom. "Mike, don't be too tough on Lincoln. In a way, he's a throwback FBI agent. It's not that he believes we're smarter than everyone else. He just doesn't like to be left out of the mix." She looked at me and her face softened. "He's a political animal. You and Harry wouldn't last ten minutes with him."

"I try not to get involved in anyone's politics. But I appreciate the warning." I made my good-byes and grabbed Hollis to head out the door. We had to wait another few minutes for Harry to break free.

I took one look at Hollis's face and said, "Pop into the bathroom, take a look at your bandage."

"Is it leaking?"

"Like the *Titanic*." In just the couple of seconds we'd been talking, a red stain had spread across the entire front of the white gauze and tape covering his nose.

Hollis hurried off. A few minutes later, Harry Grissom stepped out of the meeting. The way the FBI agents turned sharply away from him and left as a unit told me the most recent discussions had not gone any better than the one during the meeting.

I didn't even ask Harry about it. He'd tell me any information I needed to know.

He said, "Get together with Hernandez and Tunez and figure out if you have any common leads. I'll get you any help you need. How's Hollis handling himself?"

"He's smart and not lazy. That usually works out."

"Most guys would milk an injury like his and sit at home for a few weeks. I appreciate that he's not whining about it. I'll put him on background for now and then managing the crazy leads that'll come in as we get more media coverage. We'll have a couple of plainclothes help out as well."

"Sounds good, boss. Anything else?"

"Watch what you share with your FBI buddy."

"She's okay. I trust her."

"She's an FBI agent. If she's doing her job right, you *shouldn't* be able to trust her with any information. I don't care if you use her; I just don't want them screwing up our case. At this point, I don't even care if they try to steal credit. We gotta stop this guy. He's a sick and twisted bastard."

Hollis wandered back with fresh bandages around his nose. His eyes were watering, but he tried to look attentive.

Harry looked at me and said, "I need you to do your best work on this case. And that means a solve."

Hollis managed to say, "What about me?" He sounded like Rudolph the Red-Nosed Reindeer after his father covered his nose with mud.

Harry said, "Bennett's on legwork. You're on research."

My mind was already skipping ahead in the investigation. It's a double-edged sword when your boss has that much faith in you. You can do things your way, but you absolutely have to get results. And quick.

CHAPTER 11

DANIEL OTT WAS a little concerned that he was being rash. He'd finished the job at the insurance company only yesterday and was already seriously intending to make the snotty intern his next victim.

Waiting longer between victims—and distancing himself from any particular office—was meant to give the cops less to go on. But frankly, he was starting not to care. After all, no one ever remembered him. His superpower was being invisible in plain sight. He was completely and utterly unremarkable.

As a young man, that had bothered him. Now he embraced it. He was indistinctive. Even his workouts reflected that attitude. He didn't exercise to get bigger, only to get stronger and faster while maintaining his trim frame.

Now he was standing in Greeley Square Park, about forty feet from the intern, Elaine Anastas, watching her without any fear of being noticed, just as he had watched her two roommates come and go from the apartment since yesterday. Elaine's comment about how glad she was that she'd never have to do a job as lonely as his burned in Ott's brain. *The arrogance. The audacity.* He'd show her.

Elaine sat on a concrete bench in the fading light, reading a paperback of *Where the Crawdads Sing,* her dark hair draped across her pretty face as she concentrated on the book.

He'd made a study of women's clothing trends. Hers was student chic—a knockoff Kate Spade purse and an H&M jacket she wore over an AmazonBasics white T-shirt, and the Target Cherokee cross-trainers she'd clearly decorated herself with a few rhinestones and colorful laces. *Just another pretentious bitch trying to look more sophisticated than she actually is.*

Ott had already seen Elaine's tiny apartment on 30th Street, which she shared with two other girls whose work schedules he had quickly figured out. He had taped the lock on the building's rear door so it would not automatically close. He could slip in and out at any time. Now was his chance to savor and enjoy what was to come.

He turned his attention to speculating about one of the most important decisions he made for each victim: what kind of tools would he use this time?

He reached into the left pocket of his plain blue windbreaker. Would it be the twelve-inch, extra-fine, Phillips-head screwdriver? On the other hand, in his right pocket, the weight and shape of a Milwaukee brand combination wire cutter and stripper made him grin. He'd used that tool only once before, but he loved the way it made a pattern on flesh. Like someone had gnawed on it. One news report from that kill had even mentioned the police thought there might be evidence of bite marks on the corpse. It made him almost giddy thinking about it.

CHAPTER 12

IT TOOK ELAINE ANASTAS a few minutes to get moving once she put her book away in her purse. Daniel Ott barely breathed as she glanced around the park and gathered her stuff. He knew it wouldn't be much of a walk down Sixth Avenue to 30th. No lights on in the apartment. Her roommates were at work, as scheduled.

Ott watched Elaine slip into her building and, a few minutes later, the light come on in her apartment. He cut down the alley behind her building and opened the door he knew would be unlocked. He took the tape off the lock so no one would realize that's how he'd gotten into the building.

He slipped past a maintenance area crammed with broken lamps and microwaves, items the super had probably promised to fix. That was the easiest way to keep tenants quiet. Promise to do your best, but never give an exact date. It was a lot like Ott's job.

He paused at the third-floor door in the stairwell. Again, he questioned himself: Was he moving too quickly? Was it a bad sign that he was unable to control his urges? Sometimes Ott wondered if this was what a drug addict felt, though he knew his affliction was more like a mental illness. When he actually had a victim within his reach, wave after wave of a perfect balance of excitement and calmness would wash over him. He knew his mind would be clear after it was done. That's all he really needed. A clear head.

In a way, he had no choice. He'd be leaving New York City soon—well, in another few weeks. He had one more company scheduled for a complete office software installation. But if he didn't act now, he could end up lying in bed back home in Omaha thinking about nothing but this snarky intern.

No, he had to do it tonight. This girl, she'd made him too agitated. He needed to calm himself. Feel the relief. In a way, Ott was the victim. He had to kill to get mental peace.

Daniel Ott slipped on the heavy rubber surgical gloves he always wore during his murders. He also took a moment to slide fabric booties over his shoes. He felt like a surgeon. Or a medical examiner.

Then he froze, relishing the sensation that washed over him. *There it is.* The first tingling of the first wave of elation.

He found Elaine's door and gave a quick, cheerful double knock. It would sound like someone she knew. He stood there with the sharpened Phillips-head screwdriver in his hand. At the last minute he'd decided against the wire cutter.

He heard the lock turn, and the door opened wide. Elaine really didn't have any clue about living in New York.

Ott said, "Hey, Elaine, remember me?" He threw her a cheerful smile. Why not? He was in a great mood.

He enjoyed the confused look on her face. Even though she'd seen him around her office, she couldn't place his face. It was both satisfying and infuriating at the same time.

She started to say something. Before she could complete a single word, he acted. He swung the screwdriver in his right hand in a wide arc just inside the door. It pierced her throat smoothly. He let go of the handle and just gazed at his fantastic work. The black handle of the screwdriver stuck out of one side of her neck and the bloody end poked out the other side.

Elaine stood straight, just staring at him, still trying to speak. All that came out was a gurgling sound. And blood.

Ott casually stepped inside, shut and locked the door.

It took longer than he'd expected, but the shock from the deeply bleeding wound finally caught up to Elaine. The snobby intern took one step back before her legs gave out. First she dropped to her knees. Then she reached out as if she expected help from him. She didn't look quite so arrogant now.

When he didn't take her hand, Elaine tumbled forward.

This was going to be a night of confusion. At least for the cops.

Using his gloved hands, he smeared Elaine's blood in every room on almost every surface he could find.

Then he began his signature ritual. He took out a vial of blood he had been saving from a previous victim.

There were a dozen or so baseball bobblehead figurines sitting on a shelf next to the kitchen. He separated four of them and dribbled the blood from the vial over their heads. He couldn't keep from chuckling. *What will the cops make of this?* Taunting the police was part of the fun. It was a habit he'd developed over time. It made life a little more interesting. The added thrill made the taunts worth the risk.

Ott was always simple and subtle with his messages. Maybe one day someone would figure it out, though he didn't think it would do them any good. He doubted he'd ever be caught.

Now it was time for his final task. He always left this for last. Ott kneeled next to Elaine's body, now carefully positioned in the middle of a round throw rug. He pulled out his Gerber folding knife and held it in his right hand. It hadn't been terribly expensive, but he was impressed with the quality.

He studied her pretty face and admired her full lips. She'd lost so much blood that her complexion had turned sallow.

Her eyes were open, staring up at him. He plunged his blade into the left one.

CHAPTER 13

IN BED THAT night, after another long day of not-so-promising leads, I again reviewed reports and Mary Catherine tossed and turned. Finally, she sighed and said, "Maybe if I watch TV it will make me sleepy. Do you mind?" Without waiting for my answer, she took the remote.

As soon as I heard the theme music to local news, I wished Mary Catherine had never turned on the TV. The anchor led with a simple line: "With three bloody murders in less than three weeks, the city is on watch."

Well, it was clear the media had already decided our cases were linked. I tried to tune out the news segment, during which a reporter interviewed people about how they planned to protect themselves. Comments ranged from practical to blasé, and one young woman even seemed enthusiastic about the chance to defend herself: "It's kind of cool." And of course one knucklehead lodged the predictable complaint that the cops weren't doing their jobs. I wondered what he would think if he saw me covered with interview transcripts in my bed.

Mary Catherine rolled over and draped an arm across my chest. "One of those murders is your case, isn't it? You need to be careful. It won't be any fun to walk down the aisle if I have to do it alone."

Mary Catherine always had a quip to make me smile. Thankfully the news eventually moved on to other stories, and I drifted off into a deep, exhausted sleep. When my cell phone rang, I was sleeping so soundly—dreaming about my evening with Mary Catherine—I incorporated the ringtone into my dream. It took Mary Catherine's knee in the small of my back to wake me up.

She mumbled an apology as I grabbed the phone.

I heard a male voice. "Mike, sorry for the middle-of-the-night call. It's Dan Jackson down at Manhattan South."

I mumbled the standard answer: "It's okay, Dan. I was just getting up." This is old hat for any cop. Holidays, birthdays, it doesn't matter. You've got to respond.

"Sure you were. Anyway, it looks like we have a homicide down here that's similar to the ones I hear you've been looking at. Two roommates found a female victim with a distinctive facial injury. It's a very messy scene. There's so much blood, forensics isn't a hundred percent sure we're dealing with only one victim. They've just started processing the scene, but they're theorizing that the killer may have taken a second victim away from the scene."

He gave me a little more info and an address just south of Herald Square. I said, "Be there quick as I can."

I rolled over in my incredibly warm and comfortable bed,

then gave Mary Catherine a quick hug. She murmured something. I kissed her on the cheek and said I'd call her later, to which she responded with more murmuring that sounded like "Be careful."

I could get dressed in the dark as quickly and quietly as any human alive. But as I hustled out of the apartment a few minutes later, I caught the flicker of the TV from the living room.

I saw Brian on the couch, concentrating on the TV. I stepped through the dining room toward him, but his attention never wavered from the screen. As soon as he noticed me, he shut it off and slipped something under the pillow next to him on the couch. I didn't have to be a cop to notice that furtive movement. Every parent's experienced it at one point or another.

"Whatcha doin'?" I asked in a friendly tone.

Brian shrugged. "Couldn't sleep. It's so quiet around here at night. I'm not used to it anymore."

"What were you watching?"

"Nothing, really. Just flipping around the channels."

I decided the crime scene I was headed to wasn't going anywhere. I sat on the end of the couch.

Brian said, "You heading out to work?"

I nodded.

"I used to think I wanted to be a cop just like you. I guess that won't ever happen now." His voice had trailed off. With his prison record, he would never be able to get a police job. Another part of the high price he'd paid for his bad choice of working for a drug dealer.

I could sense his depression. I slid a little closer to him. "You know you can talk to me about anything."

"Thanks. I know."

"You want to tell me what's going on?"

"Nothing. Nothing other than I ruined my life and now I'm trying to fix it."

"I've got news for you, Brian, that's all any of us are trying to do, all the time. Some of our mistakes might not be as obvious as yours, but we're all out here trying to fix things."

"Even you?"

"Especially me. Don't think you're going through anything alone."

Then my son surprised me: he leaned over and gave me a hug. But for a moment, I felt like I was holding the old Brian. The cheerful kid who cared more about sports than anything else.

I left the apartment feeling remarkably good. At least as good as I could be, considering I was heading to a murder scene on only a few hours' sleep.

CHAPTER 14

WITH NO TRAFFIC, I was at the address on 30th Street in less than twenty minutes.

Brett Hollis met me at the front of the apartment building wearing a new bandage on his nose, not nearly as big and unwieldy as the previous one.

I couldn't keep from pointing and saying, "It looks better."

"I had to change it because I was having dinner with my mother. There was no way I would've survived her questioning if she'd seen a huge bloody mass on my face."

"What did you tell her happened? Not the truth, I bet. You lied to make it sound less serious, didn't you?"

Hollis shrugged. "I never lie to my mother. I told her I wasn't paying attention while running. That's accurate."

Detective Dan Jackson from Manhattan South poked his

head out of the front door. "You guys ready to come up? We're trying to limit access."

Jackson was known throughout the department for having once chased down and tackled a New York Jets running back who'd punched a woman. Jackson didn't advertise that he had played college football and was a linebacker at Notre Dame— but that Jets running back would never forget. After he spent the night in the hospital with three broken ribs, the guy had had the nerve to claim he'd been hit by a car. Witnesses contradicted him—they all said Jackson ran him down and hit him *like* a car.

I got a feel for the victim's apartment building as we climbed three flights of stairs to the crime scene. It wasn't luxurious, but it wasn't run-down either. Thin but new carpet, decent paint, and lights in the halls. Unremarkable, but better than a lot of Manhattan apartment buildings.

When we slipped out of the third-floor stairwell, I noticed two sets of crime-scene barriers. I expected the one at the door to the apartment. The other cut the hallway in half about ten feet from the door. I looked at Jackson.

The big man said, "You'll understand when you see the scene itself. There'll be a lot of looky-loos coming up here today once word gets around. I want to be able to stop them before they even get close to the apartment."

It made sense. More than one crime scene has been contaminated by inexperienced officers wandering through it.

We paused by the apartment's open front door as a crime-scene tech finished a video walk-through of the apartment. I asked Jackson the obvious questions. "Husband or boyfriend?"

"Roommates said she broke up with her last boyfriend about

five months ago. No one serious since. Coworkers and neighbors all liked her but didn't know her well."

"I guess it's too much to hope for any information from video surveillance cameras."

"No cameras in the immediate area. We're going to canvass the neighborhood in the morning when the businesses are open."

It was time for us to go inside. I elected to go in and leave Hollis behind the second barrier. Jackson had a disposable hooded biohazard suit for me to slip over my regular clothes. I'd done it enough times that it didn't take too long. The suit would keep me from contaminating the crime scene as well as protect me from any pathogens that might be present.

It's no exaggeration to say the scene took my breath away, even with Jackson's warning and my recent experience at Chloe Tumber's apartment. At first, I thought the apartment was just poorly lit. Then I realized there was so much blood smeared on the walls that it made the whole apartment appear dark. With this much blood, I understood the concern that there could be more unaccounted-for victims.

It didn't get any better as I stepped into the living room, where several crime-scene techs were photographing the space from a dozen different angles. In the middle, on a round carpet, lay the body of the young woman. She had a horrendous wound in her neck as well as a stab wound in her left eye. Blood and other fluids had pooled on the floor.

I tried to keep my composure as Jackson led me around the apartment. The victim looked so young. She must've been close in age to my oldest daughter, Juliana. All I could think about was who would notify her parents. To lose a child was horrendous. To lose one like this was unimaginable. I quickly said a prayer for her departed soul.

When we stepped back into the living room, an assortment of baseball bobbleheads caught my eye. The figurines were lined up on a shelf near the kitchen, but there was a gap between four on the right side and ten on the left side. It looked strangely deliberate. Were there some missing? I noticed blood dribbled over the heads of the bobbleheads—but only the four on the right. The application was different from the blood spread on the walls.

What did that mean? I made a note to check the crime-scene photos from Chloe Tumber's apartment, confer with Terri and Javier about any blood at their crime scenes that seemed intentionally placed.

It wasn't obvious to me yet, but the blood on the walls and tabletops and bed told a story. The message I got most strongly was that the killer wasn't finished. No way someone did a killing this methodical, this deliberately bloody, then just quit and never do it again.

This one had me worried.

CHAPTER 15

I STEPPED BACK into the hallway and lowered the hood of my biohazard suit to get some fresh air. Just like Dan Jackson had predicted, there were several uniformed officers out there already, who seemed to have stopped by just to gawk at the bloody scene. Jackson wasn't having any of it.

He barked at patrol officers, a sergeant, and even the local precinct lieutenant to get lost. None of them gave him any shit either. The lieutenant mumbled something about being the local commander on duty but still walked away as he was ordered.

I walked to the other end of the hallway, where Hollis and a couple of other detectives had set up a little command post with computers and evidence boxes.

Hollis sat on the floor at the very end of the hallway, working on a laptop. I was pleased to see he interacted well with the other detectives, gathering information we would need for a summary to our own bosses.

One of the detectives looked up from his computer screen and asked, "Is the FBI here? Someone from the mayor's office is asking."

Another detective said, "They said someone would swing by in the morning. Tell the mayor's office the FBI is in the loop. That should shut them up."

When Hollis saw me, I motioned him toward the apartment. I let him pass the first barrier and then stopped him at the door. He hadn't been issued a biohazard suit because Harry Grissom had him on data collection, but I thought he ought to take a look at this truly bizarre and horrible crime scene.

It was even worse than what we'd seen at Chloe Tumber's place.

I thought I might have to catch Hollis as he looked into the apartment. His legs got shaky and he took a big gulp of air, but he seemed stronger than he had at Chloe's apartment.

"I'm gonna say we're dealing with a true nut in this case," I said.

"That's not an official NYPD term." He tried to smile.

"It's not a term used by any professionals. But I dare someone to look in that apartment and not say whoever did it is bat-shit crazy."

I'll admit, I was creeped out. This guy was a new level of nasty.

CHAPTER 16

I HIT THE streets, and Hollis hit the books.

The next day, after spending all day interviewing techs and comparing photos of the New York crime scenes we were trying to connect, I made a beeline for the Manhattan North Homicide office, one floor of an office building owned by Columbia University but nowhere near campus.

It wasn't particularly flashy, convenient, or blessed with decent views, but I still loved my office. Its best quality was its location—nowhere near One Police Plaza. It was pure homicide investigation, no precinct built around it.

I walked in to find Hollis asleep at his desk, surrounded by stacks of notebooks and color-coded folders. After a few minutes, he popped awake and went right back to reading like he'd never been asleep. That was the mark of a smart cop.

"You ever read about serial killers?" he asked once he realized I was there. He held out a sheaf of printouts.

I shook my head. "I learn by experience."

"Never? I'd think the topic would interest you."

Now I turned to my partner. "I already have interests. Maybe you forgot that I have ten kids? I also have a full caseload. I even have hobbies. Reading about serial killers would be like a lifeguard going to the beach on his day off. Besides, I'm on legwork, you're the one on research. Remember?"

He surprised me by then saying, "Not today. I need a second pair of eyes."

Hollis explained that he had started a series of searches in newspaper databases, thinking maybe he could find a connection there that the police databases had overlooked.

I had to agree he made a good point. For the next hour we aggressively searched published records, from the *New York Times* to local papers to websites dedicated to identifying and tracking serial killers.

"I never knew all these disturbing details about serial killers, like how so many of them favor strangling and stabbing," Hollis said. "This shit is horrible."

I had to agree. The gory photographs bothered me the most. Followed closely by the knowledge that some people *liked* looking at crime-scene photographs. There were dozens of websites dedicated to serial killers that showed almost nothing but gruesome photos of their victims.

Then Hollis had the bright idea to widen the search beyond New York. We came across a news article from San Francisco dated almost a year earlier. There had been two murders there in the span of two weeks; both of the victims were women in their thirties who'd lived alone, and both had been stabbed by sharp implements with their faces "brutally mutilated," according to the article. One of the women had been slashed around the neck, but the other one was what caught my attention. She had been killed by some sort of implement driven directly through her throat—just like Elaine Anastas.

The article noted that while the murders weren't officially linked, the cops suspected it had been the same killer. Now they were both cold cases.

There's that unsolved murder rate again, I thought.

A little while later, Hollis looked up from a search of the Southeast region and said, "There could be something in Atlanta too. Looks like about eight months ago there was a series of murders there—two in apartment buildings, one in an office, and two more in nearby suburbs. All the crime scenes were noted as being especially bloody. Then the killings stopped. Nothing since."

Hollis picked up his sheaf of printouts. I could tell he was working up to a big reveal.

"I read the FBI's report on serial murder. It says the concept of the traveling serial killer is a myth."

"Is that so?" I said. I never would have consulted a report from the FBI. Not that I needed to tell Hollis that.

Hollis continued. "But there are a few notable exceptions. Such as individuals whose work involves interstate travel." He proceeded to quote from the report. "'The nature of their traveling lifestyle provides them with many zones of comfort in which to operate.'"

"I'm listening," I said.

"Ted Bundy is the obvious American example," Hollis said.

"He started in the Pacific Northwest and ended up in Florida. In Russia, a killer called the Red Ripper—named Chiclet or something like that—evaded the Russian cops for more than a decade because he traveled for his job. Killed, like, fifty people."

I thought about it. Hollis raised an interesting idea. "So you're saying we may have one of them?"

I picked up the phone.

Hollis said, "Who're you calling?"

"The FBI."

CHAPTER 17

DANIEL OTT SAT in a trucking office in Queens. This was his new assignment. He could not have been in higher spirits. It was a common state after completing one of his *rituals*. He was confident he wasn't on any police agency's radar. The fact that he never got too cocky kept him grounded in reality. Taunting the police by mixing a trail of fresh blood with cold-case evidence had become an increasingly important part of his urge.

Police officers weren't stupid. They had resources. But Ott had nothing to fear here in New York City, where the police were shackled by a mountain of rules when dealing with citizens.

He still reveled in the last waves of pleasure over what he'd done to Elaine, the intern. He'd never forget the look on her face when the screwdriver annihilated her nervous system. It had been as satisfying as anything he'd ever experienced. *Maybe* the births of his daughters had felt slightly better. But it was close.

He chuckled when he thought about the blood he'd sprinkled across the bobbleheads at Elaine's apartment. If the police believed there was more than one victim, but only one body present at the scene, they would be running in circles. At least for a while.

Ott wished he was home. He was usually more clearheaded and more focused on his family after he found a release for his fantasies. For now, he'd have to focus on work.

The new assignment looked interesting. The trucking company used radios as well as cell phones, and he would integrate them with one computer system. It was exactly the kind of issue Computelex's software was designed to handle. So far, management was no-nonsense. He'd worked a lot of places, and this company actually *did* something. It shipped goods locally and throughout the Northeast. Got results. Not like the insurance companies or medical billing agencies that provided soft services. Electronic paperwork. It seemed like this would be an easy two-week assignment.

The software finished loading, and Ott took out a sticker. Computelex required him to slap the company logo onto any computer he worked on. The two-and-a-half-inch circle showed the company name in blue beneath a smiling, anthropomorphic computer screen with two arms, one holding a telephone, the other a radio.

Ott's phone rang. It must be noon. When he looked at the phone, he saw the daily call from home was indeed right on time, as usual. He answered it with a cheerful, "Hello!"

"Hello, Papa!" His little girls' voices in unison sounded like music.

"How are my dumplings today?"

"Good," his older daughter, Lilly, said. The three-year-old, Tatyana, was probably nodding. The girls told him about a game they had made up. Every time they missed a spelling word, they had to run out the front door and completely around the house. Getting exercise while learning simple words made a good game. He approved.

Then Lilly said, "Mama is making me work on math for an extra hour today. I don't like math. I don't think Mama explains it very well."

Ott had talked to his older daughter about her homeschool classes before. In as even a tone as he could keep, Ott said, "Listen to me. Math is important in life. You're going to learn it no matter what kind of teacher your mother is. If you can't do your times tables and division by the time I get home, you'll be sorry to see me. You understand?"

Lilly said, "Yes, Papa."

Good. She was learning respect.

CHAPTER 18

OTT WAS STILL in a good mood after talking to his daughters when the manager of the trucking company introduced him to some of the employees, mostly large, unfriendly men and a few women.

One of the women caught his attention when she reprimanded two younger employees about time sheets. He wasn't looking for a victim at the moment. It was too soon after Elaine. But this woman was attractive and a little older than him, maybe thirty-eight or forty. Her reddish hair and pretty face reminded him of his first victim. He smiled at the memory.

It was not long after he had moved to Omaha. Even then, he already had started to evolve, using a few tricks of stealth and surveillance, evading detection, even planting an electronic bug or two over the years. Although he didn't like to admit how much he remained in their debt, he had his earliest employer to thank for those skills and the lessons they had taught him, many of which he still used.

Sometimes he thought about the people he used to work with. They were one of the reasons he'd moved to Omaha. In the Midwest, he was less likely to run into any of them.

All he really wanted to do was forget about that experience. He'd rather remember his first murder.

He could recall every detail. It had been a Wednesday afternoon, and he'd been looking for an office in a large building. He had his tools and software to install. He'd inadvertently walked into the wrong office—it turned out to be some kind of staffing group that handled the admin for several companies—and a redheaded woman standing at the front desk had berated him. "You're in the wrong office. They're on the fifth floor. What kind of an idiot computer guy are you?"

She clearly had more to say. But he never heard it. His hand had slipped into his tool pouch and found the handle of his box cutter. Just as the woman screwed up her face to let out another burst of insults, he'd pulled out the box cutter and swiped it across her exposed throat.

It was a natural movement and he performed it quickly. She didn't even seem to realize exactly what had happened, just that she suddenly couldn't get any air. She quickly raised both of her hands to clasp her throat. Then she staggered back, bumped into her desk, and tumbled onto the carpeted floor.

She made a few gurgling sounds and looked like a fish that had been pulled from the water. Ott stared at her throughout the whole event, still not quite realizing what he had done. That's when he felt it. The first wave of excitement and joy. The first urge. It washed over him completely as he stared at the woman on the floor with a huge dark puddle of blood spreading across the carpet.

He didn't understand at the time. It had been an impulse, completely beyond his control. He went about his day and, aside from a few news reports, never heard a word about it. Another cold case that would never be linked to him.

Fortunately, his work assignments kept him moving. He had never killed anyone in the Midwest again.

The only thing he knew for sure was that he would continue doing this forever.

CHAPTER 19

I MET EMILY PARKER for lunch at a place called Empanada Mama on Ninth Avenue just south of 52nd Street. It was the kind of place Mary Catherine would like, if we could ever take the time for a night out in Hell's Kitchen. Boldly colorful art adorned the brick walls and fans rotated along the ceiling.

Emily sat by herself in a booth near the rear of the restaurant. She wore a bright blue skirt and matching blouse. Looking at her, I could see Emily still had a sparkle in her eyes. Working for the FBI hadn't worn her down at all. Her purse, as always, sat on the bench next to her right hand. That way her gun was never far from her reach. It was good tactical sense, which I appreciated.

Emily really was the total package: smart, funny, and pretty. A deadly combination. And her easy smile was infectious. I was well aware of how close we once came to being a couple. I'm not a robot. I'd had romantic feelings for her. If it wasn't for Mary Catherine, maybe I'd still have those feelings. But this meeting was strictly business.

As for Emily's professionalism, she was tops at the Bureau. I always got the impression she was a shark swimming with minnows. And like every shark in the ocean, she was relentless, going all night, night after night, if that's what it took to break the case.

She smiled as I approached and said, "It's funny how the NYPD has no use for the FBI, until they need us."

"Hey, I'm trying to *include* you. If you're uncomfortable with the arrangement, I can find another way to get the information I need."

Emily held up her hands as I took a seat opposite her. She wore a delicate gold ring with a small emerald stone nestled in the heart-shaped center. "Wow, you're getting sensitive in your old age," she said.

"And you're getting sentimental," I shot back. "Still wearing your childhood ring." Then I softened, adding, "I know it means a lot to you."

She nodded her thanks, then leapt back into the fray. "I'm just busting your balls after the way you treated my ASAC at the meeting the other day. I should tell you he's got someone in the mayor's office listening to him."

"We didn't treat him badly. We just shot down his idea. There's a difference, whether Robert Lincoln can see it or not. And the truth is, no one in the mayor's office really listens. He might be telling them things, but they won't do anything about it unless it helps them."

"Cynical."

"Only about government bureaucracy. You have no idea what goes on with the New York mayor's office. It doesn't matter who's the mayor." I sighed, then leaned forward. "Look, we have some theories about our killer. You might be able to help us."

"Me personally? Or the FBI as an agency?"

"I was hoping to deal with you personally. At least until we figure a few things out. That a problem?"

Emily smiled, and I knew she was about to lay some kind of trap.

She said, "Let me make sure I understand. You want the benefits of FBI resources without actually dealing with the FBI?"

"I wouldn't say it quite like that."

"How would you say it?"

"I'd like to ask you, as my friend, to use FBI resources to help me. Because I'm *your* friend." I was pleased to see that my rogue diplomacy made her laugh.

When she regained her composure, Emily said, "So what can I do to help the great Michael Bennett? According to the newspapers over the years, you already have all the answers."

"If I had all the answers, I probably wouldn't still be a cop."

"Yeah, yeah. So what's your theory? I'll help you if I can."

I told her how Hollis and I had found what we thought could be similar cases in San Francisco and Atlanta. Then I said, "It'd be nice to know if the FBI was involved in those cases. It'd be great to have those reports. And most importantly, what do you think of Hollis's theory that this could be the same killer, that he travels around?"

The FBI agent took a few moments to consider everything I'd said. "Let me run it past someone I know at Quantico. The behavioral science people are in a better position to talk about theories like that. I'll keep it quiet. Nothing official."

I said, "What about the FBI's Violent Criminal Apprehension Program or the Radford Serial Killer Database?"

"Databases are only as good as the information entered," she warned. "ViCAP has been around since the 1980s. People relied on ViCAP for a long time until they realized its limitations. Also, whatever I run through the databases will track back to me. If anyone starts asking questions, an electronic trail might make it official."

"If it helps us stop this killer, I could live with that."

CHAPTER 20

BY MIDAFTERNOON, DANIEL OTT decided it was time to take steps toward making life more interesting. For everyone.

He wasn't an hourly employee, so he was free to slip out of the office early. Besides, as usual, no one noticed him leave. He headed back into Manhattan. He'd been working hard on his plan. He needed to use a computer that couldn't be traced back to him. Which was why he ended up at the main branch of the New York Public Library on Fifth Avenue.

He even took a few extra minutes to explore the iconic building before getting down to business. The woodwork on the walls and high ceilings gave it such a solemn and scholarly feel that the idea of coming here to use a public computer seemed tacky. At the same time, however, he resented the amount of money spent on a building like this. Not just the marble walls and wood carved in dramatic shapes on the ceilings and shelving and tables but also the cost of maintaining it. The money could feed half the Midwest, he assumed. He hated the obvious opulence serving pretentious New Yorkers' egos.

He pushed those thoughts out of his mind for the moment. It was time to ratchet up the stress on the cops investigating his killings. This was a wrinkle he had been considering for a long while.

He'd begun leaving messages behind, starting with the third woman he had ever killed. He liked numbers and wanted the police to know he was counting his kills. Since then, almost ten years ago, he'd found he couldn't stop. In fact, he often fought the urge to make the markers he left more and more obvious.

Ott didn't know if anyone had ever figured out any of his taunts—mixing the blood of past and present victims, stabbing them in the eye. He liked the control of puncturing the eye, the splash of the aqueous and vitreous fluids as they released from the anterior and posterior chambers. He liked the definitive proof of that final stab wound—the proof that his was the last face they'd ever see. He still hadn't noticed any mention in the media. Which was why he needed to take this extra step. Get his message heard.

He'd already prepared everything he needed. Technically, patrons were supposed to use library cards to access the computers, but Ott had noticed that if he came there in the afternoon, he could get on to a library computer without anyone caring.

He stepped into the dark paneled room and glanced around quickly. There was one librarian presiding over a computer table with five open machines. He slipped into the seat farthest away from the librarian and immediately created a new Gmail account in the name of Bobby Fisher. He'd used the name Boris Spassky once before and liked the symmetry of his choices.

It took him only a moment to find the email address he needed and another thirty seconds to upload the document from a thumb drive. If the police were too dim to notice his messages, he'd alert the media. Soon everyone would be paying attention to him, the most dangerous killer ever to hit New York. And the only one with a lesson plan.

While he was online, he couldn't help but look up a few articles and video clips featuring pundits speculating about who was behind the recent murders in New York. Ott smiled, knowing that as soon as his message was received, there was going to be a lot more of them.

He loved seeing the so-called experts talk about what the killer might do next. It was like everything else in life: no one knew anything, but they still had to talk. And people were willing to listen. The story was always the same.

Ott clicked on one article from the *New York Post*. It named a Michael Bennett as one of the detectives looking into the crimes. According to the *Post*, Bennett was "New York's top cop," and having him on the case was great news for the city. Ott smiled again. Top cop or not, this Michael Bennett was no threat to him.

More people started to file into the computer room, and Ott decided it was a good time to leave. He closed out the links he had opened on the computer, cleared his search history, and, out of habit, ran an antistatic cloth he kept in his work pouch over the keyboard. In the unlikely circumstance that someone figured out he'd used this terminal to send his message, the wipe down would be enough to eliminate his fingerprints.

As he slipped past a bookshelf, Ott found his way blocked by a pretty young woman carrying a stack of journals in her arms. She had very dark skin and long, straight black hair. She looked exotic and very un-midwestern to him.

He nodded to her just to be polite.

She smiled, revealing perfect dimples, and said, "Next time it would be better if you signed in to use the computer. It doesn't only reserve the computer; it also helps show the city how many people are using the library."

Ott was dazzled by her smile, but his anger rose quickly. How dare she confront him over a minor break in the rules.

He nodded as he slipped past her.

Then he froze.

He realized in an instant that not only had this young woman disrespected him; she also had specifically noticed him. She could remember his face. She was a loose end he would not tolerate.

Ott had a small set of tools in his pouch. Mostly screwdrivers and small wrenches. But he also had the sharp Gerber knife, the same one he'd used on Elaine, the one that came in handy for stripping wires and opening boxes.

Ott was gripped by the impulse to stick the knife into this girl's heart. He glanced around the computer room. There were a dozen people in it, but everyone was focused on their own books or screens. He wondered if they'd have enough privacy if he backed her up into the row of journals she was organizing. It would take only ten seconds. The wild card would be keeping her quiet.

He thought about slashing her throat, like he'd done to the midwestern receptionist. But if he did that, she would definitely make some noise. And there would be a lot of blood in a much-too-public space.

Ott managed to get hold of himself. This was not the time or the place. But there would be a time.

Soon.

CHAPTER 21

HOLLIS DROVE ME home that evening in a city-issued Crown Victoria. I was grateful for the ride. Driving when you're as tired as I was is as bad as driving drunk. People are killed by dozing drivers every day.

As Hollis drove, I prepped him for our morning assignment: a visit to Elaine Anastas's parents. Police procedure dictated an in-person interview with a victim's next of kin. It was going to be a rough one.

I went through the door to my apartment and gave Chrissy her daily swing in the air. Said hello to the kids who were at home. Seeing their smiling faces revived me...for about three minutes. Then I sat down to watch the news, and the next thing I knew, Mary Catherine was sitting next to me.

I started, looked at my fiancée, and said, "What are you, a ninja?"

She laughed. "A sumo wrestler could have waddled up next to you and you wouldn't have noticed."

"How long was I out?"

"About forty minutes. Dinner is in another ten. I can see by the look on your face that it's best I don't even ask you about your day."

"Thanks. Nothing worth discussing. How about you? How was your day?"

Mary Catherine frowned. The downcast expression didn't suit her. Maybe it's because I was used to her normally cheerful demeanor, which was arguably as classically and stereotypically Irish as her face.

I said, "Cut through the chitchat and tell me what's wrong." I wasn't sure I had the stamina to sit through a long story anyway.

Mary Catherine said, "Aside from Jane and her constant babbling about her boyfriend, I'm still worried about Brian. He disappeared again today. Just got home a few minutes ago."

"You can't expect someone recently released from prison to sit in the apartment all day. I'm sure he's just excited for the freedom to move around." I knew there was more to the story. I could tell by the way she hesitated.

"Trent was looking for a library book in their room, and he found Brian's savings account statement. He's withdrawn a total of fifteen hundred dollars since he's been home. I think we should talk to him about it."

This was a lot to come at me out of the daze of a short nap. I tried not to sigh as I considered potential outcomes. "I'd like to let it wait," I said. "It's important Brian knows we trust him. He's not going to like the idea that his brother was snooping on him either."

Mary Catherine didn't particularly agree with my decision. That was another aspect of her Irishness. She could not hide her emotions. Ever. From virtually anyone, and especially me.

I decided to fill her in on a little bit of my day. I jumped right in by saying, "I saw Emily Parker today. She's trying to help me with the homicide case." As I waited for a response, I felt myself tense a little bit. The beauty of the Irish soul can never be under-estimated. Unfortunately, it also encompasses an Irish temper. The problem was never knowing what would set it off.

But Mary Catherine looked calm. She took a moment, brushed some hair out of her face, and said, "Emily seems like a good FBI agent. I like to see you getting help. I know you two have history, but what's the point of marrying you if I can't trust you?"

This beautiful Irish girl never failed to surprise me.

CHAPTER 22

AT ABOUT SEVEN thirty the next morning, I stumbled into the kitchen, foggy from not nearly enough sleep. I mumbled "Good morning" to some of my family, grabbed my notebook, and slipped out the door.

And there was Brett Hollis sitting in the Crown Vic, right where he'd said he would be. I was impressed.

The second surprise was that he had stopped by Dunkin' Donuts, and had a cup of coffee and a donut stick for me.

Even so, I'll admit feeling a flash of annoyance that the young detective, who had been keeping the same schedule as me, looked so fresh and ready to go. Even the bandage on his nose looked neater and more secure than before.

I slipped into the passenger seat and nodded a greeting. "On time, ready to go, and not complaining? This already feels like it's going to be a good day."

Hollis said, "Woodstock is about a hundred miles north of the city. I have a route mapped out, and I talked to one of my buddies with the state police. I know where they're patrolling today. We'll make it in record time."

I said to Hollis, "I'd like to get there and back alive. I appreciate your interest in efficiency, but I'll make good use of the time in the car." To his credit, Hollis didn't try to make chitchat. He focused on the road and, even though it made me a little nervous, turned I-87 into some kind of speed trial.

By the time we turned west off the interstate near Hurley and I looked up from my notebook, I was rewarded with a wide-angle view of upstate New York greenery. Pastures and woods were not what I grew up seeing every day, and they were lovely to look at. I gazed out the window and said, "Not much has happened in Woodstock since the music festival."

"What music festival?"

I flinched. Surely my young partner couldn't be so cut off from the cultural past as to have never heard of Woodstock. I gave him a sideways glance, then said, "Are you messing with me?"

He smiled. "A little."

"So you *have* heard of Woodstock, right? Jimi Hendrix, the Grateful Dead, Janis Joplin?"

Hollis shrugged and said, "My grandma told me all about it."

I had to laugh at that and mumbled, "You little shit."

The home belonging to Elaine Anastas's parents sat on the edge of a wide field about fifteen miles south of Woodstock. We passed the mailbox, which leaned to the southeast like the Tower of Pisa, and bumped over the dirt road toward the house. I stopped counting abandoned refrigerators after the first seven.

The patch of grass in the front yard was covered with broken plastic toys, old tires, and a stake with a chain attached to it that I hoped was used for a dog.

Hollis mumbled, "Elaine did well to get out of here."

A woman of about forty-five answered the door. She had the blotchy complexion and red eyes of a grieving mom.

"I'm sorry for your loss," I said to Mrs. Anastas as she let us inside.

Her husband, wearing the same lost expression, answered for both of them as he wandered into the main room from the kitchen. "It was too soon."

Talking to the parents of murder victims is probably my least favorite part of my job. Having to talk to strangers about a child recently lost to a violent crime seems unusually cruel.

I sat with Elaine's parents on the couch in the front room and gave them an update on the case. The couch looked like it might have been salvaged from the woods when they dropped off a refrigerator. Two dogs barked and howled from another room, but that didn't seem to bother the Anastases.

During the conversation, Elaine's mother said, "We weren't crazy about Laney moving to the city, but all she talked about was how great living there was and how she couldn't wait to get out of school and get a job in communications."

I listened intently, then asked, "Mrs. Anastas, did Elaine know a lot of people in the city?"

"She had two roommates, and she had made a lot of friends at her internship," she said.

"How did she meet her roommates?"

"They were friends from college. Nice girls. One of them is in grad school, the other one interns for the Yankees."

The mention of the Yankees made me think of the bobble-heads I'd seen. I wondered if those had belonged to the other girl rather than Elaine.

I nodded, then followed with the crucial question. "Did she mention anyone she *didn't* get along with? A coworker, or maybe a man she met on a bad date?"

"No, nothing like that. She would have told me."

I didn't believe her. I doubted that she and Elaine discussed difficult subjects.

I looked at the weary, grieving woman and realized that she had treated her daughter almost exactly the same way our family was treating Brian. We didn't broach any problems with him for fear of scaring him away.

Maybe I needed to rethink how I was dealing with my oldest son.

CHAPTER 23

EVEN WITH BRETT HOLLIS doing his best impersonation of a NASCAR driver on our return, we weren't back in the office until the afternoon, and I felt the loss of every working hour. We were at a point in the investigation where we were eliminating possibilities rather than chasing leads. That was never a great position to be in.

I still hadn't gotten any FBI information from Emily Parker about potentially similar cases around the country, though I did request and receive crime-scene photos and police reports on the two murders in San Francisco. It was a reach to think we might link these, but I was game to try.

I looked up when I heard the booming voice of Victor Kuehne, a precinct detective who'd been in and out of our office for the last couple of weeks, working with one of our homicide detectives on a case unrelated to ours. Kuehne was known for his gregarious personality and off-color jokes. He was both loved and hated throughout the department.

He was also known for picking on detectives. And enjoying it. I thought he was a bully. Now he turned on Hollis.

"Hollis, man, are you hiding a nose job from us? That bandage seems like it's been on your face a long time."

I opened my mouth to explain that it had been only a couple of days but decided to let Hollis speak for himself.

He didn't, just smiled and shook his head.

Kuehne wasn't deterred. "Didn't you graduate from NYU before you hit the Police Academy? What are you doing, bucking to make chief before you've even gotten your hands dirty?"

Hollis still didn't take the bait.

"Lay off, Kuehne," I said. "He's working on a real case. If you're not careful, we'll get you assigned to it and stick you with a thousand crank leads."

Bullies are rarely interested in dealing with someone who stands up to them. Kuehne was no exception. He didn't say another word as he turned toward the desk he'd been using.

A moment later, Hollis stepped over to my desk and sat in an empty chair. He said, "I appreciate your concern, but I can handle myself. You stepping to my defense just convinces that moron he was right about me. He already thinks I'm not tough enough to be a cop. Now he thinks I'm not even tough enough to defend myself."

He wasn't wrong. All I could do was nod my head and say, "Understood."

What I should have said was that I'd never seen a detective make a tougher run at a fleeing suspect than Hollis had with Billy Van Fleet, but the moment had passed.

A few minutes later, Kuehne strolled by our desks. He considered Hollis for a moment, then finally said, "So tell me, is the nose job just to cover the fact that you got a small pecker?"

Hollis didn't bother looking up from his report. He said in an easy tone, "Your mom didn't mind it last night."

I didn't even try to hide my grin.

Hollis was right. Kuehne walked away, satisfied with Hollis's proper burn.

I glanced again at the San Francisco crime-scene photos I'd gotten in. The photos showed two messy scenes that looked eerily similar to the ones I'd been at recently here in New York. The savagely murdered victims, both slashed around the neck, face, and eyes—and the excessive amount of blood deliberately splashed around the rooms.

I reviewed the case file of one of the victims, a thirty-year-old tech worker who had lived alone in an apartment not far from Fisherman's Wharf. I flipped to a photo of her living room and noticed that lined up on her mantel were tiny figurines of ballerinas and musicians. Several were pushed to one side, then a gap, and then two more figurines. *Interesting.*

The separation between the two groups of figurines reminded me of the similar detail at Elaine Anastas's apartment—those bloody bobbleheads.

Was there a connection?

CHAPTER 24

DANIEL OTT REALIZED the potential risk in stalking the young librarian who'd spoken to him in the computer room in the New York Public Library.

He had only recently killed Elaine, the intern. Normally he'd pause between victims. But he felt pressed to eliminate a witness who might be able to identify him in the future.

He decided achieving that goal outweighed the risk.

Ott was surprised not to have had an instant response to the email he'd sent. It was the most daring action he'd ever taken in relation to his hobby. Although he recognized the hypocrisy between creating a meticulous crime scene and then taunting the police in private and public ways, Ott couldn't explain why he had done it. Maybe it was because they were too stupid to understand how clever he was.

He had already decided the librarian needed to go, so it was easy to forget the fact that he had rarely killed like this before, without preparing his crime-scene rituals and messages.

It hadn't been difficult to figure out which door the library staff used to exit their shifts. He got lucky in spotting the young woman after only about twenty minutes of waiting near the door.

He followed her from the library. She seemed to be a cheerful, friendly young woman. Either that or she knew an inordinate number of people. She waved and nodded hello to dozens of people in the space of three blocks. She was wearing jeans and a plain blouse, nothing remarkable, so he had to keep her long, straight black hair constantly in sight.

Ott found that the longer he followed the girl, the more she intrigued him. He appreciated how she stopped to help an elderly man struggling to get his walker over a curb. She stayed with the man until he entered a McDonald's halfway down the block.

Ott glanced around the street and didn't see many pedestrians. A taxi whizzed by, none of the passengers paying any attention.

All he needed was a quiet moment when no one was around. Just a quick blade through the throat or the chest and then he could walk away.

He thought he'd found that opportunity when she stopped to make a phone call almost twenty minutes after he'd started following her from the library. From half a block away, Ott watched her pace back and forth across an alley. He felt his pulse quicken. He slipped a surgical glove over his right hand as he made his way along the sidewalk, reaching into his tool pouch to pull out the Gerber folding knife.

He'd already decided to step up behind her and slice her throat horizontally. She would make noise and her blood would spill onto the street, but he didn't care what kind of mess he made if they were alone. *The messier the better* was his usual attitude anyway. He imagined she would just crawl into the alley and thrash around until she was dead. With luck, no one would even notice her body for a while.

He came close enough to hear her voice as she talked on the phone. The same voice she had used to reprimand him. He was almost sorry there wouldn't be time for one of his dedicated rituals.

He zeroed in on her. The librarian was facing away from him, chatting away and not paying any attention to her surroundings. Perfect.

Just as he stepped into the alley, he heard more voices. Three men dressed in white were sitting on folding chairs behind a restaurant's back exit. They were cooks, laughing and talking on a break.

All three men glanced up at him. He closed the knife and slipped it back into his pouch. Ott tried to alter his course and casually stepped back onto the sidewalk. He walked quickly out of their sight before he paused for a moment and took a breath.

About thirty seconds later, the young librarian strolled past him without paying any attention at all.

He had missed his best opportunity.

CHAPTER 25

DANIEL OTT FOLLOWED the young librarian another block until she turned and stepped into a Subway sandwich shop. The chain was the gold standard for people in a hurry or students without much money. Basic nutrition without a lot of flavor. It wasn't the flashiest business plan, but they seemed to be doing okay.

Ott was a little confused about what to do next. After feeling his excitement rise when he thought he could reach the librarian in the alley, he had calmed down.

He stopped at the door and held it open for an elderly Indian woman. The hunched woman walked in a shuffling gait. She looked up and smiled a thank-you. He nodded and helped her inside.

Ott merged into the line, putting a couple of people between him and the librarian. He glanced up at a TV bolted to the wall, where his murders led a quick newsbreak.

He wasn't the only one paying attention to the screen. Virtually everyone in line, including the hunched-over Indian woman, looked up at the newscaster. Ott waited to hear if his latest taunt had been discovered. There was coverage of Elaine Anastas's recent murder but nothing about his messages—neither the ones he'd left at the scenes nor the one he'd sent via email.

The snobby intern was garnering more attention dead than she had in her entire life. That made Ott smile. He wasn't sure what emotion it was he now felt bubbling up inside him. Then he realized: it was a sense of power. Every woman who saw that newscast was afraid of him.

As the report ended and the news moved on to the weather, Ott found himself a foot away from the librarian—only a waist-high metal rail between them.

She turned and looked directly at him.

Daniel Ott was caught between excitement and fear. This was the moment of truth. He decided to meet her gaze.

She looked directly at him, then turned back to the menu plastered high on the wall behind the cashier.

Ott stood there for a moment. She'd shown no recognition whatsoever. He had been invisible to her.

That has to stop.

CHAPTER 26

THE FOLLOWING MORNING, I stepped out of my bedroom dressed for work. Even though I'd slept a little during the night, I could feel the stress and pace of the investigation catching up to me. At least the sight of my children getting ready for school gave me some energy and made me smile.

Eddie was scribbling some sort of notes about a computer program he was working on. Fiona was reading a book about a kid in middle school. Brian was already dressed, but Jane and Juliana, the two older girls, were still getting ready. Everyone else was chatting as they ate breakfast around the long table.

I grabbed a bagel breakfast sandwich. No one made these as well as Mary Catherine. She mixed garlic and a splash of hot sauce into the eggs, which struck me as more Latin than Irish, but regardless, it was the best way to start the morning.

I slid into the chair between Mary Catherine and Brian.

Brian had a small duffel bag at his side, another habit I knew he'd picked up from prison: always keeping the things you need most with you at all times.

I asked casually, "What's in the bag, Brian?"

Brian slid his chair to the side and reached for the duffel to open it.

I said, "You don't have to show it to me. I was just curious."

Brian shrugged and set the duffel bag back down. "Just a change of clothes."

A few minutes later, everyone was in the final stages of getting ready for their day. Brian and Juliana had already left. Mary Catherine and I had a quiet moment alone at the breakfast table.

She gave me one of her classic looks for a beat, then said, "I'd have opened the bag and looked in it."

I nodded and said, "Yes, I know."

About thirty minutes later, as I was pulling into a parking spot outside my office, I got a call that there'd been a homicide on Staten Island. When the dispatcher told me the detective at the scene thought I should come, I knew exactly why—and it gave me a knot in my stomach.

I turned the car around and headed for Staten Island.

Staten Island has a special status among the five boroughs of New York. Some joke it's actually part of New Jersey. City workers are well represented in the borough's population, especially NYPD and FDNY. Many cops and firefighters rejoice if they're assigned to Staten Island.

The crime scene was in an apartment building in Emerson Hill, just off Interstate 278. Almost as soon as I stepped out of my car, I saw a familiar face and knew she must be the lead detective who'd called me in. I waited while she directed a couple of patrol officers to push the media back. I couldn't believe the number of TV trucks, until I remembered this murderer was starting to attract a lot of attention.

Detective Raina Rayesh turned to me and smiled. She was a little older than me and preferred lifting weights to running. Her dark hair had streaks of gray in it now, and I noticed more laugh lines on her face. She'd probably say the same about me. But she was the same funny, smart Rayesh, among the sharpest minds in the NYPD.

She gave me a giant hug and said, "I really hope I can find a reason to dump this on you."

I laughed and held up my hands. "I have two homicide cases of my own."

"That's why I want you to take a look at this one." Rayesh reviewed some notes. "Marilyn Shaw, twenty-six. Worked at a hedge fund in Midtown. No known current boyfriend. No one can think of anyone she ever upset."

"Elaine Anastas's mom said the same about her daughter. A young woman enjoying life in the city. No enemies. No boyfriend."

Other than Billy Van Fleet, we hadn't heard about anyone with even a whisper of motive for wanting to hurt Chloe Tumber either.

Rayesh pressed on. "This one looks similar. Like your guy."

I groaned. "First of all, please don't call this sicko my guy. Second, we don't know if he selects his victims at random. I have no third point, but it always sounds better if there are three things to bring up."

Rayesh laughed at my tired old joke. She said, "I'd still like you to take a look at this crime scene and give me your thoughts."

"Is it bad?"

Rayesh shrugged. "There's a dead girl inside. That's always bad. But I've seen worse."

That surprised me. The murder cases we were investigating all had shocking crime scenes, all the same kind of blood-soaked mess, which was part of why they all pointed to being the work of a single killer. But after I followed Rayesh through the checkpoints to Marilyn Shaw's second-floor apartment, I agreed that this one could have been worse. Yet she was also right about the similarities.

The body of a young woman with blond hair lay on the floor near the front door. She'd been stabbed in the chest. The entire front of her white blouse was stained a rust color.

"Looking at the body, it appears the killer stabbed her as soon as she opened the door. Then he stabbed her again in the eye," Rayesh said, pointing to the woman's right eye. "It has to be the same guy." A small pool of blood and fluid had dried on the hardwood floor where the victim's disfigured face rested.

I looked around the apartment. The murderer's MO ticked the same boxes, but the scene seemed...off. It was too clean, too undisturbed. It was clear that the killer had spent a lot of time at all the other scenes—this one felt more perfunctory. Had he been interrupted?

It would take time and forensics to compare all of the evidence, but my gut was telling me something was wrong here. "I don't know, Raina. Something about the scene as a whole feels different," I told her. "I'm not sensing the method behind the murder. There's no blood spread on the walls. I don't see anything else disturbed. This killer I'm tracking, he's deliberately messy. He's into grotesque displays, throwing around a lot of blood, the dramatic way he always stabs all his victims in the left eye, and so on. This seems almost tidy by comparison," I said, shaking my head.

"Back up a second," Rayesh said. "Which eye?"

"The left one. Always the left eye."

"Well, Marilyn Shaw's *right* eye is the one he stabbed this time."

Why had the killer made a change? Was he trying to taunt us?

What was it about the Staten Island case that made me so uneasy?

CHAPTER 27

IT WAS AFTER lunch by the time I got back to the office. The Staten Island crime scene still bothered me. Not the way Elaine Anastas's had, with the blood and gore, but because of the subtle changes in the killer's procedure.

The blotter on my desk was bloodstained. For a moment, I thought I was hallucinating. All the bloody crime scenes I had visited were finally messing with my head.

I used the end of a pen to touch a droplet of blood. It was fresh. I looked at the floor and saw another drop a few feet away. I followed the drops like an old tracker and was not the least bit surprised when they led me to Brett Hollis.

I stood next to my young partner's desk, staring at his bandaged nose. It looked a little worse today, even though it was healing, since now he had two black eyes to go with it.

I said, "What were you doing at my desk?"

"What makes you think I was at your desk?"

I gave him a look and pointed at his own desk, which was speckled with a design of tiny red drops that looked like the solar system.

Hollis quickly touched his nose, then looked down at the blood on the end of his finger. He mumbled, "Shit." Then he looked at me and said, "I was reading some of the reports that came in to you from San Francisco. I've also been searching the internet for similar cases, like the ones we found in Atlanta."

"Did you find anything?"

"Just that there may have been an uptick in unsolved, brutal homicides in major cities. The kind of homicides that aren't obviously related to the drug business or classified as crimes of passion. It doesn't take a whole lot of murders like that to raise the average in the whole country. That's why I think it's significant. But I can't say for sure the homicides are related to our cases."

I nodded. This kid was showing some real signs of creativity and intelligence. I could work with that.

Before I could even make it back to my desk, I noticed Dr. Jill St. Pierre barreling through the office at the only speed she knew: fast. The Haitian-born forensic scientist had been profiled by *New York* magazine for her brilliance in the lab. I'd worked with her—I didn't need to read an article to know how smart she was.

She smiled as she approached and said, "Being engaged agrees with you, Bennett."

"That's nice of you to say, but any benefit I've gotten from being engaged has been negated by these homicides. Please tell me you have something for us, that you didn't come all the way uptown to compliment me."

"Eh, I wasn't really complimenting you. It just seemed like the socially acceptable thing to say." St. Pierre let out her signature laugh. Her acerbic wit rivaled that of any detective I'd ever met.

She plopped down in the wooden chair next to my desk.

I leaned in close and said, "What's up? The look on your face tells me it's not good news."

"I deal with death and sorrow every day. I never have good news. Only news that can help an investigation or slow it down. Which some detectives view as bad."

I nodded. "So which kind of news are you bringing me?"

"I can almost guarantee this will be…confusing news."

"Let me have it."

First, she gave me a physical profile of our killer. "Forensics says he's probably a male about five foot ten, right-handed, and fairly strong based on the wounds on each of the victims. Statistics would indicate we can assume he's probably Caucasian if we're dealing with a serial killer."

I could see her hesitate, as if there was no way I was going to like what she was about to say next.

"An initial analysis of the blood found at the Elaine Anastas crime scene on 30th Street has come back."

I had to break the suspense routine. "C'mon, Jill, you're killing me. What did you find?"

"There are two different sources of blood in the apartment."

"So you agree with theories that there was a second victim?"

St. Pierre shook her head. "Not necessarily. We didn't find much blood from the second sample." She paused. "I also think that blood may have been deliberately placed rather than spilled."

Another bizarre piece of the puzzle? "What makes you say that?" I asked.

"Because of where that blood was located—we only found the second sample on some baseball figurines."

I remembered the bobbleheads that had caught my attention at the scene, and she confirmed that was what she was talking about. *Could the killer have cut himself? Was he marking his crime scene in some way?*

"Were there multiple blood sources found at any of the other crime scenes?"

"Not that we've located so far, but now that we know there might be, we'll be going back over the evidence we've collected to see if anything was missed."

"Any chance you can figure out where the blood from this scene came from?" I asked the forensic scientist.

"Once we have the full DNA profile, I assure you we'll run it through every database we can. If there's an existing profile related to our sample, we'll find it."

Even as I thanked her, my mind was starting to drift off to the endless possibilities. None of them were good.

CHAPTER 28

I WAS STILL processing the information about there being two sources of blood at Elaine Anastas's apartment.

I must've been staring off into space as I considered what this new forensic discovery meant for my case when I heard "Nice to see NYPD so hard at work."

I turned to see a man about my age, dressed in a sharp Armani suit, standing next to my desk. He had Ray-Ban Wayfarer sunglasses perched on an otherwise shiny, bald head. Just another guy trying to project that he was younger than he looked. It wasn't working.

He stuck out his hand and said, "John Macy, advisor to the mayor."

I took his hand and mumbled, "Michael Bennett."

"Yes, I know. That's why I just drove all the way uptown and waded through your maze of security."

JAMES PATTERSON

"What can I do for you, Mr. Macy? I'm a little busy at the moment."

He sat down, uninvited. "Yes, I could see you were tearing it up as I walked through the office. You looked more like a poet dreaming about the beauty of a waterfall than a detective hunting for a serial killer."

I bristled at his tone. If he was laughing or joking, I didn't mind the comment. But this guy seemed pretty serious.

I had to say, "Looks can be deceiving. I would've guessed you were a model. Maybe the *before* picture in a Rogaine ad."

He let out a forced laugh. "I love cop humor. You know I was with the NYPD."

"Sure. Remind me in what capacity?"

"I was a beat cop." He paused and smiled. "For about five minutes. Then I got smart and went to law school."

I didn't say anything.

"I don't mean any disrespect to law enforcement," Macy continued. "On the bright side, no one's trying to kill me these days."

"It's still early." This guy wasn't taking the hint. I cleared my throat and said, "Look, despite whatever impression you got, I really am swamped. Just tell me what it is you're hoping I can do for you."

Macy pulled a Moleskine notebook and a blue Montblanc pen from a leather satchel and brushed aside some papers from the corner of my desk to create a writing area. Then he looked up at me and said, "All I need is for you to bring me up to speed on the case."

"You mean our active homicide investigation?"

"You know exactly which case I'm talking about. Now give me the details."

I assessed the man. He was in pretty good shape, with only a little bit of a belly. I idly wondered if he'd be a handful if I punched him in the face. Instead, I tried to be mature. I simply said, "I'm sorry. I'm afraid I don't have that kind of time. I have more important things on my plate."

The mayor's aide straightened in his chair. "Nothing is more important than keeping the mayor informed. This newest murder on Staten Island marks a turn in the case."

I almost wanted to share my doubts about the scene on Staten Island. How I didn't think it *was* connected to the other homicides. But I decided to keep my mouth shut.

Macy was undaunted. He said, "Jesus Christ, we can't let this go on much longer. There was a shooting in Brooklyn. A woman was spooked by the murders, accidentally shot her brother coming in late. She said she thought he was the killer coming to attack her. Things are spinning out of control."

I said, "Will the young man live?"

"Probably. You know how these Brooklyn Italians are. Through evolution they're virtually immune to gunfire."

Prick.

He had the nerve to open his mouth again. "That's why you need to wrap up this case and put cuffs on this mope."

I knew he was intentionally using police slang to remind me he had once been a cop, even if it was only for *five minutes*. I said, "We're on it. That's the best I can tell you."

Macy said, "Maybe you're the wrong cop to be leading this investigation."

"Maybe the mayor has the wrong lackey asking questions." That one got a good flash of red across Macy's face.

Instead, he quickly stood up from my desk, glared at me, and said, "I'll be back." Then he turned on his heel and started to march out of the office.

I called after him, "Bring pizza. I'm starving."

CHAPTER 29

DANIEL OTT HAD followed the young librarian home from the Subway sandwich shop to her apartment in a run-down, five-story walk-up in the diverse neighborhood of East Harlem.

Overnight, he had made a simple plan.

Now he sat on the steps across the street from the librarian's building. He was dressed in a gray shirt with the name tag MITCH over the left side of his chest. He'd snagged the uniform from an unattended delivery van in Midtown. No one paid any attention to him at all.

It was early evening. From his vantage point, the street was fairly quiet. The local foot traffic seemed to have rerouted to a block party about two blocks away.

Ott was happy to sit quietly and watch the street, planning his first-ever elimination of a witness. He would forgo the rituals he loved so much. This would not be a big spectacle.

As soon as Ott saw the librarian, his loose end, walking by herself on the other side of the street, he stood up slowly and stretched. He slipped a surgical glove over each hand. He forced himself to casually walk across the empty street.

Once he reached the sidewalk, he turned and headed for the librarian. She was walking slowly, looking in her bag. Probably trying to find her keys. The opportunity was lining up nicely for Ott.

He quickly glanced around in every direction. There were kids playing on some steps a few buildings down. A woman facing away from where he was walking pushed a stroller across the street. This looked like a good window for him to act.

He reached into his pouch and pulled out his Gerber folding knife. He flicked it open with his thumb and looked up at the librarian.

Ott timed his strike perfectly. Just as he passed her, he raised his right hand and made a single, simple slash across the young woman's throat. Smooth and fast. In that instant, he caught her expression of total shock as the blade cut through the flesh and sinew of her lovely throat. She didn't make a sound.

The librarian just tumbled to the sidewalk next to the building's stairs.

Ott took a moment to make sure no one had noticed the flurry of violent action. Then he arranged the woman's body so that in the evening light it looked like she was sitting on the stoop, resting. The ruse might buy him a few more minutes to get out of the area.

Just as he straightened up, taking a moment to admire his handiwork, the door to the apartment building opened. Ott snapped his head in that direction and found himself staring at a young man with a nose stud and long black hair that hung across his face.

The man looked at the librarian and said, "Yara, what's going on?"

Ott watched as the man noticed the librarian's blood dripping down her chest onto the steps. He saw the man's face register his understanding that the librarian had been violently attacked, and that her assailant—Ott—was still standing there, facing him. The young man took a sudden leap over the railing onto the ground, about seven feet below.

Ott was on him in a flash. As the young man started to run, Ott grabbed the back of his T-shirt, swinging the knife wildly and slashing him in the arm and back.

Then the man's shirt ripped. He shot forward but lost his balance and slid onto the sidewalk.

This time, Ott didn't risk another wild slash with his knife. He aimed the point as he swung his arm and caught the man in the side. He felt the blade slip between ribs. He pulled it out with his right hand and spun the man with his left. Just as they were face-to-face, Ott plunged the knife into the man's solar plexus.

Ott left it there for a moment, then twisted and pushed the man at the same time, dropping him next to the apartment steps.

Gasping for air after the heavy physical activity, he sucked in a lungful and scanned the area. No one was raising any alarms.

He started walking quickly away from the scene in the opposite direction of the block party. He slipped the surgical gloves off his hands and into a plastic bag that he tucked into the pocket of his uniform.

As Ott picked up his pace, he couldn't get a handle on the

wild swing of his emotions. He felt vulnerable as he continued walking, but after about ten minutes, he began to feel safe. Most of all, he felt relief that a loose end was now tied up, but not the thrill he usually experienced when he had time to spend with his victims.

As he waited to catch a subway train downtown, he reviewed the events of the evening. Circumstances had forced him into eliminating one loose end, and then another one—his first male victim. There had been no time to perform his rituals. The young man and the librarian were the only two victims whose eyes he had not stabbed, and whose blood largely remained in their dead bodies. But he couldn't stop to think about this significant break from his patterns—and what response it might evoke in Detective Michael Bennett and the NYPD.

He had never planned for any of this. And now he might have to pay.

CHAPTER 30

I WAS AT home, a place where I rarely brought up work issues. But Mary Catherine is very perceptive. She badgered me until I finally told her what was wrong, the whole story about the irritating mayor's aide who'd plagued me in the late afternoon.

She smiled and said, "You'll deal with him. It's not easy, but you know how to handle people. People are like snowflakes."

I said, "Cold and annoying?"

"No, smart guy. Unique. People are unique. Having a way with them is a gift. You know how to use your gift."

"I'd like to return my gift for something else. Maybe cash. Or x-ray vision." I waggled my eyebrows.

Mary Catherine burst out laughing. "If you think that leer is sexy, you're way off. *Creepy* is a much better description for what you just did."

We laughed together and she reached out to take my hand. I leaned forward and we kissed. At first, it was just a quick peck. Then Mary Catherine lingered and I felt her tongue trace the outline of my lips. We started to make out like teenagers left alone at home. Except we were not teenagers. And we were definitely not home alone.

We were reminded of that when two of the boys, Trent and Ricky, came barreling into the living room.

"Can we go to the basketball courts at the end of the street and play with Brian?" Ricky asked.

I felt guilty, because my immediate reaction was that I wasn't sure I wanted the younger boys hanging out with their big brother. Which would mean I had to acknowledge that Brian had made some bad decisions and I was concerned he'd influence the other kids to do the same. Which went against everything I preached in telling Brian that I trusted him.

Luckily, Mary Catherine was the one who started in with the third degree. "All your homework done?"

Both boys answered in unison. "Yes."

"Room clean?"

"Yes."

"Kitchen clean?"

Both the boys stared at her, then at each other.

Mary Catherine let out a laugh. "That was just a test to see if you're paying attention. Although, if you ever want to get on my good side, cleaning the kitchen would be one way to do it."

Trent nodded and said, "Gotcha. I think we can get away without doing it tonight, though. That is, if I'm reading you correctly." He kept such a straight and serious face that it made both Mary Catherine and me burst out laughing.

Then I started thinking about the other boys who sometimes hung out at the basketball court.

Almost without thought I said, "I'll go too."

Ricky said, "Really?"

When I nodded, I was relieved to see that both boys were thrilled at the idea. It reminded me that the kids *wanted* to spend time with their parents. At least some of the time. No matter what they said or how they complained, the kids enjoyed having their parents around. Especially a supercool and athletic one like me. Or, to put it another way, they liked playing against someone they knew they could beat.

Twenty minutes later, we were on the set of four courts down the block. The courts looked like chaos to an outsider, but the kids and a volunteer from the YMCA had devised a pretty good system to make sure everyone had a chance. Two courts held three-on-three games, and the other two courts were open for general shooting and practice. People just shot around one another while they waited to get in on a three-on-three game. I made a mental note to send in my yearly donation to the YMCA.

I wasn't needed to make up numbers, so I made myself comfortable watching from the sidelines. Brian, Ricky, and Trent formed one threesome, and the team got on the game court pretty quickly. I appreciated seeing how Brian encouraged his brothers. He never got upset if they missed a shot. Which was especially good in Ricky's case. At the moment, he was shooting 0 for 6.

One of the older boys on the other team ran past Trent and threw a quick elbow. It knocked the slim teenager for a loop but wasn't anything too blatant.

A second later, Brian was in the kid's face, and I noticed my son's right hand was balled into a fist. He was taking a minor basketball disagreement to another level awfully fast. I knew, and it scared me, that prison had taught him to strike fast and first. I hustled over.

Before I got there, though, Brian had stepped away from the kid. Breathing hard. Almost panting. Actually, I realized, he was breathing *deeply*. There's a difference. I recognized it as part of the anger-management therapy he had started in prison and had continued once he was released.

I patted Brian on the shoulder and mumbled, "Good job, Son."

God bless him. He was doing his best to adjust to the outside world.

We just had to be patient.

CHAPTER 31

EARLY THE NEXT morning, I found myself at a Dunkin' Donuts on Beekman Street, a few blocks from the Brooklyn Bridge, chatting with Detective Raina Rayesh. It was nice to catch up with an old friend, even if gruesome murder was a key topic of conversation.

It was a long trip from Staten Island for Rayesh just to have a cup of coffee with an old friend. Unfortunately, a command performance at One Police Plaza was the real reason she was in Manhattan.

Rayesh said, "Pretty sure I'm getting summoned to head-quarters because I wasn't particularly patient or tactful when the mayor's aide visited."

"Was his name John Macy?"

"Yeah. Said he'd been a cop and understood what we went through, yada yada yada. So I said, 'Then you'll understand how I'm too busy to talk to you.'"

"How'd he respond?"

"Don't know. I stepped into the secure investigations office and shut the door. I ignored the receptionist when she kept calling."

I laughed loudly. "You're better than me. I tried to get rid of him and instead just made things worse. And I never did get the pizza I sent him out to pick up."

"We'll see who did a better job brushing off this jack-off after I have my meeting at One Police Plaza. How come you don't have to go?"

I smiled. "Because I have a secret weapon most detectives don't."

"What's that?"

"Harry Grissom. He's much better at these kinds of meetings than I'll ever be. Unlike me, he's smart enough to know which battles to fight. I'll just wait till he calls me after his talk with the chief of detectives."

Rayesh said, "I should've recognized the 'Bennett effect' on Macy when he came to talk to me. He was already annoyed and flustered. A sure sign someone has spoken to you first."

We both laughed.

Rayesh said, "Remember Captain Ramirez, when he was a lieutenant in the Bronx? He was quizzing us about an arrest we made and said, 'That guy was dangerous as shit. Why didn't you call SWAT?' And you said it was because we didn't have their number."

I didn't remember the exact, smart-ass comment, but I remembered Ramirez, an officious prick who used to run our shift.

Rayesh said, "He wanted to transfer you. Instead, we both got medals. I gotta tell you, Mike, you're tough on the dull and lazy."

I said, "What did Mr. Macy have to say when you spoke for that very brief time?"

Rayesh shrugged her shoulders. "Usual. Asked about the homicide. Said the mayor needed the newest information. The usual BS."

"What'd you tell him?"

"Active investigation. Yada, yada, yada." She paused for a moment, then added, "I did tell him it was too early to connect my homicide to the others. And he said he heard the killer stabbed the victim's eye. I had to tell him I didn't know why the killer did that, beyond a thirst for control."

I mumbled, "The world is full of crazy, scary people, Raina. The public usually doesn't see it. Maybe an occasional story about someone who went wild. Never the day-to-day nasty things that go on around us everywhere."

Rayesh said, "Macy's just looking to tell the mayor we've caught someone. He wants something to quiet the news media. An arrest would be just what they need. It's like in the movie *Jaws*. The administrators at City Hall just want the problem to go away before tourist season gets screwed up." She sighed, then perked up. "In all this confusion, I forgot that you're getting married really soon," she said.

"A week from Saturday. If Mary Catherine doesn't leave me before then."

"That's a possibility, because she's really smart. But I've seen the way she looks at you. You tricked her into believing all the press clippings. She's in for the long haul." Then she shook her head. "I don't know, Mike. Maybe we've been on the job too long."

"How do you figure that, Raina?"

She said, "Because all I want to do is move to Boca Raton and tell people how brave I was for the last twenty years in New York City."

"Good plan."

We both started laughing, knowing neither of us actually had any intention of leaving the job any time soon.

CHAPTER 32

I'D TOLD RAINA RAYESH the truth—that while I'd avoided an invitation to One Police Plaza for my rude behavior to the mayor's aide, my boss, Harry Grissom, had been issued his own invitation. That's why I was in the lobby outside the chief of detectives' office, waiting for Harry at about ten o'clock in the morning, a few hours after I'd compared notes with Rayesh.

When he came through the double glass doors that led from the conference room and other administrative offices, Harry shook his head at the sight of me. "I thought you understood it would be better if you were nowhere near here this morning."

"I came to support you."

Harry said, "Mr. Macy will be visiting our office this afternoon."

"What for?"

"To see how Task Force Halo is operating."

"Hollis and I, we're not really a task force. But we're happy to let the FBI call us one if we can get access to their resources as we work the case."

"It's a subtle difference we're not going to explain to the mayor's office." Harry smiled as we stopped and waited for the elevator. "We're going to convince Macy that our task force is fully staffed. We're going to grab a couple of plainclothes and pull some patrol officers to help Hollis run down all the leads we're getting from the tip line." He slapped me on the back. "You're going to make the operation look convincing, and Macy's going to buy it. Got it?"

All I could do was grin. Harry knew more about dealing with administrators and politicians than I could ever hope to understand. He also understood how investigations worked and what motivated detectives. When I thought about it, I realized what a rare combination that was. I hadn't been exaggerating when I'd told Rayesh I had a secret weapon in Harry Grissom.

Harry turned serious as he looked at me. "I will make this clear, Mike. Do not provoke this asshole when he comes to our offices this afternoon. I know he's a pompous jerk, but he's doing his job. He works for the mayor. Understand?"

I nodded. Harry was right. He's also about the only person besides Mary Catherine who can talk to me like that. Well, that's not exactly true. A lot of people can, and do, talk to me like that. Harry and Mary Catherine are the only ones I'll listen to.

Then Harry said, "Give me a rundown on the status of the case."

This was unlike Harry. He tried to keep up with investigations as they were proceeding. It worried me that he wanted to be ready for this mayor's aide. I finally asked him, "What's the real problem here, Harry?"

He looked down at the dirty linoleum floor. Then he said, "That asshole Macy's been trying to have you replaced as lead detective. I don't want to give him any reason to push for that again."

"Does he think he'd be hurting me by taking me off a case that's distracting me from my family and my wedding? A wedding that's happening in less than two weeks?"

"You and I both know it would kill you to be removed from a case. Especially this one."

I thought about it for a moment, then admitted Harry was right. As usual. So I decided to show him I was on board. I gave him a full rundown of the case. Most of it he knew already. But I wanted to underscore some important points.

I said, "There doesn't seem to be any connection between any of our victims. That doesn't mean they were selected at random, but they don't seem to have known one another. Hollis has an interesting theory that our mope travels, maybe for work. We're looking seriously at homicides in other cities that may match ours. Which also reminds me," I said, "can we give Hollis a chance to supervise the task force for real, not just for show? All he'll really do is farm out the leads. He's been running down a lot of them himself. I'm sure he'll appreciate the help."

Harry nodded. "What about the Staten Island homicide? I hear you don't think that case is related to the others. Why not?"

"The scene just feels different from the ones we're already investigating. It was orderly. There was no blood spread over the walls, and the body wasn't really mutilated. A single puncture in the chest, and a stab to her eye. But it was the right eye, when all the others have been the left."

"Any other insights on our killer?"

"Aside from the fact that he typically seems to spend hours at crime scenes? If our theory's correct, he's killed in other cities too. We're thinking it could be close to a dozen victims altogether. Maybe even more. That makes him smart enough not to have been caught already. And dangerous."

Harry nodded, then said, "About this afternoon. Answer any direct questions Macy puts to you, but don't volunteer any information, and don't expand on any points you do make." He patted me on the back. "I need you. We're making progress, even if the mayor's office doesn't believe it."

CHAPTER 33

DANIEL OTT DIDN'T mind working at a desk in the corner of the loading dock. He liked all the sound and activity at this job in Queens. He had an affinity for the workingman. Yet another lesson he'd learned from his first employer.

The men at work on this loading dock and the ones who drove the trucks were definitely hardworking men. Yet as much as he admired them, he also didn't mind lying low for a few days. He needed a chance to rest, gather his thoughts, and plan his future.

He wondered if the plan he had set in motion at the library would produce results. So far, he hadn't seen any reports about his message. Or news of the librarian's death. The police seemed to be spending all their time working a murder on Staten Island. He'd never even been there. Still, the killer seemed to have adopted a pale imitation of Ott's techniques. He was pleased at the flattery yet puzzled. If the media didn't know about the eye stabbing, how did this other killer learn his signature?

When his phone rang, Ott answered it immediately. It was noon. "Hello, my lovely girls."

On speakerphone, with the noise of the workers buzzing around him, his wife and both of his daughters giggled and chatted with him about their days. His wife caught him up on their homeschooling progress, and his daughters regaled him with a story about their cat getting stuck in a tree. The conversation kept him smiling for over an hour.

Then the red-haired woman he'd noticed the other day walked past and yelled about the computer bag lying on the floor of the loading dock, citing a safety hazard. She tried to soften the comment when she realized the bag was his, but she had already made a poor impression.

"Sorry," the redhead apologized. "When you work around messy men all day, you tend to jump the gun on little things. I forgot you were even back here. So quiet I didn't even notice you."

She stepped around the desk and stood just a little too close to Ott as she added, "It'll be nice to be able to talk to everyone over the computer. The drivers prefer radios and the office people like cell phones. You seem to be the answer to all of our problems." She gave him a big smile.

Ott nodded but didn't hold eye contact for very long. But he watched her as she walked away. She had something, some way about her, that was alluring without being wildly attractive. Maybe it was experience? Whatever it was, the image of her smiling face stuck in his head.

A shout caught his attention. Two men were standing on the

loading dock arguing about how to load tires into a long truck that couldn't make the turn to back up to the dock.

Ott stood and stretched, then walked over to where the tires were stacked and looked at the pedestrian walkway down to the street, where the truck was stopped. As much as he liked to remain invisible, sometimes it was irresistible to show off what he could do.

He turned to the loading dock manager and said, "I've got an idea."

The burly manager turned and said, "Anything's gotta be better than taking the tires by hand one at a time."

Daniel grabbed two tires and walked down the pedestrian ramp to the street. He had the driver back up a few feet, then open the side door to his truck. He set both of the tires down, one on the ground and the other propped on top of it and leaning against the truck.

When he hurried back up the ramp, the entire loading dock crew watched with anticipation. Ott thought he had it right. But what if his idea failed? He would feel like an idiot.

The loading dock crew watched silently as he ran back and grabbed two more tires. He looked up at the group staring at him. "If it doesn't work, I'll help you load the tires by hand."

He released one of the tires and watched it roll in a straight line down the ramp. By the time it hit the tire lying on the ground, it was really moving. It bounced up and off the tire that was upright against the side of the truck. It landed exactly where it needed to.

The entire loading dock erupted in applause. The manager moved his massive body toward Ott and said, "How in the hell did you figure that out?"

Ott smiled. "Simple physics. It dictates everything in our lives. I just know how to use it to my advantage."

CHAPTER 34

WHEN I GOT back to my office, Dr. Jill St. Pierre, the forensic scientist, was sitting at my desk, reading my copy of *Men's Health*. As I walked through the squad bay, her dark eyes rose from the pages of the magazine. The fact that she didn't smile when she saw me told me her new information wasn't good.

Since St. Pierre was sitting in my leather office chair, I took the hard wooden chair next to my desk. I purposely didn't say anything as I prepared for the bad news. Whatever it might be.

She said, "I heard you had to make a trip to One Police Plaza. I decided it was better to wait here in case they were sending you back to clean out your desk." Her sly smile made me laugh.

"Technically, I didn't *have* to make the trip. Only Harry Grissom did. I met him down there for support."

"Anything change on the investigation?"

I shook my head. "We have to keep the mayor's office better informed."

"Isn't that the same rule they give every time?"

"Seems like it." I glanced around to make sure no one was close by. "C'mon, Jill, you didn't come all the way up here to chat with me about my morning. Whatcha got?"

She started slowly. "I have a preliminary profile of the second blood sample from the Elaine Anastas scene."

"Could you match it to anything?"

"Yes."

I sat up straight and almost clapped. "You think it's the killer's blood?"

"Nope," she said, dashing my hopes. "But there is a connection. The second sample? It matches a homicide victim killed in Atlanta eight months ago. Hollis tipped us off to the connection and we've been working with Atlanta PD."

I was baffled by what she'd just revealed. Finally I said, "How is that possible?"

St. Pierre shrugged. "I provide the scientific data. Detectives usually do the interpretation." She handed me a manila envelope.

"What's this?"

"Atlanta PD gave us all the reports from the case. They are scanning photographs to email us. They even offered to send a detective up here. And just like here, they think this homicide could be related to several others in the Atlanta area. Apparently these cases have been bugging them for the last eight months."

I leaned back in the chair, thinking about what she'd just told me. When I looked up, the forensic scientist was glancing over one of the reports from Atlanta.

"What do you think this means?" I asked her.

"That's your area, not mine," St. Pierre said. "But I'd theorize that if your killer is getting cute like this, it's probably a sign he's bored. He has to make things more interesting. And that could be extremely dangerous."

CHAPTER 35

IT WAS LATE afternoon by the time John Macy, the mayor's aide, showed up again at Manhattan North. He wore a Brooks Brothers charcoal suit, a red power tie, and an extraordinarily smug expression.

Macy said, "I told you the mayor needs to be informed."

I wanted to reply, *And I told you I was busy trying to catch a killer. I hope you haven't endangered someone else's life by distracting me.* But in deference to Harry Grissom, I just smiled and nodded. I had promised Harry that I wouldn't make any waves.

Macy didn't help with my plan. He said, "I can't believe I had to go through that much trouble just to get a detective with the NYPD to fill me in on a case. I'm busy too. You have any idea how many people work in the mayor's office?"

I said, "About half of them."

Macy gave me a disgusted look but didn't say anything.

Then he shook his head and started marching toward Harry Grissom's office.

Brett Hollis stepped up next to me. "You just *had* to say something, huh."

"Did you hear how he set me up? If this were a criminal case, that would've been considered entrapment."

Hollis and a couple of nearby detectives started to laugh.

Harry trudged out of his office and gave me and Hollis a curt hand signal. We followed him and Macy to the conference room Hollis had turned into his tip-line headquarters.

At a nod from Harry, Hollis explained the operation to Macy. "We're getting three to five thousand leads a day over the tip line. Eighty percent of them can be discounted immediately."

"It seems a little arrogant to discount so many leads so quickly," Macy interrupted.

"Think of it this way, Mr. Macy," Hollis said. "How many calls a week does the mayor's office get about problems?"

The sharply dressed man shrugged. "I don't know. Maybe five hundred?"

"And each of those calls is equally important?"

Macy pursed his lips. "I take your point, Detective Hollis."

Hollis continued with his explanation. "About half the calls to the tip line are either encouragement—like someone saying, 'You guys are doing a great job'—or insults. A lot of those are really nasty. Let's say that leaves us with two thousand concerned citizens offering what they think is relevant information. More than half of those tips are something along the lines of 'The guy who lives next door to me is creepy.' Of the thousand or so tips remaining, about ten percent are new information. But that's still a hundred leads a day for someone to follow up on, with either a direct interview or a phone call. So far, not one lead has been useful. But we still are doing everything we can."

"Does this include leads on all the open homicides? Including the one on Staten Island?"

I stepped in on that one. "We have our doubts about whether the Staten Island murder is connected."

Macy looked outraged. "How can that be? It's clearly the same killer."

I couldn't stand it anymore. "What is that assessment based on, Mr. Macy? You don't have any experience in homicide, even if you were a cop for, as you put it, about five minutes. If we homicide detectives don't use our experience and instincts, nothing would ever get done. We'd waste our time following leads that clearly mean nothing. But we appreciate you coming from the mayor's office and telling us which homicides are related and which aren't."

Macy scowled at me for a few seconds, then looked at Harry Grissom. "Is this what you call controlling your people, Lieutenant? When we met with the chief of detectives, you assured him I'd get full cooperation. I don't think insulting me should be considered cooperation."

Harry glanced at me, then at Macy. I knew the look on his face. He was choosing his words carefully. Finally, he straightened his tie and said, in the steady, calm voice of an FM radio host, "We're trying to cooperate, Mr. Macy. You're not making it very easy."

"Task Force Halo is supposed to be a *joint* task force. Maybe you can tell me why the FBI is not involved in the case," Macy countered.

I kept my mouth shut. I wasn't about to touch this, especially given the evidence we'd been pursuing that indicated the murders might be tied to similar crimes in Atlanta and San Francisco, and that we continued to work through media and police sources—not federal channels. Which reminded me once again that Emily had yet to come through with the information she'd offered to track down.

Harry said, "That's an issue we'll discuss. We'll make a decision based on our discussions. We will apprise you of the decision once we've made it." Then he turned and walked back to his office.

I tried to hide my smile.

Damn, my boss was good at handling assholes.

Macy looked at me and said, "You don't seem to understand I speak to the mayor."

I said, "And the coroner speaks for the dead. The difference is, I listen to the coroner."

The moment I landed my zinger, John Macy stormed back into Grissom's office.

I'd launched a grenade. This meeting could have gone better.

CHAPTER 36

I SAT AT my desk like a kid in middle-school detention. I tried not to focus on Harry Grissom's closed office door, but it was tough to concentrate on anything else.

I could only imagine what the mayor's aide, John Macy, was ranting about inside my lieutenant's office. I assumed that by now he had called someone at One Police Plaza and told them how I was acting like a bratty child. I didn't have much defense for that charge.

I was kicking myself for failing to reel in the worst of my smart-ass tendencies. If one of my kids behaved like this, I'd definitely punish them for it. I didn't deserve anything less.

I noticed some members of the squad had found reasons to be elsewhere. Except for me and Brett Hollis, the office looked like a ghost town.

To help fill the time and ease my anxiety, I turned to Hollis and asked, "What are you working on?"

Hollis barely looked up. "My application to take your spot on the squad permanently."

I sat in silence for a moment until a smile crept across the young detective's face. He really was getting the hang of surviving as a cop: laugh at everything. I said, "Funny. Although it's probably not a bad idea."

"It's a waste of time."

"You don't think I'll get transferred to some precinct in the Bronx?"

"Nope. Because Lieutenant Grissom already told me I could have your spot."

That made me laugh out loud. "Seriously, are you working on anything I can help with? I wouldn't mind being distracted about now."

"I'm doing more research on serial killers. There's gotta be something in all the information and evidence gathered from the multiple crime scenes and calls to the tip line that fits some sort of pattern."

"Isn't that what the FBI's Behavioral Analysis Unit at Quantico is for?"

"From everything I've heard, the FBI doesn't always play fair. We could give them all the information we have and never hear back from them. Or we could give them all our information and then they swoop in and take over the case. I wouldn't care if it meant they caught the killer. But if you haven't noticed, their track record is mediocre at best."

"You're learning," I said to my young partner. And I meant it. I asked Hollis about his research on serial killers. Whether it was official or unofficial, his knowledge of the subject might come in handy.

Hollis lit up at the opportunity to share his research, now that he knew I was truly interested.

"Okay," he began, "so first I was looking at debunking a bunch of stuff. Like, you know how everyone assumes most serial killers are Caucasian?"

I nodded, remembering how Dr. Jill St. Pierre had said just that to me in our earlier conversation.

"Well, the truth is that as more information becomes available, it turns out that the serial killer population mirrors the diverse racial makeup of the US population as a whole. In fact, there's a black guy in his late seventies named Samuel Little who could be the country's most prolific serial killer."

"I'm almost afraid to ask—how many people do they think he's killed?"

"He's confessed to nearly a hundred murders, but they don't have enough credible details to charge him with all of them. Even so, he's still being charged with murders going back to the eighties and nineties. He is very specific in his obsession. He strangled his victims and selected them according to the shape of their neck. He also worked in gritty neighborhoods in multiple states and picked on homeless women and prostitutes, folks he believed would not be missed. Something about his theory must've held water, because it took decades to corral this asshole."

Hollis looked over at me. "It's hard to get a good sense of how many people are actually murdered by serial killers. As I'm sure you know, there are so many unsolved homicides across the country—plus deaths misattributed to overdose, accident, or undetermined causes—that no one can really say whether a serial killer is responsible for them or not."

"I don't think that's our issue here," I said dryly. "In our particular case, we have no reason *not* to believe our suspect is white and male. The forensics team says that based on the application of force, the suspect is probably about five foot ten and fairly strong. And we know he mutilates his victims, stabs their left eyes. I think he likes the feeling of power and control that comes from creating bloody, wild crime scenes. But I also think his technique hinges on how much time he has at each scene. How do you see it?"

Hollis said, "I agree with your assumptions about the time needed to create such nasty crime scenes. I think he's smart. Really smart. And clearly he travels. Probably for work, which would make him a white-collar professional. That combination is what makes him so hard to catch."

I was impressed by the young detective's curiosity. It was the sign of a good cop. "Those are some good theories. I'm proud of you." It was part joke and part serious. Regardless, I noticed it made my junior partner beam. I made a mental note to be a little more generous with the praise.

Then Harry's door opened. I was so deep into my own paranoia about the future of my NYPD career that I tried to figure out if the door had opened in an angry way or a professional way. I listened to the tone of the two men's voices as they exchanged good-byes. Not pleasant.

Macy had only a menacing glance for me as he fumed back across the squad bay floor, this time heading for the exit.

As Harry watched him leave, he ran a hand over his face, looked at me, and shook his head.

I had stepped over the line and I knew it. I also knew I needed to apologize. First to Harry, then, as much as it bugged me, to John Macy.

At the moment, though, I couldn't get a clear read on Harry. Not that it's ever easy. I slid out of my seat and started walking toward him. When I was still twenty feet away, I said, "Harry, I'm sorry. I let him get under my skin."

Harry let out a sigh. That was almost always a really bad sign that he was about to say something no one wanted to hear. I waited for the words *Go home* or, worse, *You're off the case.* I just hoped none of this problem I had created would bleed over onto Hollis. He didn't deserve to be punished for my stupidity.

I said, "What happened? What did Macy demand?"

"At first I tried to reason with the turd. Then he tried to reason with me." Harry chuckled. "Like that ever works." He looked at me in silence for a moment. "Macy came up here to see the operations of our task force, and all he saw was a junior detective pounding the books and a lead detective acting like a child. Basically, he doesn't think you're the right man for this case."

Harry looked at me. He said in a calm and quiet voice, "Get out of here. Go find some perspective. Go talk to your kids, to your beautiful fiancée, or even to your grandfather. Figure out what's more important to you: stopping a killer or annoying a minor city official."

"Should I come back tomorrow?" I wasn't being dramatic. I was dead serious.

"Yes. Unless I call you tonight and tell you not to bother. Which is a possibility." He stared at the door that Macy had raced out of. Then Harry said, "There's something about that guy I don't like. He acts a little like my first wife. He seems pleasant enough until you look a little closer." Harry looked back at me. "You remember when my wife ran off with our mechanic?"

I nodded. It's not unusual to help a fellow cop get through a divorce.

"It was tough. He was a really good mechanic."

CHAPTER 37

IT HAD BEEN months since I'd left the office this early. It was odd to see the sun still shining as I got into my city-issued Chevy Impala. I wasn't ready to explain my early arrival to Mary Catherine. Which was one of the reasons why I took a detour to Holy Name, swung by to visit my grandfather.

I was in need of counseling, or at least a little verbal abuse. Seamus was always good for both. Especially the abuse.

It took a while to get to him, though, as I first had to say hello to several different nuns I had known since I was a child. Basically, every conversation I'd had at Holy Name in the last six months had been about the wedding. And the nuns all said the same thing: "I can't believe little Michael Bennett is getting married!"

I had no trouble *not* being a smart-ass with the nuns. I didn't feel the need to remind them that *little Michael Bennett* had actually been married before, or that ever since I'd lost my first wife, Maeve, I'd been a widower with ten children—all of whom these self-same nuns had personally educated. But since happy talk of the wedding made them smile and laugh, I went along with it. I know that's what Mary Catherine (and Maeve) would have wanted.

I found my grandfather in his office, looking over the shoulder of a twenty-something African American in an Avengers T-shirt working on Seamus's computer. I knew the young man's name was Elgin Brown, and he had a degree from Stony Brook in computer technology. Elgin was by all accounts a great kid (I've noticed as I get older that anyone under thirty is a *kid*).

I said, "What's going on here? Elgin trying to erase all your gambling websites before they're subject to some kind of audit by the Catholic Church?"

My grandfather looked up at me. "Don't be ridiculous. I keep all those websites on my phone only. Elgin is showing me how we could create a website to help kids in the neighborhood who need access to tutors and after-school care."

I smiled. Not only because my grandfather was always trying to do something for the community but also because even in his eighties he wanted to learn new things. He could have just asked Elgin to summarize the information for him. Instead, he wanted to master the skills himself.

Joining the priesthood really hadn't changed Seamus at all. *Gone straight from hell to heaven,* he took to saying when he sold his Hell's Kitchen gin mill and became a man of the cloth. The first thing he learned back then was how to hide his mischievous streak in public.

I waited for a couple of minutes while they finished up their work. I had to admit, my grandfather looked pretty good for his age. At least for now. He'd had a few health scares in the last couple of years. Losing him was one of the scariest concepts I could fathom. The very idea of life without the man who raised me, encouraged me, and always kept me grounded was terrifying. For now, there was nothing I liked more than surprising him at his office.

Seamus again looked up at me. "Shouldn't you be at work rather than bothering an old man?"

Elgin stood up. My grandfather patted him on the back and thanked him. The kid slipped out of the room like a ghost.

I said, "He never makes eye contact with me."

"You intimidate him."

"How?"

"Just being a cop."

"He's never been in trouble. Why's he afraid of the police?"

Seamus shrugged. "It's just how he feels. I think the cops need better PR."

"So I've heard."

Seamus sat on the edge of his desk and said, "So what brings you over here this afternoon?"

I told him all about my struggles with John Macy. Took about five full minutes. I let my anger roll out while telling the story. When I was finished, my grandfather looked at me and said, "Ask God for strength to deal with morons."

"That's it?"

"And if that doesn't work, plant cocaine on him." Seamus waited for a response. When he didn't get one, he said, "What? Isn't that what cops do in movies to get someone in trouble?"

I kept a straight face and said, "In real life we'd plant child pornography on his computer."

"Ah, the new millennium."

"Seriously, any ideas?"

"Jerks like him almost always ruin themselves. Leave him be. Do your duty and it'll all work out. Of that, I have no doubt. Think about your wonderful family and your impending wedding. Tell me you're not just whining to your grandfather about a bully you ran into today."

I couldn't believe it, but I felt better. No one had a handle on humanity like my grandfather.

CHAPTER 38

ANOTHER RESTLESS NIGHT'S sleep did little to improve my perspective as I trudged into the office early the next morning. I was determined to go about my job as best I could. My grandfather was right. I just needed to do my duty. Forget the power play by some political hack.

Harry Grissom stood by the door reading some notice from the building manager. He looked up at me and said, in a way only he could, "Have you pulled your head out of your ass yet?"

"Hope so."

"Good. Because your new partner is on a roll and the two of us have to keep pace." Without another word, Harry led me through the office to the rear conference room, where Hollis had established his tip-line headquarters.

Hollis stood outside the room. He now wore only a simple strip of surgical tape across his nose. The circles around his eyes had turned yellow, a move up from the black eyes the broken nose had given him. He was smiling and looked like a kid bursting to show off for his parents.

He pushed open the door to the conference room, raised his arm like a model from *The Price Is Right*, and said, "Behold, Task Force Halo."

When we stuck our heads in the door, we saw a couple of patrol officers in civilian clothes and two detectives One Police Plaza had sent over. Hollis explained that he had all of them now working on the leads taken from the tip lines.

I could tell Harry was impressed, though all he said was "Halo?"

Hollis was still grinning. "The name may have come from FBI ASAC Robert Lincoln, but we've made it our own. Halo has two meanings: our task force members are angels trying to stop the devil, *and* we're going to pound that devil like in the video game Halo."

Harry nodded, though I'd put money on him never having heard of the video game.

It can be tough being honest with yourself first thing in the morning, but I had to wonder if I had resisted the idea of a task force only because someone else—specifically the FBI—had suggested it.

At least having Hollis and the task force handling all the out-there leads left me free to pursue the one from Jill St. Pierre, about the blood from an Atlanta victim somehow ending up at a Manhattan crime scene.

I connected with Detective Alvin Carter, the lead detective from Atlanta, and spent an hour on the phone talking to him about his homicides.

Carter said, "We had two similar murders in the city of Atlanta proper, but then there were another three that happened in different suburbs—and out of my jurisdiction. I couldn't get those three suburban PDs to coordinate with me. You ever try to deal with competing agencies? It's no fun."

I let out a laugh at the recognition of a kindred spirit. "I have a hard time negotiating with competing precincts, let alone agencies."

"The chief of one of the wealthier suburbs told me he didn't want city crime tarnishing the reputation of his town. He said they would handle their own homicides and basically kept me out of their investigation. The other two suburbs got in line with that stance."

I shared with him Hollis's theory that the killer may have left Atlanta for New York.

"Sorry to say it, but I agree," Carter said. "Sounds like our killer moved to New York. I hope you have better luck catching him than I did."

"It's going to take some kind of luck to figure out how he took blood from a crime scene, stored it, transported it hundreds of miles, and reintroduced it at a second scene. Even if he took the sample in a sterile vial, he'd have to have maintained it under perfect conditions for the blood to be analyzable." I then asked, "Did you get any impressions or ideas from the crime scenes? I don't mean stuff you might put in a report; I'm talking about opinions." There was a long silence on the phone and I was afraid I had lost the detective. Then I realized he was taking the time to consider every angle.

Finally, Carter said, "They were...disturbing scenes. A lot of blood, and the killer seemed to have deliberately spread it around each of the scenes. All five victims were stabbed in the neck or chest, and in their left eyes."

I was taking notes, and I triple underlined that last detail. It was all too familiar.

"Of course we kept that detail from the media," Carter said. "A signature that distinctive risks inviting copycats."

I made another note. New York was following the same plan of keeping the eye stabbing confidential. But I needed more information to be sure.

"Were there any similarities between victims?"

"They were all young women, one black and four white. The black woman was killed in her office—the only one who was—and that scene was the least bloody, as if the killer was pressed for time. The other four victims were found dead in their own homes. I suspect the killer did some surveillance before he struck."

"How long between the first homicide and the final one?"

Carter didn't hesitate. "Almost two months. Fifty-four days to be exact."

I knew what it was like to live through a case like this. It didn't surprise me at all that he knew the exact number of days it had lasted.

"Then the killings stopped as abruptly as they began. We started to wonder if maybe something had happened to the killer, if maybe he'd died. Now it looks like he moved on to New York City."

I said, "Regrettably, he seems to be alive."

Carter said, "The NYPD has serious bragging rights when it comes to the size of their force and resources, and they're not shy about letting smaller PDs know who's the biggest and the best. I hope it's true."

"I hope so too."

CHAPTER 39

DETECTIVE ALVIN CARTER from Atlanta had given me some ideas, and I was becoming convinced that these blood-soaked homicides were all related. I again compared the reports from New York, Atlanta, and San Francisco. I gathered all the files and laid them out on my desk. The crime-scene photos were horrific. I kept studying them, looking for the meaning of the killer's distinctive signatures. The blood. The stabbing of the eyes. The arrangement of knickknacks at the scene. And now the introduction of the blood of a previous victim.

I made a list of follow-up questions for Carter. I wondered if there had been more than one blood sample found at any of the Atlanta crime scenes, and if so, if we could find out whether that blood had come from either of the San Francisco victims.

Hollis approached my desk. I looked over my shoulder at

the conference room where Task Force Halo was operating and asked him, "Any new leads coming in?"

"There are new leads, but a lot of wacky leads, and the hardest thing is trying to organize them all," Hollis said.

That's the way it always happened. Someone above you in the chain of command had the idea to open up phone lines for some tips, and the next thing you knew, all you were doing was listening to crazy people jabbering about their weird neighbors or how they were "psychic" and wanted to help the case.

I didn't miss the irony that we were actually using a task force that had been designed to fake out and shut up the mayor's office. Hollis showed me that the tips weren't only coming in via the phone lines—some helpful citizens were even sending in pages of Cutco and L.L.Bean catalogs with circles around pictures of knives that might be the murder weapons.

"One caller said he has a strange, secretive neighbor in Red Hook who gave him a weird vibe, and who had girls coming and going all the time," Hollis continued. "It turns out that the neighbor is a photographer of high-end nude models. The local precinct detective followed another lead, up in the Bronx, and uncovered a counterfeiting operation. Turned out to be pretty big-time. The detective is going to be recognized by the commissioner."

I could see that the young detective had done a good job managing the onslaught.

"That's always the way—poke around places we normally don't and find all kinds of shit. Opening cases NYPD doesn't even know they have. And then we end up clearing everyone else's cases but not our own."

I was starting to get back in my groove when I noticed someone skulking through the office.

It was the mayor's aide, John Macy.

CHAPTER 40

AS SOON AS I saw John Macy, my mind raced. How to handle him? Should I simply pretend yesterday's encounter never happened? Ignore him and hope he did the same with me? Then I started thinking reasonably, like an adult human being.

He seemed to be walking directly to my desk. Before he reached me, I said, "Hello, John. I'm sorry about yesterday. My jokes got a little out of hand. I was wrong, and I apologize."

Macy was dressed in another stunning designer suit and carried a leather satchel. I wasn't sure what his reply would be. Would he apologize in return? Strike back savagely and inform me I'd been removed from the case?

But Macy's choice was essentially to ignore me. He nodded in acknowledgment that he'd heard me but said nothing. He walked right past my desk and took a seat in front of Brett Hollis.

Hollis looked as surprised as I was.

Macy didn't waste any time. "As I understand it, Detective Hollis, you are now my contact on this case and, for all intents and purposes, the lead detective. At least as far as the mayor's office is concerned."

Hollis started to answer, but Macy cut him off.

"First, I'd like to have an overview of the case. Second, I'd like you to show me exactly how the task force is working. This afternoon I will have a photographer from the mayor's office with me to take pictures, which we will make available to the media."

Hollis fumbled for a reply. I had to bite my tongue. Literally. What kind of moron exposed an active investigation and its tactics while a killer was still out there targeting victims? Politicians and the news media didn't care about the consequences when there was a chance to make a splash or grab a headline.

Macy kept the freight train rolling. "I'm going to check in with you at 10 a.m. and 6 p.m. every day," he told Hollis. "Before each check-in, I expect to have received from you by email a one-page memo summarizing your investigation during the preceding hours."

"I don't have access to the entire case," Hollis demurred. "I'm just running leads off the tip line."

I was impressed at Hollis's misleading statement. The young detective was learning the ways of bureaucracy. I felt a little like Yoda.

Macy didn't miss a beat. "You will confer with Lieutenant Grissom as needed to fill in the gaps in your knowledge."

Hollis sat there, unsure what to do or where to turn. Every cop has been in this spot: a superior from the police department, or a local political hack, pressuring you for information you're not comfortable disclosing.

Macy's face turned more severe as Hollis hesitated in his response. "Was there anything I said you didn't understand?"

"No."

I was secretly glad Hollis didn't add a *sir*. Macy didn't deserve that kind of respect.

Macy eased up and said, "I'm trying to help you, Son. Right now the police have a serious PR problem in this country. The public doesn't rate them as highly as they used to. I want to fix that."

Hollis gave Macy another confused look. "We may have bad PR right now, but we're still way ahead of politicians and lawyers. So at least the people have *some* common sense."

It was hard not to cheer when I saw the scowl on Macy's face. I was also thrilled to witness that my new partner could handle himself just fine.

Macy said, "It won't take much for this killer to push the city into an all-out panic. We need to calm people down and catch this guy before he takes another victim. And smart-ass comments from the local cops won't help the situation. You have your orders. I expect you to carry them out."

On that subject, at least, I agreed with this pompous ass.

CHAPTER 41

MY ALARM CLOCK went off before sunrise, and I groggily faced the new day. Last night I'd gotten home after dark. It had been too late for dinner, and I'd barely had the energy to interact with my kids. I missed them, and I missed Mary Catherine. This was not how I wanted to live.

I jumped out of bed quickly and got dressed. I wanted to spend at least some time with the kids this morning. When I stepped into the living room, though, it took me a few moments to process an astonishing sight: all six of my daughters—Juliana, the oldest, plus Jane and the twins, Bridget and Fiona, even Shawna and Chrissy—were lined up facing Mary Catherine.

They were standing at attention, looking like marine recruits about to be inspected by their drill sergeant. All six wore flowy yellow dresses with white lace around the neck and the sleeves.

Only the two youngest, Chrissy and Shawna, looked happy about the exercise.

I said, "What's this? Am I having a dream where there are nothing but beautiful women in the world?"

The older girls did not appreciate my comment. Shawna and Chrissy giggled.

Mary Catherine said, "It's so much easier to coordinate bridesmaids when your groom can provide the entire wedding party. The girls and I have been getting separate fittings, so this is my first chance to see what they look like as a group."

Juliana said, "Like a cluster of grapefruits waiting to be picked."

Jane said, "Please don't take pictures, and if you must, don't let anyone see them. I'd die if Allan ever saw me in this dress."

The twins were caught between the more sophisticated, grown-up girls and the cute, silly little girls. They wisely decided to skip commentary.

Shawna stepped out of line, turned, and looked at her sisters. "I think we all look soooo beautiful. I am so excited about being in the wedding!"

That was all it took to shut down Juliana and Jane. If their little sister was this excited, they weren't going to complain.

Mary Catherine said, "Is everyone happy with her dress? Do they all fit well?"

The girls all nodded or mumbled that they were satisfied. Mary Catherine clapped her hands and said, "Then go change and off to school, all of you."

As the girls scampered away, Mary Catherine turned to me. "Good morning. You seemed so exhausted, I would've bet you'd sleep right through till noon. At least you look better this morning."

"Is it getting that bad?"

"This is the worst I've ever seen a case drain you. Anything new on it? I knew better than to ask you last night."

"I spoke to a detective in Atlanta yesterday. It seems very likely our killer was there too, though about eight months ago. After committing five murders, he abruptly stopped killing there. Maybe we've heard the last of him here too."

"You really think so?"

"No. No, I don't."

Mary Catherine looked around to make sure none of the kids was close by. "Can we talk about Brian for a minute?"

I felt a sudden flutter of panic. *What has my oldest son done now?* I gave a silent nod, steeling myself for what disturbing news might possibly follow that cold open.

"You know I've been curious about where Brian goes every day."

"*Curious, intrusively paranoid*—they're all just words."

She punched me in the arm playfully. For the record, *playfully* doesn't mean it didn't hurt.

"I followed him yesterday morning."

"You conducted surveillance on Brian?" My tone indicated exactly what I thought of the idea.

"I know, I know. It's shady and shifty and I shouldn't have done it. But I'm worried about him. God knows what he's doing. Or who he's meeting with."

I hated that I had to ask. "So what did you find out?"

"I followed him to the subway. He got on the 1 train headed downtown."

"You didn't follow him to see where he was going?"

"I think he might have spotted me. I'm not sure, but I thought it'd be best if I didn't continue."

I let out a smile and said, "Brian was running countersurveil-lance. Interesting. You got burned and returned to HQ."

Mary Catherine said, "That's all you have to say? *Interesting?* Aren't you worried about your son?"

"You know I am, but he's not breaking any laws by hopping a train downtown. We've got to have some faith in him. On the basketball court the other day, a boy tried to pick a fight with him, but Brian wouldn't engage. I saw how hard he's trying to stick to his anger management program. I'd like to give him a little more of a chance. Let's have breakfast."

I put my arm around Mary Catherine as we walked from the living room into the kitchen. I saw the New York *Daily News* on the kitchen counter, stepped over and picked it up. It was still rolled with the rubber band the doorman used to make the papers easier to deliver.

Mary Catherine grabbed a cup of coffee and headed into the dining room. She took a seat at the end of the dining room table. I sat down next to her and unrolled the paper.

My eyes locked on the headline blaring in bold type: LETTER FROM A KILLER. At that same moment, my phone started to ring. I knew there had to be a connection.

The entire front page of the New York *Daily News* was a letter from the person claiming to be our killer.

To the Women of New York:

Now that you see what I can do, you are right to be afraid. Respect the fear.

I know how to watch. I know how to kill. I know how to evade the police.

Your arrogance has been your downfall. I am the one in control, not you.

Think of the one who has killed the most. I am better than him.

And I'm about to prove it. Again. And again. And again. And again.

Bobby Fisher

The NYPD hadn't gotten any heads-up about the publication of this letter. My phone kept ringing and ringing. I was getting multiple calls from management.

The only one I answered was from Harry Grissom.

CHAPTER 42

DANIEL OTT WALKED the streets of Manhattan. He had to get to work in Queens, but that could wait.

Now that his letter was finally out there, he sensed people were acting differently, and he wanted to experience how it felt to walk among them. As he walked, he noticed that the crowds still bustled about, bumping and pushing, but their overall energy felt more tentative. He also noticed more people reading actual newspapers. Ott realized he was starting to get quite a kick out of seeing how others reacted to his hobby.

How scared they seemed.

He couldn't suppress his smile. *I did this.*

Ott pulled a copy of the New York *Daily News* out of his bag. He'd already read the article that accompanied his letter to the paper. He'd read it six times. Every time, he'd gotten even more excited. He loved that the reporter called him a "maestro of death" who played "a genius game of cat and mouse with the police."

Ott contemplated sending another letter, maybe to a national newspaper, like *USA Today*. He wondered if he should mention the other cities he'd visited, then he hesitated, concerned that someone might piece together his travel itinerary. It was a long shot but one he'd rather not risk. Maybe he'd just point out how clever he was in arranging his counting messages. He couldn't deny the thrill he got from boldly taunting the police.

His phone rang. It was too early in the morning for his usual call with his wife and daughters, but Lena said she needed to talk to him. After Ott spoke to his two daughters for a few minutes, and listened to their stories about the neighbor's dog and how they were learning to use computers almost as well as their dad, they gave the phone back to his wife.

Lena seemed upset. She told him that this morning an older woman had bullied her at the grocery store.

"I was standing in the meat aisle when she reached over and pulled a package of pork chops right out of my hand. She looked at me, then walked away with the pork chops in her basket."

"What did you do?"

"I let it go. I decided it wasn't worth arguing over pork chops. Plus, she was old."

Ott said, "That's what makes you so special. You're not an arrogant bully like so many American women. You stay exactly the way you are. I hope we can raise our daughters to be just like you."

"Aren't you sweet," Lena said. "Do you know yet when you'll be home?"

"I have a couple more things to do here in New York City. I'll head back probably sometime late next week."

"The girls and I can't wait to see you."

"I can't wait to see all of you."

After he finished the call, Ott contemplated his next move.

Helping his wife through a trying experience made him feel that he was repaying part of the debt he owed her. He owed her at least as much as he did his former employers, and that bothered him a little bit.

But his kind, quiet wife would never bother him the way brash, opinionated women did.

Ott was starting to feel like he was doing the women in this city a favor by instilling a little more civility among them. Maybe his lesson plan was more than just a hobby.

CHAPTER 43

MY MORNING COMMUTE was a crazed montage of phone calls and texts as I reread the killer's letter over and over at every stop in traffic. In the letter, the killer had made it clear he was no phony. And he was not done teaching New Yorkers a lesson in civility and manners.

The letter was short, to the point, and clearly designed to cause panic and confusion. Was he trying to gain attention and notoriety, like the Zodiac Killer, Jack the Ripper, and the Golden State Killer had all done in the past? All of those criminals had reached out to the press. He had also raised a challenge. *Think of the one who has killed the most.* I considered the prolific serial killer Hollis had mentioned, Samuel Little.

Which killer was *Bobby Fisher* trying to top?

I was getting sucked into the puzzle. Exactly as the killer wanted me to do.

I had already been on the phone to the NYPD tech department. They were busy talking to the newspaper's computer staff, trying to figure out the origin of the email.

I decided to make a personal visit to the New York *Daily News* building to see the individual in charge of editorials and letters to the editor. I drove directly to the paper's offices, way down by Battery Park and about a mile from One Police Plaza. The editor didn't seem surprised to see an NYPD detective in his office. He also didn't seem to care.

The editor was in his early thirties and was dressed surprisingly casually, given his title. I looked over the framed diplomas hanging on the wall: an undergrad degree from Northwestern's Medill School of Journalism and an MBA from NYU. There were also several trophies on a low, oak bookshelf—though as I slipped past, I saw one was a soccer trophy with a plate that read FOR PARTICIPATION.

With a murder investigation at stake, this guy was going to have to do better than that.

He had the air of a sharp Wall Street banker working for a fraction of the salary—and, by the look of his degrees, a lot more student debt. His slicked-back dark hair and wire-frame glasses made it seem like he couldn't decide if he wanted to be a hotshot media guy or an intellectual.

I skipped the pleasantries and went straight for the confrontation. "I can't believe you wouldn't at least call us for comment before you printed a letter from what could be our lead suspect. What kind of journalism is that?"

"Welcome to the new millennium's journalism, Detective. In today's media world, speed is everything. Look, we weren't trying to screw up your investigation. Fact is, the email sat in the general folder for days before anyone even looked at it.

When our techs confirmed it was sent from a New York–area IP address, we became convinced that he'd sent the letter to everyone in town, so we decided to run it before we could be scooped. And the proof is in our circulation. It's skyrocketing."

"The NYPD isn't trying to censor you or inhibit any First Amendment rights. We're trying to catch a killer. This is an active investigation."

"Which is going nowhere." The young editor made a face, but truthfully, I couldn't read his expression. "When are you going to start doing something about this freak?"

I realized I was getting tired of this kind of conversation, of answering the only question anyone ever asked. "We're approaching this case from every possible angle," I said. "Doing everything we can."

"I admit, Detective, I might not have your experience, but I have a good education and common sense. What about rounding up some suspects? Doing some quick searches? No one cares about search warrants anymore. This shit has got to stop. The people have a right to know that the killer is taunting everyone in New York, including the police. And now that they do know, it's only a matter of time before they start taking matters into their own hands."

I chuckled.

"What's so funny?"

"Your belief system. That the Constitution matters only when there is no crisis. That's not how the world works. We can't all be hypocrites. We have to follow policies and rules set down for legal investigations."

The editor said, "I'll put this argument down to a draw. But the next time the asshole kills someone, Bennett, this conversation goes on the record. And 'Doing everything we can' is going to sound a lot like 'We're not doing anything.'"

CHAPTER 44

AN HOUR LATER, I met Brett Hollis in front of the main branch of the New York Public Library. His face looked much better today. That single strip of tape across his nose didn't seem so out of place. Maybe I was just getting used to it.

The editor at the New York *Daily News* was right about one thing: circulation. And not of library books. Everywhere I looked I saw people with a newspaper under their arms or reading news stories on their phones. A cab rolled by with its windows down. I could hear one of the local AM radio hosts—a well-known sports commentator—talking about the letter from the killer.

Hollis had been busy. He'd gotten a report from the NYPD's Computer Crimes Squad, who had worked with the *Daily News* IT staff and improved on the staff's initial findings. They'd figured out that the email's IP address had originated from a computer inside this library building. The email address provided to the paper was traced back to a newly opened account in the name of Bobby Fisher, no other identifying information attached.

In short, the letter didn't seem to provide any new information on the killer, other than the challenge he had posed. How was that possible?

"By the way," Hollis told me, "I also heard that a staff member here was the victim of a homicide up in East Harlem, just a few days ago. But her case doesn't seem similar to ours. No mutilation, none of our guy's markers."

I asked Hollis how he was doing, dealing with John Macy.

Hollis sighed and looked up at one of the pair of giant marble lions, Patience and Fortitude, that flanked the building's stairs. "He was the last person I saw last night and the first one to call me this morning. But if I'm working with the great and famous Michael Bennett, I guess I should expect a few rough patches."

"Funny."

Hollis asked me, "How'd the meeting with the editor at the *Daily News* go?"

"About like you'd expect. It's very clear to me that they're only interested in the number of papers they sell or clicks the story gets online, not in helping out our homicide investigation. I swear, sometimes it feels like there are some awfully blood-thirsty people in the media who want more murders so they can have juicier stories that sell more papers."

Hollis shook his head in dismay, then said, "So what're we hoping for from our visit to the library?"

"Ideally, a description of some kind. We have the date and time the email was sent. Maybe a security camera got a useful image of the killer. We should be able to narrow down the hours of footage. Maybe a member of the staff even spoke to him. We can get a forensic artist if we have to make a composite."

"I hope we find something. We got nothing useful so far from the tip line."

I turned and looked at the crowds of people passing the library or congregating in front of it. I was struck by the fact that we were looking for a needle in a haystack. A giant haystack. And a needle that moved from city to city.

Patience and fortitude. That's what it would take to catch this killer.

CHAPTER 45

DANIEL OTT STOPPED in front of the main branch of the New York Public Library, contemplating the new research he needed to do today. As before, he preferred to use someone else's computer when looking up anything…unsavory. If anyone searched his laptop, they'd find only his work-related materials and Google searches having to do with the best homeschool curriculums.

The most important part of today's research was not electronic. He was interested in the reaction of the other librarians to the death of the librarian he had killed, along with whoever that other man was.

That's why he was back here today.

He was already wondering about his next victim. He'd be leaving New York in about a week, and it would be nice to enjoy one last night of rituals and excitement in the big city.

Besides, he'd promised the *Daily News* that he would claim another life. And he didn't want to let his readers down.

He looked in the faces of the women striding past the library and saw half a dozen who might fit his needs. Women who looked like they would ignore him if he spoke to them. Women who thought they were better than him, better than everyone.

As he stood for the moment next to the stairs leading into the main entrance of the library, however, he glanced down and saw a frail-looking woman with a child sitting in her lap. She wore a floral dress that looked vintage 1970s. Next to her sat a wire shopping basket holding a stack of clothes with some chips and a half eaten Clif Bar balanced on top.

The woman spoke with a heavy accent. "Can you help us? We need money to get upstate."

She had big brown eyes and seemed completely defeated. The little girl in her lap was about three. Her curly hair was dirty, and she wore a T-shirt stained with grape juice. She gave him the briefest of smiles.

Ott pulled his wallet from his back pocket. When he opened it, he realized all he had was a single ten-dollar bill. He'd meant to stop at the ATM but had forgotten. Ott looked down at the sad pair and handed the woman his ten dollars.

The woman squeezed his hand and said, "Bless you. May God bless you, sir."

"I'll be happy if you use the money to buy that little girl some food. I believe I'm beyond God's blessing. If there is a God," Ott said. He realized that some of the lessons of his childhood had definitely stuck with him. He had nothing against churches, but that wasn't how he'd been raised. Aside from his wedding, he had never been inside one.

Ott left the woman and went into the library. The first time he had visited, he'd made a quick note of the security. Frankly, he'd expected more cameras. There were a few around, but he also noticed several dummy cameras, fake cameras positioned to make security appear beefier. Ott glanced up to make sure they had not installed video cameras since his last visit. His eyes quickly moved up the walls and around the decorative crown molding. There was nothing. No cameras or sensors of any kind.

He walked directly to the computer room and looked up and around. No new cameras there either. He knew the idea was to make the room as inviting and unintimidating to people as possible.

Two staff members were in the room. One was organizing magazines in the corner, and the other sat at a desk, sorting through books that had recently been returned. She paid no attention to who was at the computers, or whether they had signed in.

Like he belonged there, he settled into his place at the third computer from the door. The same one he'd used to send his letter to the New York *Daily News*. He wanted to see the story online even though he'd already read it so many times in print. Often the online stories were accompanied by photos or embedded videos not available in the print edition.

Ott then moved on to other local media stories about the murders. He was interested in learning more about the detective on the case. There were photos of this Michael Bennett in several different settings. Ott didn't think the man looked like a cop. He looked more like an actor. Then Ott did a search on Bennett.

He couldn't believe the number of articles that had run over the years. The man had been lead detective on several major investigations. There were also several human-interest stories about his personal life. He was a widower with ten adopted children. Ott wondered if he'd adopted the children before or after his wife died.

He glanced up from the computer at the two women working in the room. They both appeared subdued. Ott assumed that was because of him, because he had murdered one of their colleagues. He smiled. They had no idea it was her conduct on the job that had put their friend at risk.

The woman behind the desk had a beautiful face and long, lustrous blond hair that flowed over her shoulders. He wondered how much money and effort it took to keep her hair looking like that. Probably enough to feed a poor family in other parts of the world. Just the thought of it made him a little angry.

Ott stretched his neck to get a better view of the woman. He was hoping to read the name tag she wore on her blouse.

Then he got hold of himself. He returned his focus to the computer and started doing a little more research. He wanted to know more about this Michael Bennett before he did anything else. His idea to stir things up might have to wait.

164

CHAPTER 46

YOU KNOW, I'VE lived in New York my whole life and I've never been in here before," Brett Hollis said as we entered the library. He looked awestruck by the marble walls and high ceilings of the scholarly locale.

"Impressive, isn't it?" I said. "As a tourist destination, it even makes a little money for the city." And as we walked through the famous library, I felt a familiar pride and appreciation for this monument to learning.

I waited while Hollis phoned a tech agent from the NYPD, gathering a few more pieces of the puzzle. Then we continued on to the admin office, where we identified ourselves and were led to Carolyn Richard, a confident older black woman in charge of public services, such as the computer room. Ms. Richard was imposing and elegant, and as soon as I saw her, I thought, *She could be one of the nuns from Holy Name*—especially the way she had her arms folded across her chest when she told us to come in and sit down.

Ms. Richard said, "I assume you're here about Yara Zunis."

Is that the murder victim I just heard about from Hollis? I thought so but wasn't sure, so I kept quiet, let her talk.

"Yara Zunis, one of our librarians. She and her boyfriend were victims of a terrible crime. They were both stabbed to death outside their home in East Harlem."

That didn't fit our killer's MO—as far as we were aware, he only ever killed young women, not couples, and he never killed out in the open. Still, what were the chances that a serial killer uses a specific library's computer and then one of that library's staff is murdered? Was it just a horrible coincidence? Or could there be some sort of connection?

I gathered my thoughts and said, "My utmost condolences to you and your staff on the tragedy you've all suffered. But we're actually here investigating an email that our cyber forensics team believe was sent from your computer room."

"Oh my—is this related to that awful letter I read in the *Daily News*?" Carolyn Richard asked. She was a smart woman, and I could see her quickly reassessing the situation, even as I demurred, citing confidentiality issues.

During the walk to the computer room from her office, I asked Ms. Richard more about Yara Zunis.

"How long had she worked here at the library?"

"Yara was one of our newest and brightest," she said, "a recent graduate from the prestigious Master of Library and Information Science program at Simmons University in Boston. She was making significant contributions. It's such a terrible shame."

She shook her head and sighed. "Is there anything you can tell me about the investigation into her murder? I know it's not your case, but I assume there's communication between precincts."

"I'll have the detectives handling the case get back to you," I told her. I was pretty curious about it myself, to be honest. "For now, our primary concern is the email."

Ms. Richard nodded, then said, "With all these murders in the city, I've been starting to wonder if our staff needs to commute using some kind of buddy system."

The marble floor of the entrance hall gave way to the high marble walls of the periodical/computer room. The two young women working there immediately looked up when Ms. Richard entered.

I quickly scanned the room to get a sense of the security measures in place. I saw a few cameras, but they were mainly dummies. I wondered about the computer sign-in procedures.

I saw a quick movement to my right. I turned but caught only a glimpse of a man wearing a white, short-sleeved shirt and a tie leaving the room.

Why had he caught my attention? Call it instinct.

I glanced back to Hollis. He hadn't seemed to notice the guy, and Ms. Richard was intent on introducing me to the blond woman behind the desk.

Even though the blonde was the person I needed to talk to about the email, I had to excuse myself. "We need to go talk to someone for a minute."

I grabbed Hollis by the arm and pulled him with me out the door, saying, "I saw a man wearing a white, short-sleeved shirt and a tie. As soon as he saw us, he popped out of the room with his head ducked down."

As Hollis kept pace, I added the kicker: "I have a strong feeling that we gotta find this guy and talk to him right away."

CHAPTER 47

SET PERIMETERS AND *start a methodical grid search.*
I knew the routine for searches, honed during my days as a
uniformed officer in the Bronx and as a homicide detective,
hunting everyone from drug suspects to bank robbers.

But that approach took manpower, at least twenty cops to do
right. Right now it was just Hollis and me, and I was hesitant
to call in reinforcements based on nothing more than my flimsy
hunch and a fleeting image. Besides, it would take too long to
get backup here and organized.

Instead, I sent Hollis toward the main entrance as I rushed
down a hallway in the opposite direction. My last words to the
young detective were "Don't do anything stupid. Just hang back
and call me on the cell if you see him." I knew advice like that
was difficult for a young hotshot like Brett Hollis to follow. He
was wearing the damaged proof on his face.

I loped down the empty hallway with my right arm loose at my side so I could reach my Glock if needed. I should've come to a complete stop and *sliced the pie* by looking around each corner, but there wasn't time. Smart policies are all well and good, but no bad guys would ever get caught if we officers followed every policy to the letter, every time.

Sweat slipped down my forehead as my pulse picked up.

To my right was a marble staircase that headed down, away from the main floor. I took the steps two at a time. Just as I skidded onto the tiled floor of the lower level, a figure moved to my right.

I saw a flash of white shirt and dark tie.

I let out a quick "Freeze!" as I reached for my pistol, and in the same instant, I recognized the uniform shirt of a security guard. The man flinched and scooted away from me.

I flashed my badge. "NYPD. Did anyone else come down here?"

He hesitated, then said, "I thought I heard footsteps, but it might have been yours coming down the stairs."

A door down the hall was cracked open. I indicated it with a lift of my chin. "Where does that go?"

"Lower-level maintenance. Nothing there but conduits and heating units."

I raced to the door without another word. The guard called after me, but I didn't have time to waste words. I was hoping for action. I almost hoped he'd call for more security people. A group following me could be useful if the chase ended in a show of force.

I reached the open door and discovered that it led to a narrow, metal staircase descending into a dark, tunnel-like passageway filled with electrical boxes and abandoned computers stacked haphazardly against whitewashed cinder-block walls. Tracks of wires seemed to guide me in one direction. At the same time, something told me to slow down and make every move deliberate.

A light flickered a dozen feet down the hallway. I flipped my coat away from my right hip and slid my hand onto the butt of my duty weapon.

I pulled my phone from my pocket to check on Hollis. No service.

Could Bobby Fisher be down here, setting up for his next match?

CHAPTER 48

FIFTEEN MINUTES EARLIER, Daniel Ott had looked up from the public computer to see the same man he'd just read about on the internet standing by the door. He had done a double take, stolen several more peeks, then was certain. It was that detective, Michael Bennett.

For a moment, Ott calculated the odds of this being a coincidence. No: the police had to be here because of the dead librarian. But did Bennett know that the librarian and her friend were connected to his handiwork? It hurt his brain to think too much about it. He had to slip away. Fast.

Even if Ott hadn't just been reading about the detective, he would have suspected something. Bennett and the other guy he was with just *looked* like police officers—fit, well-dressed, and alert. They had come into the room with an older black woman. Ott watched as the three of them stepped over to the information desk, and while they seemed distracted, he used his soft cloth to wipe the keyboard of prints, quickly gathered his things, and slipped out the door. Almost involuntarily, he'd picked up his pace to a near run.

Mistake. The detective had noticed him leaving.

At the bottom of the marble staircase, Ott fingered a screwdriver in his pocket. A screwdriver through the neck or in an eye would definitely slow down anyone chasing him.

He considered his next move, zeroing in on another stairwell that didn't look public. No marble or frills. He raced for it.

Ott found himself in the lowest level of the library. The Ghostbusters may have prowled the subbasement stacks, but not the maintenance corridors. The stark layout here meant some part of him would be visible anywhere he crouched or lay down. There was no place he could hide.

Then he saw a junction box built into the wall. One of those big industrial suckers. It had to be four feet tall and two feet wide. It was a screw model with no handle.

He had an idea.

He snapped his head in every direction. His heart beat hard in his chest. His hands shook. He used his cheap tie with the Computelex logo to wipe sweat from his face.

The first screw at the top of the box was hard to reach. He was able to remove a couple more screws, but then they slipped from his hand and scattered on the rough concrete floor.

He wasn't sure what he'd find when he opened the box's door. Would it be a mess of wiring inside? Luckily for him, when he finally yanked the door open, he discovered there were no breakers or other more complex electrical connections. This was just a pass-through that redirected most of the wires up to the main floors of the library.

It would be tight, but he could fit inside it if he contorted his body just so. Ott hopped up, then pulled himself all the way into the box. He kept the screwdriver in his right hand. If someone opened the box while he was inside, he'd take a mighty swing at their eyes, leap into the passageway, then run.

With his left hand, he pulled the door shut behind him. He crouched uncomfortably inside the box, perspiration running down his back, ears straining to hear any noises outside.

CHAPTER 49

I MOVED CAUTIOUSLY. The heat down here couldn't account for all the sweat in my eyes. Some of it was nerves.

I had no cell service. No radio. I had to admit that I'd put myself in a stupid situation. If the guy I'd seen was the killer, and if he was down here and managed to get the drop on me, I wasn't sure anyone would even know to look for me here unless the library guard had sounded the alarm.

This area of the library was creepy. The flickering light down the hallway reminded me of the horror movies my older kids were just about brave enough to watch through half closed eyes.

I thought I heard something. A shift. A slight metallic noise. Now I was studying shadows in the poorly lit corridor. My mind was starting to play tricks on me and I was freaking myself out.

Keeping my right hand on the butt of my pistol, I moved

slowly. Once I passed the flickering light, I paused and listened again. I leaned against the wall next to some kind of giant circuit box. I really thought I heard something moving inside.

Mice? Squirrels? Or worse—rats?

I looked down at the concrete and noticed a single screw sitting in the middle of the corridor. I kneeled down and picked it up. Before I rose again to my feet, I rested in a silent crouch. Listening. Feeling like there was someone close by. I cocked my head like a curious dog. But I couldn't pick up the sound again.

Then I heard a noise. It registered on several levels inside my head. I listened and realized it was footsteps. Not someone trying to hide.

Then a voice called out, "Officer! Are you still down here? Officer?"

I called out, "Over here."

The security guard I had seen on the upper level swung into view. He was winded and overheated. His sweaty hair was plastered to his forehead, and he was panting from exertion.

He had to lean down with his hands on his knees and take a couple of gulps of air before he could stand upright and speak. "The cop with the broken nose? He told me to come find you," he said. "He needs you at the main entrance. He said to hurry."

I kept the screw I found on the floor. For no reason that I can explain, it struck me as a potential piece of evidence. I shoved it into my front pocket as I started to jog ahead of the security guard.

CHAPTER 50

AS I BURST OUT of the main doors to the library, I held up my hand to protect against the glare of the sun; though it wasn't all that bright out, my eyes had quickly grown accustomed to the gloom of the basement. I felt relief to have gotten out of there.

Crowds washed by on the street. The security guard directed me to a bench just past the edge of the stairs to the right, where Brett Hollis stood next to a man of about forty-five wearing a short-sleeved shirt and a gaudy purple tie. His thinning hair hung in a loose comb-over. He was sweating in the midday sun. The fact that he was thirty pounds overweight probably didn't help the situation.

The man was not in custody, I noted, and he and Hollis were talking casually. Hollis saw me coming down the stairs and gave me a quick headshake. This wasn't our suspect. As I walked up, Hollis told me, "This gentleman is a vending machine rep who was meeting with the library staff. I already confirmed it. I sent the security guard to look for you before I checked out his story."

I looked at the pudgy, red-faced, balding man. He looked pissed off.

"Do we need to hold him any longer?"

Hollis shrugged. "That's sort of the problem. He won't leave."

The man looked toward Hollis and said, "I'll have your goddamn badge over this." Then he looked at me, making the assumption that, as an older detective, I was probably in charge, and said, "He arrested me without a warrant! I know my rights. I know how you guys operate."

Arrested? I turned to the man and said, "I'm sorry. I'm not sure what you're talking about."

Hollis said, "Sir, you were never under arrest. All I did was talk to you for a couple of minutes about a matter that needed clearing up, and you didn't argue."

"I was too scared. You intimidated me."

All I could say was "C'mon, sir, you got misidentified. We cleared it up in a couple of minutes. Won't you just go about your business?"

The pudgy man barked again. "Bullshit. I want your names and badge numbers. Why are you bothering me when you should be trying to catch that nut cutting up women all over the city?"

I could sense Hollis losing patience with the man. We needed to de-escalate. I reached into my wallet and pulled out a business card. I wrote Harry's name and phone number on the back. I handed it to the man and said, "That's our lieutenant. If you have any complaints, talk to him."

"I'll go straight to the *Post.* I know you cops all watch each other's backs. I'm a US citizen."

I'd had enough. I gave the man a hard look and said, "You have the right to get on with your life. I would recommend you exercise that right as soon as possible. Frankly, I've heard all the shit I want to out of you."

The man started walking away on the sidewalk, muttering to himself. He stopped twenty feet away and shouted, "Cops suck!"

It wasn't original, but he got his point across.

Hollis looked at me and said, "What now?"

"We work with what we have. I was chasing ghosts beneath the library. At least you got to talk to a real person."

"Enduring that conversation was more painful than breaking my nose," Hollis said, and I laughed.

"Now we need to meet with library IT so that we can check the video surveillance to see if our runner shows up."

CHAPTER 51

HOLLIS AND I turned the corner from the library entrance to find a coffee shop on 41st, just off Fifth Avenue. The place was nearly empty of customers. We headed toward the rear and commandeered two wide tables, where we spread out our papers.

I had a cup of plain black coffee and some kind of cruller. Hollis opted for a healthy and hydrating bottle of water. He never would've made the grade when I was a rookie. Back then, drinking coffee during our shifts and alcohol in the evenings felt mandatory. Frankly, I don't miss the old days.

We'd spent more than an hour talking with the head of library security and his IT guy. We'd searched through the available video feeds. I'd noted the dummy cameras, but I was still surprised at how few active feeds they actually maintained.

The head of security had looked at me and shrugged. "We're a library, not a central bank. We have a decent budget, but it's not spent on security cameras. Our biggest expense is staffing exhibits of our permanent collections. Some of the items—like first-edition books by famous authors, or one-of-a-kind photographs and artwork—are quite valuable. We have to prevent tourists from trying to steal a piece of library history. On the flip side, we also need to patrol the quiet spaces where homeless people sneak in to sleep during the day and overnight. But if the guy you're looking for passed by any of the display areas, we may have captured his image."

Not likely, I thought, but I thanked the security head for his time.

At least we had a little more information to work with.

The outburst from the concerned citizen outside the library underscored my biggest worry. New Yorkers aren't shy about criticizing the police, and that guy had felt free to curse us out. God knows an ass like John Macy would use any public outcry as a reason to screw with me, especially as the unsolved murders kept mounting.

I slapped a legal pad down on the table and started writing. The lists of what we were missing and what we still needed to do were far longer than the list of what we had.

When I wondered out loud if I'd caught a glimpse of the killer at the library, Hollis talked me down, reminding me that there was no reason to assume the killer had even been there today, only a case of mistaken identity with the vending machine rep.

With an audible sigh, I conceded his point and then said, "So what's our next move?"

"Maybe the answer lies in the earlier murders. We need to work those connections until we forge a clear link."

It was as good a plan as any. And one that would take us back to the office.

As we started to gather up our stuff, the manager of the coffee shop, a well-built young black man, approached. He said, "I noticed your badges. I was wondering if you guys might help me out."

I said, "What's the problem?"

"There's a homeless guy who sits for hours right in the doorway of my shop. The guy's killing my afternoon business. I called the local precinct a couple of times, but one of the cops I talked to said that the truth is, they don't consider loitering or harassing my customers for change enough of a crime to warrant an arrest."

The manager blew out a frustrated breath, admitting, "I once made the mistake of paying him off. I gave him five dollars to find another spot. But he was back the next day, and he told me it would take ten if I wanted him to move again. He just sat down now. Is there anything you guys can do?"

I looked past the manager to see a white guy with a scraggly gray beard who'd propped himself right in the coffee shop's doorway. He wore an old olive-drab army-surplus jacket. As I watched, two different customers walked toward the front door. First one, then the other, turned away and left rather than step over the man's legs. I could see the manager's point.

I turned to Hollis and said, "This is a good lesson for us as members of the NYPD. The store's owner has made a legitimate request, and I'd like you to handle it. The faster it's taken care of, the faster we can get back on our case."

I purposely hadn't offered any advice to Hollis, and he didn't say a word. He simply jumped to his feet and headed to the door of the coffee shop.

So far, I'd been impressed at how Hollis handled difficult coworkers and even an ass like John Macy, but I wanted to see more of how he dealt with the public. This was a sensitive, potentially volatile situation. He was on his own. I just hoped his solution wasn't too harsh.

The way he barreled through the front door and spun on the sidewalk to confront the man didn't give me much hope. Then the homeless man stood up and faced Hollis. I wondered if I might need to go defuse the situation. But I waited.

Just as he had done with Van Fleet, Hollis put his hand on the man's shoulder. He spoke to him quietly. I saw the man's head nod, and then he shook Hollis's hand. I also noticed something Hollis probably didn't want me to see: my young partner slipping the man a card for the VA New York Regional Office on Houston Street and some cash as he was walking away.

Hollis had done some practical problem-solving. And shown some compassion. I was impressed.

CHAPTER 52

BACK IN THE office, I looked like a crazed hoarder with towering stacks of paper and crime-scene photographs piled high and spread around my desk, on my guest desk chair, and all over the surrounding floor. Other detectives veered around me and avoided eye contact. I'd have to remember this trick in the future when I didn't want to chat.

I was comparing five case files. The two San Francisco homicides were on the desk directly in front of me. I had three of the five total Atlanta-area homicides on the chair next to my desk—two from Detective Carter and one from his cooperative suburban counterpart. Neither of the agencies investigating the other two murders down there were interested in sharing their files with the NYPD. Fine. I didn't have time to argue.

And I didn't have any more time to spare making certain that the killer who'd likely hit first San Francisco and then Atlanta was probably the same one still at large in New York. The one who in a published letter had threatened the entire city that he would kill again.

The city was in a panic, and John Macy was breathing down our necks.

I had a full range of law-enforcement tools at my disposal. Photographs, forensic reports, interviews, even security footage, though nothing identified the killer. The local agencies had also done video walk-throughs of each crime scene. Some were excellent and gave complete views of every surface and angle. Some were rushed and cursory. Not that the detectives and PD photo techs could have ever imagined that the images they were capturing might prove part of a multistate serial-killing spree.

I stared at a set of novelty shot glasses in the crime-scene photos from one of the San Francisco victims. Souvenirs, I assumed, from the victim's travels, advertising Cancún, Kingston, and Key West. One lone shot glass stood about a foot away from five others. Once again, my mind went back to the strange, asymmetrical arrangement of the bobbleheads in Elaine's apartment here in New York…and the ballerina and musician figurines in the other San Francisco victim's apartment.

Once I started searching, I discovered similar arrangements in the other crime-scene photos, from the Bronx and Brooklyn, and in the three Atlanta-area scenes.

For instance, in one of the Atlanta crime-scene photos, I spotted a shelf where three teacups were lined up on the left, and nine were on the right, with about a foot-wide space between the two groups. In one of the other Atlanta victims' homes, a collection of small vases was divided into clusters of two and seven.

There's always a certain amount of luck and chance involved in any investigation. And this methodology of dividing the victims' collections seemed too deliberate not to be significant.

Looking for more evidence to bolster my theory, I brought up the walk-through videos from the third victim in Atlanta. The footage did a pretty good job of covering her entire apartment, though the detective working the camera had been more focused on getting close-ups of the victim's injuries and body than views of the crime scene. I could understand this victim-centric technique, but for my purposes, it was frustrating not to see more of the house.

I let out a short groan of annoyance that caught Brett Hollis's attention.

He stood up from his desk and stepped over to mine. "What are you looking for? Anything specific?"

I pointed to the crime-scene photos. "See those bobbleheads? And these shot glasses? The vases, the teacups, and the figurines? A number of similarly strange-looking setups at different crime scenes, and I'm wondering if the items might've been separated like that deliberately."

"You think the killer was sending a message?"

I made a face. "That's what I'm starting to think, yeah. But I'm just not sure what."

Hollis looked intrigued. He stood behind me as we watched the Atlanta video again. We divided the screen so he looked at the right side and I looked at the left.

About two minutes into the video, Hollis yelped, "There. There it is. Hit Pause." His finger tapped the screen of my laptop.

On a windowsill in the far background there was a barely

noticeable line of grayish dots. We froze the image and tried to enlarge it. There was one dot to the left, and three to the right, a gap of about five inches between them.

Hollis stared at the screen. "What are those? Buttons?" After a second he said loudly, "Coins! Those are dollar coins."

"Nice catch. Good eye."

Hollis said, "We still have no idea what the killer is trying to tell us."

It was something about staring at the dollar coins that made my swirling thoughts click into place. It was as close to an epiphany as I had ever had, at least in police work.

I said, "He's counting his kills for each location." I quickly grabbed the Atlanta-area crime-scene photos. "See? The video is of the first crime scene in the Atlanta area. Look at the date. Then it's three weeks before the next crime scene, in the actual city of Atlanta. That crime scene shows these two little vases on the left. The next crime scene is in some place called Dunwoody, about six days later. It's the set of teacups with three on the left and nine on the right. His third murder in the Atlanta area. Now it all makes sense. Like the bobbleheads at Elaine Anastas's apartment. She was the fourth murder in New York."

It felt right, like we had solved one important piece of the puzzle.

Now I had to find out if the other cases also fit the pattern.

CHAPTER 53

DANIEL OTT SAT in a McDonald's on 42nd Street, a few blocks from the New York Public Library. About every ten minutes, waves of customers entered and exited, effectively switching places. That's what Ott wanted right now: a lot of people around him. He looked at the crowd. He listened to their conversations.

A TV sat high on the wall, playing the news on channel 1. The anchor was quizzing someone from the mayor's office about the investigation into the murders. *His* murders. The city staffer, a man named John Macy, didn't sound particularly confident that an arrest would be made any time soon.

Ott sipped a Diet Coke and realized the sweat that had soaked his collar and under his arms was now dry. No one seemed to be looking for him. He was safe—at least for the moment. He swiveled his head, trying to work out one of the kinks he'd developed after hiding in that junction box for over twenty minutes. Then he straightened out both legs and heard his knees click with relief.

He smiled at a very cute Asian child whose mother had her strapped in a harness, with a leash attached. An older daughter carried shopping bags from inexpensive chain stores, like Claire's and H&M. The little girl on the leash paused right in front of Ott's table, level with his french fries. Her eyes cut from the fries to Ott, and back again.

All Ott could do was smile and nod his head. The little girl snuck two fries and rewarded him with a beautiful smile.

That happy smile reminded him of his own young daughters, waiting for him at home. He would be there with them soon. Now he was starting to feel normal. He relaxed slightly, allowing himself some perspective on the uncharacteristic stumble he had made back at the library, the moment the police had gotten close.

He was still a little freaked-out to have been reading an article about one of the city's best detectives, Michael Bennett, the one working his cases—only to look up and see the man in person. But even the so-called great detective hadn't been able to find him in the lower level of the library.

Daniel Ott sat at the table, finishing the last of his Diet Coke and fries and thinking about what needed to be done. Maybe he'd been thinking too broadly. He didn't need to send more emails to other newspapers. He could stir things up *and* disrupt the police investigation via more decisive and specific action.

He got out his burner smartphone to do a little research. There was one plan of attack that would surely rock the city. Killing Michael Bennett.

He knew the detective worked out of the Manhattan North Homicide office. Had to look at a few city maps to find the exact location of that office, but he was able to discover that the NYPD operated that department from a rented floor and four extra offices in an office building owned by Columbia University on upper Broadway near 133rd Street. Bennett's home address was unlisted, but Ott was good…and smart enough to know that hunting a target who lived in a city apartment with eleven other people was too risky. And he didn't like the idea of threatening children to incite panic.

He reassessed. Okay, maybe killing Bennett was too complicated.

Briefly, he thought about Bennett's family. Ten kids was a lot of children. Ott didn't care what culture you were raised in or how big a farm you had to work—he didn't see how raising ten kids was viable. Especially for a NYPD detective with a high-profile caseload. But Ott dismissed the idea of harming the kids. Besides, if Bennett were sidetracked by a personal issue, another detective would just take his place. And Bennett would probably still be available to consult.

He just needed to get Bennett off the case for a while. If Ott succeeded in injuring the detective or one of his colleagues, he could really throw a monkey wrench into the investigation. If he could do it without making it look like an intentional act of violence, no one would even connect him to the sneak attack on the NYPD.

He enjoyed having a problem like this to work on. His engineering background helped with almost any decision.

CHAPTER 54

I FELT LIKE a Christian walking the halls of the Roman Colosseum on my way to judgment in the arena. Every pair of eyes that set on me made me feel uncomfortable. For some reason, all FBI offices made me feel this way.

A lot of people don't realize that when it comes to law-enforcement agents and employees, the NYPD is much larger than the FBI. We number almost forty thousand cops, while the FBI has only approximately fifteen thousand agents active at any given time. The NYPD even has offices outside New York City. After the 9/11 terrorist attacks, NYPD and city officials felt the FBI could have done a better job providing them with information prior to the attacks, so now NYPD detectives are in several Middle Eastern cities as well as European cities. There's even a contingent of uniformed officers at the Vatican so visitors from New York City can feel reassured if there's a problem and they need to turn to a trusted element.

I was here at the FBI offices today to meet with Emily Parker. She knew my preference was to meet at a restaurant or coffee shop so I didn't have to venture into federal offices like this, but today she'd forced me to come here. Her "invitation" was making me feel like she was playing a prank on me.

Emily greeted me with a hug as she met me in the hallway and led me back to her cluttered cubicle. Before I could sit on the hard plastic chair next to her desk, I had to move aside a pile of files and notebooks. Though who was I to criticize, given the unruly stacks currently covering my desk and floor? Especially since I understood she probably knew exactly where to locate everything she needed. With a mind like hers, filing systems were a waste of time.

Emily smiled and said, "What's so important that I got Michael Bennett to actually come to the FBI office voluntarily? Honestly, the only thing that surprises me more is that you're not in custody."

"Ha ha," I replied. "All jokes aside, I need a sharp brain like yours to consider something we discovered about the killer."

"I can't wait to hear this one." She scooted her chair away from her desk and closer to me.

I cleared off a space on her desk and carefully laid out copies of the crime-scene photographs from New York, San Francisco, and Atlanta. I explained in great detail exactly what Hollis and I had discovered, not only about the bloody crime scenes but also the deliberate arrangement of the collections of objects found inside the victims' homes in each location. I explained our interpretation of them as the killer's way of tallying up his murders.

Emily was attentive but silent, never interrupting me as I explained our theory. That was a sign of a professional law-enforcement agent. Too bad more FBI agents didn't follow her example.

When I was finally finished, she looked me in the eye and said, "Impressive. I usually only hear about a personality mosaic this elaborate being pieced together by one of our people down at the Behavioral Analysis Unit at Quantico."

"What do you think of our theory?"

"It's pretty convincing," she said. "And I'm even more impressed knowing you guys came up with it on no budget, very little time, and using only crime-scene photos and public newspaper databases. But not all of the crime scenes have these messages. Like the one on Staten Island."

"That bugs the shit out of me. I've been over those crime-scene photos and back to that apartment several times. Nothing. I don't know if the killer was interrupted and had to leave or if there's some other explanation. But I still think we're onto something."

Emily said, "Maybe the message at the Staten Island crime scene is tiny. Or just not as obvious as these, like a handful of buttons or some grains of sand. Something someone could have accidentally swept up or knocked over. Based on your theory, this guy clearly needs to taunt us. That's ballsy."

I smiled at her dispassionate evaluation of our killer.

She said, "So what do you want from me?"

The research you promised me, I thought, but before I could answer, I heard a voice.

"Detective...?"

I turned in my seat and recognized FBI ASAC Robert

Lincoln from our previous meeting at One Police Plaza. He wore a gray suit with a red power tie and stood at the entrance to Emily's cubicle, snapping his fingers like he couldn't remember my name.

I recognized it as an old trick meant to put me in my place, but I fell into the trap anyway. I offered, "Bennett."

"Yes, of course. What brings you down here? I was under the impression that the NYPD had no use for the FBI."

Emily saved me. God bless her. She said, "Detective Bennett was just updating me on their multiple-homicide case. He's linked the killer we're investigating here to previous homicides in San Francisco and Atlanta."

That caught the FBI supervisor by surprise. "Really? Do you have all his reports, Emily?"

She nodded.

Lincoln said, "And you've confirmed this?"

Emily nodded again.

"Open an FBI case on it. Get in touch with the other jurisdictions. They may be more interested in our help than the NYPD has been." He looked at me. "We'll keep you up-to-date on our case." He paused and threw in a quick, "As time permits."

I smiled and said, "Of course."

Lincoln asked, "Who will be my contact?"

I didn't hesitate. "Macy, John Macy. Technically, he's with the mayor's office. You two should hit it off." I gave him John Macy's card and Lincoln walked away without another word.

Emily looked at me. "You handled that pretty well. You're full of surprises today." She pulled out a blank notepad and said, "I think I have an idea of what I can do for you. I'll run everything in your reports, and in the forensic reports, through every database. I'll also see about getting police reports from the two Atlanta suburbs who refused to cooperate with the NYPD. I'll even see if I can find some travel patterns."

I said, "Emily, you are absolutely the best." And then, "What took you so long?"

She gave me a perfect smile and said, "First, tell me something I don't know. Second, I think we just made it official. We're both on the same case."

CHAPTER 55

SOMEHOW, EVEN AFTER everything I'd dealt with during the day, I made it home with energy to spare. I felt excited to engage with my children or even go for a bike ride with Mary Catherine, if that's what she wanted. We hadn't been riding quite as much as the three times a week she'd intended when we bought the bikes, though we'd ridden enough that I could tell the difference in my endurance.

As usual, as I walked to my apartment, I looked forward to experiencing one of my great joys in life: a greeting from my beautiful children. I didn't care that as they got older, fewer and fewer of them physically met me at the front door. Tonight I just wanted to be with them. Any of them.

So it was a major disappointment when I opened the front door and found no sweet little ones there to greet me. No one at all. Not even the littlest girls, whom I could usually still count on to be excited to see me.

The apartment felt eerily quiet. Something was different. I called out, "Mary Catherine? Chrissy, Shawna?" But I got no response.

I wandered into the kitchen, expecting to find someone in there, but even that was empty. Then I heard someone shout in the living room. Actually, it sounded like several people shouting. Was it an argument? I hurried out of the kitchen, cut through the dining room, and froze at the edge of the living room.

Three of my boys—Trent, Eddie, and Ricky—were all engaged in some kind of monumental battle on our Nintendo gaming system. I watched over their shoulders for a few moments. I couldn't tell who was represented by which avatar on the screen. There was an ogre, a guy in green tights, and what looked like an elf, all fighting with crazy-looking monsters. I'd issued a partial ban on realistic shooting games when the boys were younger. As they grew older, I used the excuse that I didn't want their little sisters exposed to the violence.

These characters may not have had guns, but there was definitely violence. Still, I withheld any comments. Honestly, I was glad to see the boys all playing so well together. I raised my voice to be heard over the clamor of the battling warriors on the TV. "Hey, guys. Where is everyone?"

Immediately, Trent pressed a button and the action froze. The three boys looked up at me like they had been caught stealing cookies.

I assured them that they weren't in trouble. "I'd prefer a game that taught you something, but at least I'm not seeing any brains being splattered by a sniper here."

Ricky gave me a wide grin. "We *are* learning all kinds of things, Dad."

"Like what?"

"How to fight with swords, what magical spells work best, and most importantly, how much fun it is when the girls all go out for a while."

Trent chimed in. "And Eddie figured out how to hack the game to give us access to more powerful weapons."

Is it wrong to be proud of your son when he uses his incredible ability with computers to hack a stupid game like this? It didn't matter. I'm proud of them all.

I said, "Where are Mary Catherine and the girls?"

They said in unison, almost like they had practiced it, "Wedding stuff."

I chuckled. "What about Brian? Have you seen him?"

"Mary Catherine left some money, so he went to go pick up pizza," Eddie said. "He should be back pretty soon."

My stomach tightened when I heard that Brian had some extra cash and had volunteered to go out. I was more worried about him than I'd let on to Mary Catherine. Before I could start my interrogation about how much cash and where he'd said he was going, the front door opened and Brian walked in holding two large pizza boxes.

He looked at me and simply said, "Hey, Dad." No subterfuge, no hiding anything. He put the boxes down on the dining room table, then joined his brothers in the living room.

All four of my boys together, playing a game and getting along. No scene could have made me happier.

I decided to throw caution to the wind and took a slice of pizza into the living room, breaking one of Mary Catherine's most sacred laws: all food must be eaten at the dining room table.

I felt emboldened, but as soon as I sat at the end of the couch with a slice of mushroom and onion pizza in my hand, I considered my actions and quickly asked, "What time did Mary Catherine say they would be back?"

"The girls said they were going to grab something to eat while they were out," Trent said. "I doubt they'll be back before nine o'clock."

I relaxed and took a big bite out of the slice. I was excited to spend an evening with my boys, playing some kind of stupid video game. It was every father's dream.

"Am I allowed to join the game?" I asked.

The boys were delighted at my request. They immediately stopped the game and restarted it to add me as a player. As I basked in the unanimous acclamation, I felt like a celebrity.

Before I could start my turn, though, my phone rang, and I dug it out of my pocket. It was Detective Dan Jackson. All he said was "Looks like we have another homicide."

"Where?"

"SoHo. I'll text you the exact address."

"I'll be there as quick as I can." A tiny part of me shriveled up when I had to inform the kids I was going back to work. It hurt like hell to leave my boys. Especially with those looks on their faces.

A classic example of a cop leaving his own family to protect someone else's.

CHAPTER 56

I FOUND THE building in SoHo, one with three apartments above an Asian grocery offering certified organic produce. The kind of place young hipsters love.

A small, anxious crowd had gathered behind the yellow crime-scene tape. About a dozen people watched intently as NYPD personnel came and went from an unmarked blue door on the right side of the market. It was a mild evening with a cloudless sky. New Yorkers will do anything to get outside for a few minutes in nice weather, but I wished they would move along to a park or the waterfront instead of worrying about a serial killer.

I immediately spotted Detective Dan Jackson's broad form in the shadows next to the building's door. He looked up from where he was directing some NYPD forensic investigators and held up a hand in greeting as I walked toward him. Jackson was sufficiently imposing to stop a fight with just a look. But he also got the most out of the people he worked with. The talent that came naturally to him was a difficult skill to learn, much less to master.

After we slipped hooded biohazard suits over our street clothes and walked up a straight staircase with thick carpet that muffled our steps, Jackson pulled out his notepad. "Lila Stein, twenty-six, didn't show up for work at the county courthouse on Centre Street. She's reliably held her position as a court clerk for the past four years. One of her coworkers stopped by to check on her and got no answer at the door. The coworker called 911, and first responders entered the apartment and found the body. Seems to be in keeping with our serial killer's MO. Dispatch called patrol. They called me. I called you. And here we are on this fine evening."

"You know, Dan, I had other plans for 'this fine evening,'" I said. "They involved video games, pizza, and my teenage sons."

"I feel ya, brother. I was going to watch *Frozen* with my five-year-old twins."

I slid on my filtering mask and followed Dan Jackson through the door. I immediately saw Lila's body, lying on the linoleum floor at the edge of the kitchen, her long brown hair spread out around her head. She almost looked like she was sleeping.

She wore a bathrobe over a sheer nightgown. Blood stained the front of her garments. The stab wound indicated that a blow from a sharp instrument had struck very close to her heart. There was also a puddle of blood and fluid near the right side of her face.

Jackson said, "This scene isn't nearly as bad as the one on 30th, but like that poor vic, this one's also been stabbed in the eye. That's why I figured it was connected to our serial killer."

I glanced around the apartment, careful not to touch anything. I looked down at the victim again, realizing she had been stabbed in the right eye, like Marilyn Shaw. And this apartment was less of a hellscape than some of the others, more like the scene on Staten Island. Not much seemed to have been disturbed beyond the murder victim.

So now we had four victims who'd been stabbed in the left eye and two stabbed in the right. Was I placing too much emphasis on which side the killer chose?

I continued to walk carefully around the apartment. Jackson followed as I explained the working theory Hollis and I had come up with after our examination of the previous scenes in the other cities. About how the killer arranged objects to keep count of his victims. No matter how hard Jackson and I looked, though, we didn't find any of those markers here.

Are Hollis and I on the wrong track? What the hell does this mean?

CHAPTER 57

DANIEL OTT FOUND an internet café in Midtown Manhattan. The little spot served coffee and stale pastries at high prices in exchange for the privilege of signing on to their lightning-fast Wi-Fi. On a busy day, the place resembled a fancy communal diner, the café's three long tables crowded with as many as fifteen customers, mostly younger people with lots of piercings and tattoos.

Ott used a VPN—a virtual private network—to conceal his identity and location after logging on to the Wi-Fi. It might've been overkill, but given his internet research, Ott didn't want to risk anyone accessing his online history from this café.

He hadn't finished his research on Detective Michael Bennett. At the library, he'd found out that the Bennett children went to a Catholic school called Holy Name on the Upper West Side. Ott hacked into the faculty chat room, where the most popular topic of conversation was *Michael Bennett's getting married!*

Now, this was a pleasant surprise. Finally, a personal commitment guaranteed to take Bennett's mind off the case. Ott took a few handwritten notes rather than risk saving any of the hacked links to his computer. He had no real plan just yet. But he trusted one would come.

Just as Ott reached for his overpriced, bitter coffee, a muscular young man in a black T-shirt and baggy black pants turned to him. Ott tried to decipher the tattoos curling around the man's neck and up his face but couldn't tell what any of them meant.

The tattooed man said, "Yo, dude, nice computer. Why don't you let us use it for a little bit?"

One of the man's tablemates, a scrawny young guy about six feet tall, added, "I promise we'll only keep it for a couple of days." The three girls they were with all laughed at his wit.

Ott didn't think this was funny at all. He hated men like this, almost as much as he hated arrogant American women. He decided the best course of action was to ignore them, and purposely focused his attention back on the screen of his tricked-out Lenovo laptop.

The tattooed man wouldn't leave it alone. He stepped in close to Ott. "I was trying to be nice. Let it seem like you were being generous by giving us your computer. Now I'm just going to take it." He reached for the laptop.

As he did, Ott casually drove the point of his steel tactical pen straight through the middle of the man's hand, pinning it to the wooden table. The tattooed man's eyes popped wide and he gasped.

Ott said in a low voice, "Shout or do anything stupid and this pen goes into your throat. Do you understand?"

The man barely nodded. He was so scared he couldn't even

reach across to pull the pen out of his hand. Ott did it for him with one quick jerk. A tiny spout of blood shot into the air and landed back on the man's hand.

Ott said, "Usually my lessons in manners are more severe and intensive. Did this one do the trick? Are you going to bother people you don't know anymore?"

The tattooed man shook his head.

Ott pulled a wad of napkins off the short stack directly in front of him. He handed it to the man, who wrapped it around his hand. Ott calmly used another napkin to wipe up the blood on the table.

Ott said, "Gather your friends quietly and leave. Right now. If I have to deal with you again, you're going to lose an eye. Understand?"

The man nodded again and did just as he was told. He turned to his friends, cleared his throat, and said, "Let's go."

One of the girls said, "I'm not done yet."

The tattooed man snatched her coffee off the table and they all followed him out the door.

Daniel Ott felt very satisfied with himself.

CHAPTER 58

TO A COP in the middle of a serial killer investigation, sleep is a precious commodity. Which is why I felt frustrated when I sensed a movement near my feet that dragged me out of my dream. I mumbled Mary Catherine's name. Then I heard a man's voice. *What the hell?*

I sprang up, completely disoriented. I wasn't in my bed. I wasn't even in my bedroom. I shook my head, then rubbed my eyes. I felt like a toddler waking up from a nap, unsure of where I was.

Finally, I realized I was lying on the couch in our living room. Remnants of the boys' game night were still evident. Extra chairs were pulled around the Nintendo system, which was still hooked to the TV, and two empty pizza boxes sat neatly stacked on the floor, waiting to be recycled.

I looked to the foot of the couch and realized it was Brian who'd brushed my feet as he gathered up some papers and stuffed them into his backpack.

Brian said in a quiet voice, "It's just me, Dad. My phone was stuck in the couch and I needed some of these papers. Sorry." He stood up and slipped on the backpack. "Why are you sleeping on the couch? Did you have a fight with Mary Catherine?"

I shook my head, actually had to think before I answered, as if I'd been drinking the night before and everything was confused. "I got in late, didn't want to wake her, and the next thing I knew you were here." I looked at the blinds and saw slants of sunshine pushing through the slats. "What time is it?"

"About six thirty in the morning. I think everyone else is still asleep. They've all been really quiet."

That quiet was shattered a few moments later as my other sons all came tumbling out of their rooms. I looked at Brian and said, "Thanks for the gentle wake-up, as opposed to the cymbal clash of our very own Bennett family percussion section."

I stood up and realized I was even still wearing my shoes from the night before. My body was stiff, and I tried to shake out my shoulders. I felt like I was doing a walk of shame when I shambled into the dining room. The girls all smiled. Chrissy jumped up and gave me a hug.

Mary Catherine said in a flat voice, "You need more sleep."

I wanted to say, *No shit.* Instead, I just nodded.

Mary Catherine was serious. "The wedding is sooner than you think. I don't want you making yourself sick from not eating or sleeping right." She walked across the kitchen into the dining room, then kissed me gently on the forehead. "The boys told me you got called out again last night. Did you get a break on the serial killer?"

I shook my head and mumbled, "Just another body."

Mary Catherine spoke up so everyone could hear her. "That's why I instituted a no news policy in this house. There's nothing else on the news these days but the murders. CNN is even starting to cover them." She looked at the bright faces around the dining room table and said, "Does everyone understand?"

There were nods and mumbling as Mary Catherine returned to the kitchen. Not watching the news wasn't a particular hardship on my kids. I plopped into the chair at the end of the table and just listened to the simple chatter between the kids. It was nice to get a sense of what was going on with my family.

Jane looked at her phone and frowned. "Allan didn't text me good night."

Juliana teased her sister. "Give it a rest, Jane. We all know you have a boyfriend."

Fiona added, "And we know he's cute."

Bridget chimed in. "And he plays on the lacrosse team."

Jane knew they were winding her up but couldn't help throwing in "*Captain* of the lacrosse team."

Mary Catherine came back out of the kitchen. "That's enough, girls. Leave your sister alone."

I closed my eyes for a moment and immediately felt myself start to doze off. Instead, I stood up again. "Gotta shower and get back into the office. Lots to do." I clapped my hands together as if I was excited about the prospect.

Mary Catherine gave me a stern look. "You can't sleep for a couple more hours?"

"Afraid not."

"This case won't affect our wedding, will it?"

"No way."

She seemed dubious.

I added, "I promise."

Mary Catherine knew I wouldn't break a promise.

CHAPTER 59

I'D LIKE TO say I was more than ready to face another day when I sat down at my desk in the Manhattan North Homicide office. But that would be a lie. Almost as soon as I sat in my new rolling leather chair—Mary Catherine had ordered it from Office Depot after I complained one too many times about city-issued furniture aggravating my aching back—all I wanted to do was put my head down on the desk and go back to sleep. But a twenty-minute nap would do nothing for me. What I really needed was a two-week nap to get back to normal.

To make matters worse, Brett Hollis seemed to be in a very chipper and pleasant mood. He was wearing an even smaller bandage strip across his nose, humming the theme song to *Game of Thrones* as he reviewed tips that had come in overnight.

I sighed as I looked down at the crime-scene photos from the homicide in SoHo, very impressed that Dan Jackson had already gotten someone to print the images and leave a duplicate set on my desk. It was that kind of cooperative attitude that made the NYPD so effective at solving homicides.

Hollis stepped behind my chair and looked over my shoulder at the photographs. "What did you think of the latest scene?"

"It was most similar to the Staten Island crime scene. Definitely a homicide by a sharp implement of some kind, and the killer stabbed the victim's eye—but her right one, *not* her left. And there was blood around the body, but not spread on the apartment walls. No idea yet if any of the blood came from a second sample either."

"Did you find any rearrangement of the victim's collectibles, any sort of counting message?"

"Nothing at all."

Hollis patted me on the back. "It's all going to work out. You keep saying if we all do our jobs we'll catch this guy. We're all doing our jobs now. I'm going to run down a couple of leads from the tip line in an hour or so. That's *my* job."

I let out a chuckle. He was a good kid. Hollis gave me a wave as he walked toward the conference room.

I looked down at my notes from all the homicides in every city we'd identified and then at the new crime-scene photos from Lila Stein's apartment.

I said a quick prayer for her soul. It was probably the fifth time I had prayed for her since last night.

I craned my neck to glance across the wide squad bay, past a dozen desks with empty chairs. Brett Hollis stood in the conference room, organizing the leads with Task Force Halo. I noticed that Hollis was dressing sharper on the days he worked with the task force. Today he wore a nice Arrow dress shirt with a subtle blue tie. He looked good. I was impressed.

Harry Grissom wanted to recruit the best and brightest into his homicide unit, and as I had already told my boss, Hollis was a keeper. He had that little something extra. He could deal with people. He wrote good reports. And he didn't seem to get overwhelmed by assignments that were outside the box. This was part of what I, like a football scout, was supposed to do in my role as a senior detective: Identify needs and then find the right personnel to fill them. Keep management in the loop.

I couldn't suppress a cringe when I noticed the door to the squad bay open and John Macy stalking through the office. That couldn't be good, though since news of another homicide had broken, I'd expected to see him at some point.

He glanced in my direction but ignored me completely.

He marched past me and into the conference room like a member of command staff. I looked over and saw Hollis, whose expression quickly shifted from pleasant to annoyed and then to angry. He gave me a look I had to interpret through the conference room glass. It was definitely something along the lines of *Please come in here.*

Which was just about the last thing I wanted to do. If I never had to interact with John Macy again, I'd consider the rest of my career a success. But I couldn't leave my partner alone. Especially not when he had made it clear he needed support.

I only hoped not to embarrass Harry again.

CHAPTER 60

I STOOD UP, straightened my shirt, and walked to the conference room with purpose. As soon as I opened the door, I heard Brett Hollis say, "Ask him yourself," as he cut his eyes to me.

I looked at John Macy and said, "What can I do for you?" It was as professional and direct as I could manage.

Macy fumed and did little to hide his annoyance at having to acknowledge I was a living, breathing person. Finally, he stood tall and puffed out his chest a bit. He said, "I need details on the latest homicide in SoHo from our man."

I had to think about how to respond. After a moment, I shrugged and said, "There are certain aspects of the murder that make it appear to be the work of the same killer as in our other cases. However, there are also several details that don't match up. We're going to have to wait for forensic reports to come back before we can say anything definitive. And even then, we're still dealing with a killer who's proven adept at not leaving behind any identifying evidence at crime scenes."

Macy shook his head in disgust. "Typical."

"Typical of what?" My voice was taking on a sharper tone already. "Typical of the cop who doesn't want to be skewered for rushing to judgment? You're not a fellow cop I can discuss theories with. You're a politician. I don't trust you not to run off and tell the mayor about a theory I later discover was mistaken. So all I can do is tell you the facts as I know them."

Macy folded his arms in front of him and cranked his condescending tone up to say, "What if you took a guess? Something no one can hold you responsible for." He deliberately slowed down and over-enunciated each of his next words. "Do you think that this homicide is the work of the same killer?"

I looked at Hollis, took a deep breath, and said, "No. I don't think it's the same killer." There, it was out in the open.

For a moment, Macy just stared at me. Then he argued, "I read the initial memo. The victim was fatally slashed and then stabbed in the eye. It *has* to be our killer."

"Wrong," I shot back. "It doesn't *have* to be anything. Look, you asked for my opinion and I gave it. Overall, that whole crime scene just doesn't feel like the work of our killer."

Macy was incredulous. "Now crime scenes have emotions?"

"Credit me with some experience."

Macy nodded his head reluctantly. Arms still folded across his chest.

I continued. "Crime scenes usually show the underlying personality of the killer, especially when we're dealing with serial killers."

Hollis chimed in. "That's correct. My research has shown that a particular killer's MO is often reflected in the scene he leaves behind. Some killers rush, and others take their time. Some killers have serious OCD and the compulsions are reflected in their murder scenes. Maybe the victim's body has to be laid out in a certain way, or the wounds must be inflicted at exactly the same angle every time."

I picked the thread of the conversation back up. "And in this case, while the crime scenes in SoHo and Staten Island seem similar to each other, they don't really seem like any of the others. The differences are significant enough that we can't discount the possibility that they are the work of a second killer."

Macy said, "Are you shitting me? Now you're saying not only that you don't think this most recent murder is part of the pattern but that you don't even think the Staten Island murder is related?" A vein on his forehead started to throb. "A second-killer theory is not going to fly. Do you have any idea what kind of panic that will cause?"

I didn't know what more to say. "Just giving you my experienced opinion. Obviously you're going to have one of your own."

"This is no time for a standoff, Bennett," Macy said. "We need results. Go get some. Now."

With that statement of the obvious, Macy was out the door.

Hollis was next. He sighed and wiped his face. "That was a serious dick-waving contest," he said. "I gotta get out of here for a few minutes. I'm running down those leads I mentioned. All of them are fairly close by and shouldn't take me too long."

"I'll go with you."

Hollis shook his head. "I got this. I can handle a simple lead or two." He winked and patted me on the shoulder, leaving me in charge of the Task Force Halo headquarters.

Four victims—six, if I was wrong about the second killer—and zero suspects. The numbers didn't look good.

CHAPTER 61

DANIEL OTT FOUND himself in the Manhattanville neighborhood of West Harlem, standing outside the building that housed Michael Bennett's Manhattan North Homicide unit. He stood next to a steel support for the elevated train that ran directly across the street from the building.

There were cars parked under the track for blocks in each direction. Many of them looked like police vehicles. A lot of Ford Crown Victorias and Chevy Impalas. He supposed that was one of the main perks of working this far uptown: parking. Apparently free parking. Something that was pretty much lacking everywhere else on the island of Manhattan.

Ott had handled quite a lot of surveillance over the years. With the exception of his first, spontaneous kill and the librarian's unexpected friend—his loose end's loose end—he always researched his victims' movements and habits. But none of them had ever had the slightest idea that Ott was watching them. None of that was as serious as what he was doing now, surveilling a police officer.

He stared across the street at the entrance to the office building. There was a furniture truck in the midst of a delivery. The crew had set several temporary ramps next to curbs so they could roll all kinds of office equipment into the building. There were three stacks of chairs on specialized dollies, each stack more than six feet tall. On separate dollies rested two desks, turned on their sides so that they too rose almost six feet in the air. Everything on the sidewalk was some sort of obstruction.

Great.

Daniel Ott didn't want to be here, watching the building. He was supposed to be at work in Queens, though really, he was ready to get home. He wanted to see his girls. But Bennett was getting too close to identifying him. And he had to admit he did feel a twinge of excitement as he bounced several plans through his head. What could he do to disrupt the investigation, starting right now?

As he watched, he spotted the young detective he'd seen with Bennett at the library, the one with the broken nose, stroll out the front of the building. Today the man wore a blue shirt and tie, and was walking with a woman in a bright yellow skirt. Ott could tell by their body language that the two young people were attracted to each other.

They stopped on the sidewalk near all the office furniture. They stood right on the curb as a bus whizzed past them, yet they barely noticed. The detective said something and smiled. The young woman laughed and placed her hand on his arm.

Another bus rolled past. Ott lost sight of the couple for a few seconds. Then an idea popped into his head.

He crossed the street quickly. He had to balance patience with speed. He wove through the office furniture deliveries, using them as cover to obscure his approach, though they also blocked his vision. Each time the couple shifted position as they continued their animated conversation, Ott lost sight of them.

Ott pulled from his pocket a pair of rubber surgical gloves and, with his gloved right hand, extracted his Gerber folding knife and opened the blade.

Then he heard the hiss of air brakes and a diesel engine. Another of the fast-moving buses coming this way. Ott couldn't believe the timing. He closed the knife and stepped over one of the small ramps lying on the sidewalk. He took a moment behind one of the chair stacks to calculate how fast the bus was moving. The big diesel unit looked to be gaining speed quickly.

All Ott had to do was knock the detective into the middle of the street, where the bus would have no choice but to make him a headline in tomorrow's paper.

The time was now. Ott stepped quickly from behind the stack of chairs, his head down and his legs driving. But he lost his bearings slightly when sidestepping a ramp, and realized that instead of the detective, he was about to run into the woman in the yellow skirt.

Ott tried to redirect or slow his charge, but it was too late. His shoulder connected with the woman's midsection and she let out a loud gasp as he knocked the wind out of her. The woman staggered from the blow and stepped awkwardly from the curb onto the asphalt.

Ott had screwed up. There was no other way to view it. He just stood there, frozen.

Then, unexpectedly, the young detective darted off the

sidewalk and jumped into the street, pushing the woman out of the path of the bus.

The bus driver stomped on the brakes. The big vehicle skidded sideways.

The detective barely had time to look up as the flat nose of the bus struck him squarely, sending his body flying a good fifteen feet, arms and legs flailing as if taking flight…before hitting the ground with a tumbling thud. The bus managed to stop about five feet from the spot where the young man's body now lay in the middle of the street.

The detective's left leg was bent at a sickening angle. His right arm flopped behind his back.

Ott didn't wait to see anything more. He casually turned and walked away from the bus. He didn't rush—remembering how his mistake in the library had gotten him spotted by Bennett—but he didn't waste time either.

He was more than two blocks away when he heard the first siren rushing to the scene.

CHAPTER 62

IT'S NOT EXACTLY unusual for cops to get hurt—
or worse—on the job, so this was hardly my first time at the
Columbia University Medical Center. But getting exiled from
the emergency room and sent to the waiting room was new.

I had raced downstairs from our offices as soon as I'd heard
the sickening sound of the bus hitting something, then skidding
to a stop. Not that I'd expected to find my partner, of all people,
flat on the ground in the middle of the road, limbs akimbo.

I rode in the ambulance with Brett Hollis and had been
raising hell to make sure he got the best care. Though maybe I
raised a little too much hell, actually, since an Asian American
doctor told me that if I didn't get out of the ER, she'd cut the
tendons in the back of my leg. I didn't believe her completely,
but then again, I wasn't going to bet my mobility on it.

The waiting room seemed especially crowded. Mainly with

patients, but there was also a large contingent of NYPD people in one corner, including a couple of eyewitnesses to Hollis's injury who were saying the incident was no accident. I would need to interview them later.

I saw Harry Grissom talking to a twenty-something woman in a vibrant yellow skirt, whom I vaguely recognized as someone who worked on one of the lower floors in our building.

I also spotted a woman who appeared to be in her mid fifties sitting on the outskirts of the NYPD crowd. She had dark hair and was using a Kleenex to wipe her eyes. She looked familiar, and I realized I recognized her from the family photographs Hollis kept on his desk.

I stepped over to her and said, "Excuse me. I'm Michael Bennett. Are you related to Brett Hollis?"

The woman looked up at me, nodding, and said, "Ann Hollis, Brett's mom. He's told me all about you." She clearly didn't want to say too much for fear of breaking down.

I sat in the empty chair next to her. "I'm so sorry about Brett. I rode in the ambulance here with him, but he was only conscious enough to hold on to my hand."

"The ER doctor gave me a list of his injuries, but I haven't heard anything more. Have you?"

"She didn't even tell me that much, but I'm only his NYPD partner. You're his next of kin."

A tear ran down her left cheek as she looked at me and said, "It's about what you expect from this kind of accident. Shattered pelvis, broken leg, broken arm, concussion. Plus he cracked a front tooth and broke his nose again."

She seemed on the edge of a meltdown. I understood. I would have already melted if this had happened to one of my kids.

She started to sob, and I put my arm around her. Most veteran cops have done some time in a waiting room, comforting the loved ones of fellow cops who'd been injured on the job.

As I sat there, holding my partner's mother, my mind drifted. First, to Hollis's injuries, and his chances of recovery. Yet with the pressure from the mayor's office mounting, it was hard not to make a mental to-do list of next steps in the investigation. Even as a woman literally cried on my shoulder.

Harry caught my eye, and I excused myself from Mrs. Hollis. The lieutenant led me into the hallway, away from the commotion of the waiting room.

Harry nodded over at the woman he'd been talking to earlier, who was now also dabbing her eyes with a Kleenex. "The young lady in yellow over there, Kelly Konick, tells me that Hollis jumped into the road to save her when she was knocked into the street, and he got hit instead."

I was not surprised to hear that Hollis had been injured in an act of bravery. He had already impressed me, and I'd told Grissom as much, but his actions today were in line with the best of the NYPD.

"Ms. Konick says she thinks someone pushed her. Intentionally. But she didn't get a good look at who it was." Harry paused. "It's all speculation right now. But do you think this might've had anything to do with your case?"

I thought about it for a minute and said, "I have no idea. But if it *was* related to us, why would the guy push her and not Hollis?"

I couldn't help but wonder if it was a simple accident. Were we being paranoid? I thought back to the man I saw rushing from the computer room in the library, the strong feeling I'd had that he might be the killer. He had evaded detection that day, but he may have changed course. Instead of trying to outrun the investigation, maybe he was attempting to derail it. But that was crazy talk.

Wasn't it?

CHAPTER 63

BY THE TIME I left the hospital, I was emotionally spent. I'd stayed with Brett Hollis's mother while her son was in surgery. Mrs. Hollis had told me what a good soccer player and student he'd been in school. She dropped in that the only thing he'd ever wanted to do was be a detective. Even after graduating from NYU and getting job offers in the private sector for more money, her Brett wanted to feel like he was contributing.

By the late afternoon, a surgeon who hadn't bothered to change her bloody blue scrubs found Mrs. Hollis in the waiting room. I stayed with her to hear the news.

The doctor had sharp, clear eyes that focused solely on Mrs. Hollis. She said, "We've done everything we can do for today. We stopped all the internal bleeding and set some of the simple breaks. Tonight, an orthopedic surgeon will set his pelvis and left leg. And his nose is going to need plastic surgery. You can go up and visit him in a few minutes, but don't expect much in the way of conversation."

I appreciated the doctor's direct, comprehensive delivery. Hollis's mother and I walked up to the recovery room together. My partner, prone on his hospital bed, looked wrecked. He'd live, thank God, but he was facing a brutal recovery. I stood with Mrs. Hollis for a few minutes while she navigated the tubes and machines, held her son's hand, and spoke to him quietly.

I said a few silent prayers over him, then eventually slipped out to return home to my own family, where I spent that evening laughing and playing games with Mary Catherine and my children, grateful for every minute of it. But even through my happiness, an unease took hold in the back of my mind, and it only intensified overnight.

I woke up troubled, staring at the white ceiling as Mary Catherine snored peacefully next to me. The familiar sound was calming.

The first rays of sunlight crept through the blinds, and then stark reality flooded in.

We had a copycat killer on our hands.

It was the only explanation. This killer had at least two victims. Maybe more. There could be more bodies that hadn't been discovered yet.

I managed to get up, dressed, and out the door without waking anyone else. Which in my apartment is a real accomplishment, no matter what time you attempt it.

I was at my desk, going over everything I had on the Staten Island and SoHo homicides, when Harry Grissom walked into the office.

He stopped and looked at me. Then he checked his watch. "What the hell are you doing here so early?"

"Me? What about you? I thought elderly people needed as much sleep as they could get."

"Funny. I wonder how hard you'd be laughing if I had you organize all the files according to suspect description and number of reports written."

I patted the wooden chair next to my desk. He took a seat cautiously. Then, without pretext, I explained my copycat killer theory.

I pulled out the photos of the two victims from Staten Island and SoHo, Marilyn Shaw and Lila Stein. I set them on the desktop so Harry could see them clearly. "We have to be sure."

Harry shook his head. "I never have to worry about much. You take on enough for both of us."

CHAPTER 64

I DIDN'T WASTE much more time around the office. I was in my car, headed to Staten Island, just as the morning rush hour was picking up.

Detective Raina Rayesh was on the scene of a shooting in the Elm Park area and couldn't meet me at Marilyn Shaw's apartment, but she gave me her blessing to do a follow-up. I appreciated it. In police work, you never want to do anything that gives the appearance of trying to steal someone else's case. So if a colleague gives permission for a follow-up, it signals complete trust.

I was standing outside the apartment, trying to get a feel for what the killer might have seen when looking at the building. As I stood there, a tall Hispanic man stepped out of the main door and walked right up to me. "Can I help you, Detective?" he said with a light accent.

I gave the man a bemused look. "How'd you know I was NYPD?"

"Since that poor girl was killed, most all of the people coming around here are detectives or media types, or rubbernecker creeps. Besides, you look like a cop. And you're driving an Impala."

I laughed. The friendly man turned out to be the building super, and he gave me a tour of the building before we went to Marilyn's apartment.

We stepped around the crime-scene tape, and as the super opened the door, he said, "Nothing's been touched. Once the investigation wraps, I don't know how I'll ever rent this apartment again. Landlords are supposed to tell potential tenants if a violent crime happened in an apartment. It's a tough sales pitch."

"Can't argue that," I said.

"I get it, of course. And God knows I'm not the only one struggling with that these days," the super said ruefully, raising his eyebrows in acknowledgment of the recent murders all across the city.

He told me to pull the door shut when I was done, and I thanked him, then suddenly found myself alone in the apartment. Once again, I noticed the relative tidiness of the scene, especially compared to Chloe's and Elaine's apartments—no blood smeared on the walls, nothing really excessive aside from a significantly sized rusty-brown stain on the hardwood, about six feet from the door.

Such death markers always saddened me—the loss they represented, the people who would miss out on the rest of their lives. If I ever stopped feeling that way, I'd retire. The desire to obtain justice for these victims is what gets homicide detectives like me out of bed in the morning. Unfortunately, it's also what keeps homicide detectives like me awake at night.

I checked the apartment thoroughly but didn't see anything that looked like it could be one of the *counting messages* Hollis and I were sure our killer had left at the other scenes. Marilyn Shaw would have been the fifth victim in New York, after Elaine. The super said nothing in the apartment had been touched, and I believed him, so I couldn't attribute it to anything having been accidentally disturbed either.

I wandered over to inspect a huge array of framed photographs sitting on a shelf along one wall of the living room, all in artistically jumbled rows, with no obvious gaps visible. Marilyn Shaw appeared to have been a very pretty brunette who was present in most of the pictures, along with people I guessed were her parents, her friends, her siblings, and presumably a bunch of nephews. She looked like someone with no worries. These are the kinds of photos that make a homicide detective even more determined.

One photo in the back caught my attention. It was of Marilyn wearing a New York Giants jersey, standing in a sports bar with a TV playing a baseball game directly behind her. A light-haired man was standing next to her, his arms wrapped around her and his smiling face half hidden by her shoulder.

I was surprised to recognize the bar—a place far from Staten Island, much closer to my place on the Upper West Side. It was a spot near Morningside Park on Manhattan Avenue. I used to take my kids there. They had decent food, but the real draw was their collection of old-fashioned games like Skee-Ball and pinball, which the kids loved.

I pulled out my smartphone and took a picture of Marilyn's photo for my records. Who was the man with her in the picture? Why had this photo meant enough for her to print and frame it?

Something told me this could be important.

CHAPTER 65

I DROVE DIRECTLY from the crime scene on Staten Island to Lila Stein's apartment in SoHo. I'd called ahead, and Detective Dan Jackson was waiting in front of the Asian grocery store as I pulled up. The big detective was chatting amiably with a shorter man, the store owner.

Jackson introduced us. The man's name was Tom, and he was a second-generation Chinese American with a little bit of a New Jersey accent he joked he'd picked up while in college at Rutgers. Tom was also the apartment manager, so he gave us a key. As on Staten Island, this apartment was still an active crime scene so had not been touched.

"You really think there's a copycat?" Jackson asked me as we climbed the stairs.

"I wouldn't be here talking to you if I didn't."

We ducked the crime-scene tape and entered the apartment.

I went straight to the long library table in the main space that held Lila Stein's personal mementos: a glass plaque she'd received for being court clerk of the year; a ceramic dog that looked like a niece or nephew had made it; and half a dozen framed photographs.

As at Marilyn's apartment, I could find no evidence that any of Lila's possessions had been grouped in any sort of deliberate way by her killer. I looked over the photographs on the table. I saw Lila and her parents, the older couple standing proudly on either side of their pretty daughter. Lila and her sorority sisters, all cheering for something together. Lila and the Eiffel Tower, the Grand Canyon, at the beach—all trips she'd taken. But when I spotted another photo in the back, I thought I was suffering déjà vu. I reached back and picked it up, immediately recognizing the background—*and* the man standing beside Lila, again with his arms around her, but turned in profile.

Jackson said, "Of all the photos, what's so special about that one?"

I pointed at the photo, running my finger along the upper edge. "See all the NFL logos around the mirror? I know this place," I said, explaining that it was a restaurant/sports bar uptown where I took my kids to play games. I took a photo of Lila's picture, just as I had the one on Staten Island, then set the frame back down.

Jackson said, "You think it means something?"

"I'm working on a theory." I didn't fill Jackson in just yet, or tell him about the other photo I'd found at Marilyn's place. I told him I might call him later.

Jackson slapped me on the back and said, "There's nothing I would rather do on my twins' birthday than follow you around on interviews. I'll leave my phone on."

CHAPTER 66

I WASTED NO time speeding uptown. Neither photograph seemed to have been taken very long ago. Maybe someone at the bar would remember seeing the same man there with two different women. You never knew until you asked.

I parked on the street. It was a little before noon, so when I went through the open door, the place was so empty I thought they might still be ‘closed. Then the portly manager, whom I used to see all the time, wobbled into view from the kitchen.

He looked at me for a moment, then recognition dawned on him. A broad smile swept across his face. "Here by your-self? Where are all those beautiful kids of yours? I'm lucky I didn't go bankrupt when you stopped coming by." He let out a good cackle.

I approached him and stuck out my hand. As we shook, I said, "We'd still be coming, but you know how it goes—as they get older, there are more and more school and sports events we've got to go to."

The manager grinned. "Maybe I can lure you back with a good hamburger for lunch."

I started to shake my head.

The manager said, "Some homemade lemon chicken salad?"

"I'm actually not here to eat. You remember I'm with the NYPD, right?"

He nodded carefully. The kind of nod cops get from people who think they might be suspects and start doing a mental rewind of their recent past. That kind of self-censoring slows down investigations.

I eased his mind. "I'm looking into a pair of homicides. The one thing they had in common was a photograph taken at this bar." I showed him both photos on my phone. "The same man appears in both of them, though it's hard to get a good look at his face."

The chubby man studied the photos carefully, then looked over his shoulder to confirm exactly where in the bar they'd been taken. He wasted no time in leading me over to a hallway that featured a couple of Pop-A-Shot games. "Here's where one photo was taken. I can tell by the TV in the back. The other was obviously taken near the bar. You can see the mirror and all of our NFL gear."

"Do you think we could figure out *when* these photos were taken?"

"I dunno…maybe you can figure out the date of the game going on behind the girl? I can see it's the Yankees and the Red Sox."

I sat at the bar, checked a few websites, and made a few calls.

I was able to figure out the six dates when the Yankees and Red Sox had played recently. All of the games had broadcast on the same channel here, and all had started at 7 p.m. And all the dates were within the last two months. I was onto something.

Lunchtime business in the bar picked up while I was busy on the phone. To his credit, the manager kept himself free to help me if I needed it. We searched through the security videos he had on hand. Of the six dates, he still had security videos from four of the nights.

He set me up in his rear office with a computer. He even brought me a Coke and a sandwich. We both figured I was going to be here awhile.

I started watching the first security video, and fast-forwarded to 7 p.m. I couldn't believe my luck—I struck pay dirt within two minutes. I was easily able to identify Marilyn Shaw from her photograph, and barely another minute of searching turned up the man who appeared in both Lila's and Marilyn's photos. He was a tall white man with sandy hair and an athletic build, and looked to be in his mid to late thirties.

I tried to get a feel for their relationship. They held hands and laughed together, and while the video wasn't perfect, I was at least able to pull some full-face stills of the mystery man off of it and run them through the state photo-ID database.

Then fate stepped in.

CHAPTER 67

AS A PHILOSOPHY major, I've read dozens of quotes about fate. How it favors one person over another. Some sayings assert that fate favors the prepared. Or the determined. Or the virtuous. But often it simply favors the lucky. There's no other way to explain it. And every homicide detective in the world will admit to having a number of cases solved by lucky breaks.

I'd just gotten back to my car when my phone rang. The number was an NYPD exchange, and it turned out to be main dispatch sending through a call from a uniformed patrol officer named Janelle Gibbs.

Officer Gibbs said, "Detective Bennett, I'm sorry to bother you, but I just heard something odd at a domestic and I thought I should pass it along to you."

"It's no bother. Whatcha got?"

"I'm in Brooklyn, in Cobble Hill, at a nice brownstone. Like I said, I got called to this domestic. The husband left and the wife is really, really pissed off."

"I'm listening."

"She confronted her husband about some burner phones she found in the house. He threatened her and stormed out. But the wife's no dummy. She knew they were phones he used for girlfriends." Officer Gibbs sounded sharp. "Anyway, she found out one of the girlfriends' names, and when she told it to me, I recognized it as being the same as one of the victims murdered by that serial killer you're investigating."

"What was the victim's name?"

"Marilyn Shaw."

I felt a rush of excitement. *Can this be the mystery man from Marilyn's—and Lila's—photo?*

"I'll be right there. Don't leave and don't give any info to the wife."

"No problem. I told her I'd be writing reports in my car for a little bit. She's busy with a toddler anyway."

Officer Gibbs gave me the address and I was on my way, yet another trek from one end of the city to the other. I was starting to feel like an Uber driver. In this case, I caught a lucky break and found the FDR open all the way down to the Brooklyn Bridge.

Officer Gibbs was a tall, attractive black woman who seemed way too young to be a cop. Or maybe I was just getting older. I could tell by the look on her face that Gibbs was shocked I'd gotten to the brownstone in Cobble Hill so quickly after her call.

But she had her shit together. She had the info all ready and laid out for me as I walked up.

"The wife is inside with the kid. I haven't reached out to the husband," Officer Gibbs said as she concluded her report.

"You've done a tremendous job. Do you mind coming up to the house with me? Sounds like you and the wife already have a rapport. I don't want to intimidate her."

As we climbed the stairs to the top of the stoop, a woman with messy brown hair stepped out of the open front door with a little boy in her arms.

"Mrs. Cedar, this is Detective Bennett," Officer Gibbs said.

"Please, call me Lauren," the woman said. She hefted the toddler on her hip. "And this is Tyler."

Tyler had blond hair and big, beautiful brown eyes. He smiled, then giggled when I tickled his bare feet.

"Come on inside," Lauren told us.

As soon as I stepped into the living room and looked at the photos lined up on the small fireplace mantel, I had the confirmation I needed, that Lauren Cedar's husband was definitely the same man from the sports bar.

I talked to her for a minute more but didn't want to give out too much information. She was still shaken.

Lauren sniffled, recounting for me the outburst from her husband that had prompted the call to the police. It had started when she found a couple of burner cell phones and confronted him with them, accusing him of cheating on her. Instead of denying it, he'd gone on the offensive, yelling and throwing things around.

She said, "I told him he was being too loud and that he was scaring Tyler. That he was even scaring *me*. You know what he said?"

I shook my head.

"He said that Tyler and I *should* be terrified of him. Then he grabbed my arm and jerked me back into the kitchen." She pulled up the sleeve of her blouse and showed me her right arm, where a perfect imprint of a large hand was already turning into a bluish bruise.

I asked a few more questions and wrote down the information she gave me.

Her husband, Jeffrey Cedar, was an attorney in lower Manhattan, and according to his wife, he was a lying piece of shit.

Which certainly seemed true.

But I was growing more and more convinced that this lying piece of shit might actually be a killer.

My only real question was whether he'd killed them all.

CHAPTER 68

JEFFREY CEDAR SAT in his law office not far from the criminal courthouse in lower Manhattan. He was finding it difficult to concentrate on the client sitting across from him. He'd had an argument with his wife that morning after she questioned where he went at night when he said he was working. Then she accused him of cheating on her. She'd found a couple of the burner phones he often used to stay in touch with the different women he met. He always took care to bring these women to places far from Cobble Hill or lower Manhattan—anywhere, really, as long as it wasn't the kind of spot his wife would ever have any interest in going.

But this morning, no matter what he said or how loud he said it, his wife just wasn't buying it. She seemed to be spinning off the rails, she was so upset. He even had to grab her arms and hold her still just to get her to listen to him. That, added to the sound of his son wailing, had started his day off on a sour note. And it didn't feel like it was getting any better.

Once, about three years ago, Jeffrey had smacked Lauren in the face after she refused to stop nagging him. The blow had left a mark on her cheek for over a week, and he'd had to keep her at home for fear of getting arrested for domestic abuse. Even worse, she'd been pregnant with Tyler at the time. But he'd learned from his mistake. Now he was always careful. Subtle. Never did anything that would show up on his wife's face.

Jeffrey returned his focus to the client sitting at his desk. He twirled his pen in his left hand as he listened to the young man across from him explain that he wasn't actually "dealing" drugs so much as he was "redistributing" them for someone else.

Jeffrey felt like his degree from Syracuse put him a notch above a lot of the other bottom-feeders in the criminal justice system. He did admit to some jealousy at the NYU and Columbia grads working at the big firms. But he'd found his niche and was doing fine on his own. He usually wouldn't even take on a low-end dealer client like this kid, except that said kid's parents had plenty of cash and had thrown a big chunk of it at Jeffrey to clear their son of the drug charges against him.

He tuned in to hear some of what his client was droning on and on about. "The damn cops took my entire stash. All of it. I couldn't believe what dicks they were."

"It sounds like we're going to have to cut a deal, Jason," Jeffrey told him. "It's too hard to explain why you were holding so much heroin and four thousand dollars in cash."

"All I was doing was helping someone out. They needed this stuff delivered. I didn't negotiate with no one. I didn't force no one. All I did was deliver."

"And now, unfortunately, that solid work ethic is going to have to be put on hold for one to five years."

Jeffrey wrapped up that meeting with his disgruntled client and, a few hours later, found himself listening to another douchebag talk about how he had been railroaded. He felt like he'd been listening to this particular pitiful client all day, though they'd been meeting for only about forty minutes.

The client insisted on sticking to the story that his eight-year-old niece was making a wild and unsubstantiated accusation against him. He was outraged that the police had arrested him on the word of a child. He never brought up the fact that forensics had found semen on one of the girl's dresses and that two different psychological assessments had determined the niece was rational and telling the truth.

Jeffrey put on a show for the client, who was already paying an exorbitant rate for his services. "I think we can work this out. It's going to take some extra time on my part. And I'm afraid I can't make any absolute promises. I will, however, need a much larger retainer to pursue the case the way I think it should be pursued."

Without a word, the douchebag client reached into the front pocket of his baggy pants and pulled out a checkbook. Jeffrey had already run the guy's credit score and talked to him about what assets could be open to a civil judgment if his wife's sister's family sued him. Using that as a cover story, he'd learned the guy had more than three hundred thousand dollars in a 401(k) plan and another thirty-five thousand dollars in liquid investments. The only real calculation Jeffrey made was how much he could ask for without scaring the client off. It was almost like betting on a hand in Texas hold 'em poker. If you raised too much, the suckers at the table tended to fold.

When he saw the hesitation on his client's face, Jeffrey said, "I can almost guarantee, no matter what happens, you won't do any jail time. I can point out your record of employment, no previous convictions, and I assume you will be able to get character witnesses to speak on your behalf."

The client nodded solemnly, his long brown hair flopping in front of his face.

Damn, Jeffrey Cedar thought, *this bluff is almost too easy.*

CHAPTER 69

ONCE AGAIN, I was back in my car, returning to Manhattan. Between using my phone, speeding, and no doubt driving recklessly, I was violating a few traffic laws.

I wanted to wait to call in backup until I verified a little more information. I contacted the analyst in our squad and had her run the name Jeffrey Cedar in every database she could access. I had to learn everything I could about this guy before I pulled up to his office.

What I got back was the information that Cedar was thirty-seven years old, had worked as a prosecutor for one year, and then had moved to private practice in the same office for almost nine years. He had been disciplined twice by the state bar, once for misrepresenting his relationship with a witness and once for trying to keep money the government had seized when they agreed to return it to his client. But as was the case with most bar complaints, not much had been done about either ethical lapse. Both times he'd just been put on probation for three months.

He'd also received a number of traffic violations and a bushel of parking tickets, but nothing outstanding.

None of this painted a picture of a homicidal maniac to me. But I did recall the fear in Lauren Cedar's eyes when she talked about her husband. To me, any kind of domestic violence is an indicator of a much more serious problem.

Cedar's office was a few blocks west of the criminal courthouse. Although the twelve-story building looked well-maintained, it had an older fire escape that wrapped around the sides of it like an awkward, rusty snake. To update it would cost a fortune, but it might be worth it. I wouldn't have called it a luxury or high-end building, but it was clearly occupied by professionals.

I lingered in the lobby for a moment and looked at the tenant listing, which was displayed in a glass-paneled case by the elevator. There were at least a dozen attorneys, a couple of architects, an accounting firm that looked like it took up an entire floor, and a couple of administrative offices. I found a listing that had several names on it, including Cedar's. He was on the fifth floor, so I took the elevator up there and found another door with the same names on it when I exited the elevator. As soon as I opened the door, however, I figured out it wasn't a firm—it was just three attorneys sharing a receptionist.

The receptionist looked up and smiled, giving me a very professional "May I help you?"

I smiled back. I wanted to keep this friendly—at least for now. "I need to speak with Jeffrey Cedar."

Her eyes darted to her appointment book, then to the closed door on my left. "Do you have an appointment?"

"I do not." I pulled out my badge. "I just need to ask him a couple of quick questions."

She made no pretense of hiding her phone as she texted someone and received a message in return. She then smoothly informed me, "Mr. Cedar is with a client at the moment."

"I'll wait." I suppressed a smile at the receptionist's uncomfortable squirm in her desk chair.

The receptionist texted some more. I was only mildly worried about Cedar trying to avoid me. My bet was that he would definitely consider himself more than capable of talking his way out of the domestic dispute he probably assumed I was here regarding.

A few minutes later, the door opened and I saw a middle-aged man with long brown hair walk out. He turned in the doorway and said, "Thanks, Jeff. I feel a lot better now."

I popped up before the lawyer could close his door. I could hear the receptionist calling out to me as I pushed Cedar's door open.

I found myself inside a large, comfortable office, staring right at the man I'd seen on the video from the sports bar, in photographs at Lila Stein's and Marilyn Shaw's apartments, as well as at the home he shared with his wife and son.

I still had my badge in my hand. I held it up and said, "Are you Jeffrey Cedar?"

He tried to smile as he stood up. "Officer, is this about my argument this morning?"

"With your wife?"

I could see the relief in his face. What criminal defense attorney couldn't talk his way out of a domestic dispute? I let him relax. His confidence would be his undoing.

I waited a moment before I burst his bubble, then said, "No, this is not about your wife. It's about Marilyn Shaw."

For starters, I thought. This man had a lot to explain, or he'd be pinned for multiple homicides. He was an attorney who'd thought he could walk a tightrope. He had just fallen off, and there was no safety net.

Cedar said, "Who?"

I held up one of the still photos I'd gotten from the sports bar security system. It clearly showed Cedar and Marilyn holding hands.

He tried to act casual. "Oh, you mean Mary. I'd be happy to talk about anything you want. I'm just a little busy right now." He casually picked up his mug of coffee from his desk. "Maybe we can schedule a meeting later."

"Nope."

"Excuse me?"

I spoke slowly. "I want to talk to you right now."

That frustrated Cedar. He sighed and looked away. Then he said, "Not without my attorney."

"Okay, who's your attorney?"

That's when Cedar surprised me. I mean, big-time. By committing the fresh offense of assaulting an officer.

With his left hand, he flung his warm coffee in my face in a smooth motion, then used the heavy mug to swat me across the temple. It felt like a bomb going off right next to me. I saw streaks of light and heard the heavy ringing of a head injury.

Yet even as I felt myself falling, I knew to block Cedar's exit. I felt for the door and shoved it closed as I hit the thick carpet. With what energy and clarity I had left, I rolled toward the door so Cedar couldn't open it.

I kept my right eye open as I reached for my Glock. I couldn't risk him coming at me again. If he managed to kick me in the throat, I'd be done.

Once again, I was surprised by the guy.

Cedar saw my movement as I reached for my weapon, and he panicked. He raced across the room, opened a tall window, kicked out the screen, and jumped.

CHAPTER 70

JUST AS I managed to get to my feet, the receptionist burst through the door.

"Jeffrey!" she called, rushing to the open window. Her voice was filled with emotion—not shock, but something deeper. Her boss's bizarre exit meant something more to her than just a disappearing paycheck.

I was right behind her. I still couldn't believe that the low-rent attorney had jumped. Not far, though, it turned out. The fire escape was less than three feet below the windowsill.

Craning my head—still dizzy from the blow Cedar had dealt—out the window, I saw my assailant making his way down the old fire escape. He was already two floors below us and moving fast.

I didn't like the look of the drop from the fire escape. But I had no choice. I couldn't risk him escaping arrest. Not if he was our killer.

I got on my phone and called dispatch directly. As soon as someone came on the line, I said quickly, "This is Detective Michael Bennett of Manhattan North Homicide. I have a suspect on the run. His name is Jeffrey Cedar, thirty-seven years old. White male, over six feet, sandy hair." I gave my location and told the dispatcher to get some patrol cars headed my way. Immediately. And to have the office building locked down. The receptionist could not be allowed to leave the premises.

My forehead was throbbing. I'd definitely have a bump where Cedar had hit me. I crawled out of the office window and onto the fire escape. I immediately regretted it. My acrophobia kicked in big-time. I'm not fond of heights. As soon as I took a few steps down the fire escape toward the fleeing man, I realized I could have taken the internal stairs. But on the other hand, if I didn't keep Cedar in sight, who knows what direction he'd run—and then I'd have no chance of finding him.

I focused on making sure my feet connected with each metal step as I carefully but quickly climbed down the fire escape. I had a little spin in my vision, the world swirling as I took in the distance to the ground. The sounds of the city faded to a soft white noise. My determination to get justice for Cedar's victims pushed through any fears I had.

I'd just about reached the third floor when Cedar managed to make the jump down to the narrow road below.

He never once looked back, although he must have heard the clattering sound of my footsteps in pursuit. I guess he thought he'd hit me hard enough to slow me down. Like I said, his confidence would be his undoing.

CHAPTER 71

MY LEGS WEREN'T quite as shaky by the time I made it to the fire escape's second floor. I had just seen Jeffrey Cedar running through the street and around the corner of a building. I knew he was headed west.

Once I landed on solid ground, I felt my stomach rumble like I'd just gotten off the Cyclone in Coney Island. I was panting. I swallowed the feeling and kept going.

My rubber-soled work shoes are not dedicated running shoes, but I made it to the street and turned the corner in an all-out sprint. I didn't shout or draw attention to myself. Cedar wasn't going to stop at the command *Stop! Police!* Instead, I relied on my running ability to close the distance.

My plan went into the toilet once Cedar looked behind him and saw me gaining ground. Then he shoved aside a couple of people next to him and picked up the pace from a fast lope to a mad dash.

I looked around, hoping one of the patrol cars I had called for would come roaring up and save the day. That didn't appear likely at this moment. I had to keep running. I could feel the sweat bead on my forehead and my lungs start to burn as I pushed my own pace.

Cedar was almost a block ahead of me now. All I could do was look for his white shirt. Then he came to a sudden stop. I thought he might be surrendering. Or maybe he pulled a muscle. Instead, he turned to his right and grabbed a messenger just getting on a bicycle.

Cedar threw the guy to the ground, then jumped on the bike awkwardly. The seat was set to the messenger's much shorter height, not Cedar's large frame, but he still got moving pretty fast. There was no way I could catch him.

Just as I came to this conclusion, I reached a stand marked CITI BIKE. A woman was sliding one of the blue unisex bikes popular with commuters and tourists into one of the slots. Before the locking mechanism could click into place, I shouted, "Excuse me! I'm sorry!" as I grabbed her bike and hopped onto it. It was a little low for me as well. But I stood on the pedals and started pumping for everything I was worth. I called over my shoulder to the woman, "I'll return it, I promise!"

I had to dodge two men who tried to gallantly stop me. I didn't even bother yelling *Police* or *NYPD*. I just threaded the needle between the men trying to grab me, and found myself about a block behind Jeffrey Cedar.

I fell into a rhythm on the bike and realized once again how much riding with Mary Catherine had helped my stamina as well as my leg strength. I started to close in on Cedar. Now we were almost to the Hudson and it looked like he was turning south.

He cut across West Street without even looking for oncoming traffic. The man was desperate. And I had no idea where this idiot was headed.

I put my head down and pumped the pedals hard.

CHAPTER 72

THERE WERE A lot more pedestrians here. Mostly tourists looking at the waterfront. That didn't help me in any way. Now I could only see Jeffrey Cedar every time his head bobbed up from a pedal stroke. But he was definitely riding south as hard as he could.

Eventually he slowed his pace, and again I closed the distance between us. Once I had to slam on the brakes and throw the bike into a slide to avoid hitting a woman with a double baby stroller. For all my effort and a scrape on my ankle, all I got was a dirty look from her.

Now the crowd had thinned, but I don't think Jeffrey Cedar had any idea I was behind him. He had definitely slowed down and was sitting comfortably on his bike seat instead of pumping the pedals from a standing position.

We weren't too far from Rockefeller Park. I couldn't think

of any place near there that would be of use to Cedar. If he really wanted to escape, he needed to be headed to the Staten Island Ferry or finding some other way off Manhattan. The Holland Tunnel was north of us, but he'd need a vehicle to get through that.

My heart and legs were burning. I had no idea where this asshole was going, or if he even had a plan. Billy Van Fleet had run, even though he wasn't guilty. I couldn't let those circumstances repeat with Cedar.

I was surprised how quickly I'd caught up to him, and I was beginning to contemplate a wild leap from my bike to his when he must've sensed me closing in. He dared a quick peek over his left shoulder, then he swerved right. Hard. Now we found ourselves in the grassy picnic area of Rockefeller Park.

It wasn't that busy on a weekday, though I still heard squeals and shouts as Cedar cut between people lounging on the lawn.

He risked another look over his shoulder, but it was poor timing. He struck a giant man wearing a red Nebraska Cornhuskers shirt. They both went down onto the thick grass. The man in the red shirt snarled as he tried to rise to his feet. He was older than Cedar but looked like he could rip the attorney in half. Cedar popped up onto his feet, though, and abandoned the bike, setting off toward the water. But the Cornhusker reached out and somehow managed to grab Cedar's foot as he was fleeing.

I successfully turned my bike sideways and skidded to a halt just in front of them.

Cedar kicked the man with his other foot and freed himself. He bolted toward the seawall.

I started running after him. The sun was bright in the cloudless sky, and no breeze came off the water. I realized right then that the heat was going to get to me quickly. I still had my phone but hoped one of the patrol cars I'd asked for earlier would show up. There really isn't a cop around when you need one.

Cedar was running along the low seawall and had a good stride. I saw one of the smaller tour boats, about forty feet, cruising parallel with the wall. I couldn't imagine what they were looking at around here, but I could hear the guide's voice over a tinny loudspeaker.

Cedar took one more look at me over his shoulder. He must've realized at that point that I wasn't going to give up. I sure hoped *he* would. But, of course, he didn't.

Instead, he sprinted hard and leapt off the seawall. I slowed my run and watched as he timed his jump perfectly. He landed on the rear section of the tour boat. He was on the deck behind a gaggle of elderly women, who all shrieked when he landed.

I watched as Cedar wobbled for a moment with his arms outstretched. He scrambled for a handhold at the stern of the boat but, when he didn't find one, started to lose his balance.

I stood at the seawall along with a couple of other pedestrians who had stopped to watch the show, feeling helpless as we watched in horror as Cedar bobbed and slid on the rear deck…then tumbled over the stern.

I already had my phone out, ready to call a rescue boat, when I saw the position of his landing—almost directly behind the stern. The anguished sound of his screams will be etched in my memory forever as I, and everyone nearby, witnessed Jeffrey Cedar get dragged underwater and chopped to bits by the boat's propellers.

Ten seconds later, it was all over. The captain of the boat had raced to cut the engines when he realized what was happening, but it was already too late. A red film spread across the surface of the water like something out of a horror movie.

I was frozen, staring at the gruesome scene. So was everyone else. Aside from a couple of people crying on the boat, no one nearby made a sound.

I had to sit on the low seawall for a moment. Everything caught up to me at once. The stress of the last weeks. The exhaustion of chasing a murder suspect. The grisly murders of at least six young women here in New York. The concern over whether Hollis would improve. And now the macabre scene in front of me.

There was nothing more anyone could do except wait for the cavalry, the first responders activated by dozens of eyewitness calls to 911. And try to keep from vomiting, and embarrassing myself and the NYPD.

CHAPTER 73

WHILE I HAD been chasing down Jeffrey Cedar, his receptionist had been brought by patrol car to Manhattan North Homicide. Her name was Olivia Green, and I paid her a visit in the interview room where she'd been waiting with her attorney—conveniently, one of Cedar's former colleagues.

Judging by the look of shock on her face, she was struggling to absorb the disturbing events of the day. Not only had her former boss struck and then fled from a detective, but she herself was being held in custody.

"Ms. Green," I said, "do you know why you're here?"

She shook her head.

I remembered the emotional look on her face when Cedar jumped out his office window. I needed to determine the nature of their relationship.

"Ms. Green, you worked for Mr. Cedar. Did you date him too?"

She looked genuinely stunned by the accusation, and so did her attorney.

"Never," she said. "I'm an old friend of Lauren's. I babysit Tyler all the time."

"Did you know that earlier today Lauren called the police?"

"No," she said. "Is she all right? Is Tyler hurt?"

"Tyler is fine," I said. "But Lauren showed me a bruise on her arm in the shape of her husband's hand. She said he hurt her when she confronted him with evidence he'd been cheating on her. Both of the women he'd been seeing are dead. And he may have had other victims."

"Jeffrey may have a temper, and I believe he may have cheated, but he's not a killer," the receptionist protested.

Olivia Green was quite insistent. She was also wrong.

"A killer is exactly what he *was*," I said. "And note my use of the past tense. I'm sorry to inform you that Jeffrey Cedar is dead. He died trying to escape arrest for the crimes he committed. And in order to avoid your own arrest, I need you to corroborate Mr. Cedar's whereabouts on the dates of multiple homicides currently under investigation by the NYPD."

She opened her mouth to speak, until her lawyer cut in.

"My client has nothing to say at this time."

A uniformed officer brought in boxes containing the contents of the receptionist's desk and placed them on the table.

"You're a meticulous record keeper, Ms. Green," I said. "We've collected paper calendars going back years. Show us the current one. And the mileage logs on the car Mr. Cedar claimed as a business expense."

With a trembling hand, she opened the boxes, looking

through the contents until she found the requested documents and set them on the table.

"Did Mr. Cedar travel much?" I asked.

"Before Tyler was born, yes," she said. "Not so much recently. But he did drive his car all over the city."

And there, in Olivia Green's perfect handwriting, was all the proof I needed. Cedar had almost certainly murdered Marilyn Shaw and Lila Stein—but on the evening Chloe Tumber was killed, he'd been in court, awaiting the decision of a deliberating jury. And the records showed equally airtight alibis for the murders of Elaine Anastas and the other two victims in Brooklyn and the Bronx.

Now I was positive. Jeffrey Cedar was a copycat. We still had the real killer to catch.

CHAPTER 74

AS I CAME out of the interview room, I ran into Harry Grissom. He had been observing my questioning of Olivia Green.

"Great work, Mike," my lieutenant said. "Now I need you to go home and get some rest. You're no good to me or the investigation if you're exhausted and distracted."

"I've been exhausted and distracted for over a month."

"Well, I don't want it to go any further. Take tomorrow off if you need it. Spend some time with that beautiful family of yours."

I took his word as command.

I came in the front door just before dinnertime, about the same time as Brian. He was carrying his small duffel bag and nodded hello. He shrugged when I asked how it was going. Was this the new normal in communication with my oldest boy?

Before I could get into any further questions with him, we

both heard crying. When you have ten kids, the sound of crying isn't immediately concerning, since it's not all that uncommon— it's likely that someone's just annoyed with someone else.

Brian followed me into the dining room, where we located the source of the crying: Jane, at the end of the table, sobbing hysterically into a very wet paper towel. Mary Catherine sat on one side of Jane, stroking her hair. Juliana sat on the other, holding a roll of paper towels. There was a pile of crumpled towels in the middle of the table.

In between sobs, Jane said, "I-I-I just can't believe he would do this!"

I'd been around long enough to guess almost exactly what had happened.

Brian was still new to this game. He said, "What who did?"

Juliana looked up at her brother and explained, "Allan broke up with Jane. No notice, nothing. When she tried to talk to him, he just told her it was over."

That set off a new round of wailing from Jane. "And-and we were supposed to go to the school dance this weekend!"

Brian muttered, "That asshole."

Instinctively, I placed a hand on his shoulder to calm him down.

Brian jerked away from my touch and stormed out of the room.

I stepped to the dining room table and gave Jane a kiss on the top of her head. I wished I were better at this kind of thing. I knew I'd have to deal with it a lot more as the girls got older. But I was at a loss. I did my best to teach the boys to always respect women, and at least, from the little bit I heard through gasps and crying, I didn't get the impression Allan had been disrespectful. Just thoughtless. But I still wanted Jane to feel better.

The front door slammed. Hard. I looked at Mary Catherine. She said, "Has to be Brian."

I rushed out the front door, but he had already caught the elevator down to the lobby. An angry Brian roaming the streets and hunting a clueless Allan Martin III made me very nervous.

CHAPTER 75

I TOLD THE girls I was going out to catch Brian. I grabbed my keys and raced downstairs. The doorman said Brian had turned left after he'd burst through the doors onto the street.

Sure, Jane was upset, but that was part of life. She'd get over her first breakup. I hoped Brian realized the same thing.

I couldn't see him in either direction. I jogged toward the left. Now my imagination started to kick in. I felt my stomach begin to burn as I considered all the terrible things Brian could do to an unsuspecting high schooler.

Before I knew it, I was three blocks away from the apartment. I thought of the basketball courts a few blocks from here where Brian liked to hang out. I broke into an all-out run. This was not the family time I had envisioned.

A quick overview of the courts did not produce Brian. I was

at a loss. Then I spotted one of the young men who coordinated the leagues.

"Have you seen Brian?" I asked.

"Not in a couple of days."

I groaned in frustration.

"Have you checked Holy Name? I know he likes their courts. Don't you guys have some relative who works there?"

I thanked him and burst into a sprint I didn't realize I was capable of after my draining chase of Cedar. Clearly the bike riding with Mary Catherine had had more effect on me than I'd thought.

I slowed as I approached the church and called my grandfather. He didn't answer. Seamus wasn't big on cell phones. He thought they caused cancer. On several occasions he had claimed he would start using his cell phone around his ninetieth birthday. He figured by then it wouldn't matter.

When I got to campus, I threaded my way through the courtyards that led to the basketball gym. A couple of the nuns tried to engage me in conversation. They were still full of questions about the wedding. I was as polite as possible without ever stopping, not even for a moment.

Brian was taking anger management classes, but he also had strong protective instincts. And right now, the two might be about to combust. If someone had wronged his sister, no training could keep that primal rage in check.

The image of a bloody Allan Martin III, beaten, or with a shiv stuck in his stomach, popped into my head. I could also imagine Allan's father in court, disparaging my son as a bad influence and a danger to the Martin family. The final part of that equation was Brian being locked away like a rabid dog. I was panicked. It made me run faster. Much faster.

I burst through the doors on the upper deck of the gymnasium and heard the sounds of a pickup basketball game in progress. There were voices and a few hoots and hollers.

I froze at the sight of Brian playing one-on-one with Allan Martin. My other boys, Trent, Eddie, and Ricky, sat in the front row, cheering their brother on.

No one was dead. There wasn't even any blood. I eased onto the very top bleacher. I realized my legs were shaky. I wasn't sure if it was from the sprint or the fear I'd had about what Brian could've done.

I watched silently. Both of the boys were better than I'd thought. Allan sunk a three pointer. Brian hit three fifteen-foot jumpers. On the last one, after the ball had slipped through the hoop and bounced on the hardwood floor, the boys stood face-to-face.

Brian called out, "Game." He stared down the younger boy and said, "Do it. Do it right now."

I was intrigued, but also ready to intervene if Brian was ordering Allan to do something out of line. I watched as they both stepped over to the bleachers. Allan retrieved his phone, and the other boys gathered around him.

I made my way down the bleachers until I was in the lower level, not too far from the boys. None of them noticed—they were all too focused on Allan's phone.

Ricky said, "Put it on speaker."

Allan said, "Don't you trust me?"

"Not even a little. Now put your phone on speaker so we can all hear it."

Allan pushed a few buttons.

"Hello?" said a voice I immediately recognized as Jane's.

Allan didn't waste any time. "I'm sorry for breaking up with you, Jane. It was a mistake. Is there any chance you would still go to the dance with me?"

There was almost no hesitation on the line as Jane answered. "No." Then she hung up.

I couldn't keep a wide smile from spreading across my face.

My three younger boys all started to hoot and chide Allan.

Trent said, "She's already over you, loser."

Eddie said, "Can't play basketball, don't know women. Good luck in the future."

All four of my boys walked out and left the entitled little shit standing in the gym by himself.

CHAPTER 76

THE NEXT MORNING, I lingered long enough to eat breakfast with the family. Jane looked much better. Being able to turn Allan down had meant a lot to her.

Mary Catherine lingered over our kiss good-bye at the front door. It'd been so long that I'd forgotten what a good mood felt like. She made me promise to call her soon with an update on Brett Hollis. I hopped into my city-issued Chevy Impala and made the short drive to the Columbia University Medical Center.

Outside Hollis's room, I took a moment to compose myself. As I opened the door, I heard a voice behind me. I turned to find a tall nurse with reddish hair.

"What are you doing?" she demanded.

I closed the door. "I was going to visit my partner, Brett Hollis. Isn't this his room?"

"He's resting right now. They set his pelvis last night. Come back sometime after lunch and he'll be ready for visitors."

I knew not to argue with the nurse. Nurses are right up there with nuns, judges, and teachers.

It took almost no time for me to make it back to my car. I had a number of assignments I wanted to cover today.

Mainly, I was checking with employers of the victims from our homicides, my own follow-up to the initial Task Force Halo outreach.

It took me less than an hour to visit the workplaces of the victims in Brooklyn and the Bronx, as well as Columbia Law School, where Chloe Tumber had been enrolled. No one had any new information. I would hit the rest after I saw Brett Hollis this afternoon. I might even get home before dark again.

Almost as soon as I settled at my desk, I saw John Macy trudging through the office, straight toward me. "I heard Hollis is out of action," he said. "I guess we're stuck with each other."

I thought about that for a moment. I looked up at the well-dressed mayor's aide and said, "Let me just wash up. Have a seat and make yourself comfortable."

Macy seemed to appreciate my new attitude. He smiled and pulled a notebook out of the leather satchel he always carried. He settled in at Hollis's desk, not thinking twice about reorganizing Hollis's papers.

I went to the bathroom and washed my hands. I didn't want to lie.

Then I left the office. I decided it would probably be a good idea to finish my visits with the other businesses before I went back to the hospital.

I smiled as I drove away, wondering how long Macy would sit quietly at the desk before he started asking about me.

CHAPTER 77

THE PEOPLE AT Manhattan Family Insurance, where victim Elaine Anastas had interned, were pleasant and tried to be helpful. They all spoke highly of her.

Not that I'd expected anything else—most people only seem to recall a homicide victim's positive qualities, although someone's bad traits are more likely to have led to their death. Not that that necessarily applied when we were talking about a serial killer. Still, I tried to hide my impatience when I heard on endless loop: "Elaine was so bright." "Elaine was so driven." "Elaine came from someplace upstate but managed to make it in the city." High praise from fellow New Yorkers.

About the fifth person I spoke to was a man named Luis Munoz. Munoz was dressed in a black suit with a yellow tie and acted more like he owned the place than managed it. He also made sure to tell me that he'd gotten his MBA at Columbia.

We sat at adjoining empty desks. After Munoz went on and on about what a good intern Elaine had been, I said a little harshly, "C'mon. It's just us. I'm not going to make any notes. And I promise I won't remember who tells me what. But this bland information about Elaine won't help me capture her killer. I need to understand who she really was. Can you help me?"

Munoz considered my position and finally said, "Okay. Truth is, I knew Laney reasonably well. I even met one of her two roommates at an office happy hour. I can't remember the girl's name, but she interned with the Yankees. She loved baseball."

I had spoken to that roommate. It had been her bobbleheads I'd first noticed.

Munoz continued. "Laney was highly social. Almost had, like, a phobia of loners or of being alone."

I asked a few more questions and was impressed by how forthright Munoz was being. He even admitted that Elaine had once turned him down for a date. *Not that, as her supervisor, he should have been asking,* I thought, keeping the future working lives of my daughters in mind.

As I started to wrap things up, I noticed a sticker, then saw that duplicates had been applied to the frame of every computer monitor and landline phone in the office. The stickers showed a cartoon computer, its long arms holding a radio in one hand and a telephone in the other. Underneath it was a company name: Computelex.

The branding struck me as unusual so I took a picture of it with my phone.

I thanked Munoz and decided it was time to head over to the hospital.

CHAPTER 78

THE NURSE CARING for Brett Hollis recognized me from this morning, nodded, and waved her hand toward his room.

I opened the door quietly. Mrs. Hollis looked up at me from where she sat by her son, holding his hand.

As I stepped farther into the room, I saw Hollis was awake. He even managed a smile. His face didn't look too bad, though he was back to bandages across his nose. I guess I was used to it. He also had one arm in a cast, and one leg as well. He didn't look very comfortable lying in the bed.

Hollis managed a weak, "Hey."

"Hey," I said back.

Mrs. Hollis stood up. She said, "Brett's been through a lot. They set his pelvis late last night. The doctor seems happy with his progress."

"I'm just here to say hello," I assured her.

She gave me a stern look. "Three minutes. That's it. When I come back from the bathroom, you've got to go."

I nodded my agreement. I liked her. I could see where Hollis got his smarts.

I sat down in the same chair his mother had been in. I wanted to chat with Hollis. Cheer him up. But the truth was, I had an agenda.

I leaned in close and asked, "Remember anything?"

Hollis smiled. "All business. I respect that." His voice faded out. I handed him the cup from his nightstand and helped him sip some water. Then he started again. "A guy tumbled into Kelly and I just reacted."

I remembered Harry Grissom telling me that Kelly Konick was the pretty girl in the yellow skirt who'd been there with Hollis. "Can you remember anything about the guy?"

"I never got a good look at him. From what I saw, he looked average. Exactly average. I wouldn't be able to identify the guy if he walked in with a sign that said, 'I pushed your colleague in front of that bus.'"

I laughed dutifully. But the idea of a man being invisible because he was so unremarkable—that stuck in my head.

"Any thoughts on why he might've pushed Kelly? We have a couple of witnesses who said it looked deliberate from a distance."

Hollis shook his head. "I was kinda distracted, and a little nervous because I'm really into Kelly. I wasn't paying attention to anything except her."

The door opened and Mrs. Hollis walked in. I stood up and told Hollis, "I'll be back tomorrow. Rest and do what your mom says."

Hollis gave another weak smile as he said, "I always do."

CHAPTER 79

AN UNEXPECTED CALL diverted me from following up with Ms. Richard at the New York Public Library. Instead, I met FBI agent Emily Parker at a Starbucks not too far from the hospital.

Emily had requested the meeting but hadn't explained the reason behind her invitation.

She was already seated and pushed a plain black coffee toward me. "Hail the New York hero. You single-handedly prevented Jeffrey Cedar from killing again."

As I slid onto the opposite chair, I said, "I appreciate you not making me visit the FBI offices again, especially to congratulate me on a case that seems to be only partially solved."

She couldn't hide her own smile. "As much fun as that was, I'd rather Robert Lincoln not see me with you." She took a quick sip of her own coffee. "I'm sure you get that a lot. People saying they'd rather not be associated with you. People avoiding you. The usual."

I had to smile as I replied, "Actually, I get it more than I care to admit. Though hopefully all that will stop once I'm happily married."

We both let out a good laugh at that.

Emily plopped down two thick case files on the table between us. "Time to talk shop," she said, turning serious. "Tell me what you've found on the killer remaining at large."

I told her about my unorthodox briefing with Hollis from his hospital bed.

"Hollis gave me the idea that he could be someone so unremarkable he's virtually invisible," I said. "That's not to say it was our killer who pushed Kelly Konick in front of the bus, but I'm open to the possibility. If he blends in everywhere, there's a likelihood he's quite ordinary-looking."

"Interesting," Emily said. "Maybe that's why we've got no reports of anyone noticing anything strange near any of the crimes. Not in any of the businesses where the victims worked or around where they lived."

I had to admit it was gratifying to hear the nation's "premier" law-enforcement agency agree with me.

Emily leaned in close. "The people at Quantico believe our killer targets women he feels have disrespected him."

I related my interview with Luis Munoz, Elaine Anastas's manager at Manhattan Family Insurance, that he had mentioned she'd had a phobia of loners. Maybe she had encountered one and somehow insulted him.

"Could a loner also be a ghost?" I wondered aloud. "Or a killer?"

CHAPTER 80

I DROVE HOME after my meeting with Emily Parker. Traffic was slow, and I was grateful. With ten kids and a busy office, sometimes it's hard to find a quiet place to think. Like a lot of cops, the best place for me to mull things over is in my car.

For once in the progress of this case, I felt pretty good about my day. Brett Hollis seemed stronger than I'd expected, and I'd gained some valuable information that had been validated by the FBI.

Stopped at a light on Amsterdam Avenue, I tried to put all the pieces together. I believed our killer was a traveler. I didn't think he was from New York. But how to find out more? There were no databases for *jobs with travel*. No businesses were going to come forward and suggest one of their employees was a killer.

I had two more employer interviews scheduled for the next morning. I thought I knew all the right questions to ask.

It felt like things were back to normal when I walked through my front door. Chrissy and Shawna gave me a hug. The other kids were doing their homework at the dining room table. There was very little drama.

Jane looked reserved, but not melancholy. I didn't want to make a big fuss over her. Juliana had told me that the boys had circulated it at school that Jane had been the one to dump Allan. The story of her saying no to him over the phone was true enough. I guess it's all in how you spin it. And, apparently, in how many brothers and sisters you have to tell the story.

The front door opened and I smiled at the sight of my grandfather, Seamus. A moment later, his IT guy, Elgin, followed. Seamus introduced Elgin, then let the kids introduce themselves to him. It was no small feat.

Seamus pulled me into the kitchen and said, "I hope you and Mary Catherine don't mind that I brought Elgin over for dinner without checking first."

I said, "You know I don't mind. I also know you don't care whether I mind or not."

Seamus chuckled. "Just trying to follow social convention, my boy."

My grandfather, Mary Catherine, and I stood in the kitchen for a moment. Elgin seemed amazed at the number of people at the table. I smiled at the gangly young man as he took in the group.

I called from the kitchen, "Yes, Elgin, this is normal."

He managed a shy smile as he looked up and said to all of us, "Usually, it's just me and my mom at home."

Having Elgin at the dinner table helped take the focus off Jane and her funk. For a quiet computer nerd, Elgin didn't seem to mind the attention.

Of course, he and Eddie bonded over computers, losing everyone else at the table as they dove deep into the details of networks and hacking. Elgin reached into his backpack and pulled out a magazine called *2600*. He handed it over to Eddie.

Eddie's eyes lit up. "Wow, the latest issue. Thanks!"

Mary Catherine inquired, "What kind of magazine is that?"

"It's a magazine for hackers. Really cutting-edge stuff," Eddie blurted out.

Elgin looked down at the table but added, "There's nothing in it Eddie hasn't already seen. I just thought he'd get a kick out of reading it."

Mary Catherine nodded, trying to avoid openly endorsing hacking.

After dinner, Seamus took me aside. In a low voice he said, "I wanted Elgin to see you as a real person, with the family. He's been following the investigation, and he mentioned that it's difficult for him to think of cops as regular people."

There were two sides to every story, and I took the NYPD's. "The news always avoids any talk of a cop's family or the kids left behind when a cop is murdered. I'm glad you brought him. He seems like a good kid." I smiled. "He's smart and gets along with the others."

Seamus clapped his hands together and rubbed them. "Great. Now for the next order of business: your wedding. Specifically, you need to write your vows."

"I'm working on it."

My grandfather winced and said, "That's a tired excuse. How hard can it be for you to write four or five lines?"

"Can it be a limerick? Mary Catherine *is* Irish, after all."

"So are we. If you do a limerick, she'll slug you. After I get the first crack at you."

I tried to hide my smile as I said, "There once was a girl from Tipperary. Her body was not terribly hairy. She—"

My grandfather punched me in the arm and walked away.

CHAPTER 81

THE NEXT MORNING, my first stop was the bustling medical supply office near Columbia where Chloe Tumber, the third New York homicide victim, had worked part-time while she was in school.

The manager, a pleasant woman, was clearly busy but didn't rush me or my questions, though she didn't have much information either. No one in the office did. There was no one as forthcoming as Luis Munoz here. Even when I made the offer to go off the record, no one had any information to give me about Chloe other than that she was twenty-six years old and a whiz with data entry. But apparently she'd kept to herself and also kept unusual hours due to her class schedule.

I thanked the manager but mentally wrote this place off as another dead end. Before I gathered my things and stood up to go, I took a moment to check my phone and messages.

Then I saw it: the same sticker I'd seen at the insurance company yesterday. Stuck on the front edge of a computer monitor. The cartoon of a computer with rubbery arms holding a radio and a phone. Computelex.

It took a moment for it to register, then a thousand new questions rushed into my brain. I reached up and stopped the first person walking past me.

"Excuse me," I said, putting my finger on the sticker in the corner of the computer monitor. "Do you know what that is?"

"Oh, yeah, it's from the company that installed computer software to coordinate our phones and radios and some of our vans. There's a sticker on every piece of equipment that was updated."

"When were they here?"

"Maybe three weeks ago?"

I did a quick calculation and realized that was shortly before Chloe Tumber had been murdered. "How many people from the company were here to install the software?"

"I think it was just one dude. Honestly, I don't remember much about him. He was only here for about a week."

He was a ghost, I thought.

CHAPTER 82

DANIEL OTT WAS essentially finished with the software and hardware upgrades at the trucking company in Queens but was enjoying hanging out with the men on the loading dock. They'd come to him for a couple of other engineering issues after he'd impressed them with his system of loading tires so quickly. They'd even invited him out for a beer one evening after work. He'd never experienced this kind of friendliness before.

Now he was just wrapping up the last few issues before heading home to Omaha. Ott wasn't quite sure he was ready to leave New York. He was reveling in the media attention, and he doubted he'd get the same amount of news coverage anywhere else. Reading the articles and hearing the TV stations relentlessly covering his crimes tickled him.

Ott wanted one more notch in his belt before leaving New York. That would be his last word to Detective Michael Bennett.

Since he had not seen any news stories about the bus hitting the younger detective, he assumed the investigation was ongoing. If the detective had died, there would've been a report about it. Perhaps injuring him was just as good. Maybe even better. It would distract other people in his unit. They would visit him in the hospital, wasting time.

He had heard a couple of the truck drivers talk about the excellent hamburgers at a sports bar on Greenpoint Avenue called The Queen's Castle, and he decided to go for an early lunch. The place looked a little hokey on the outside with fake towers and turrets, but Ott felt his stomach rumble, looked at the menu posted outside, and then stepped through the door.

He glanced around the dimly lit sports bar and noticed that the half dozen flat-screen TVs hanging on the walls were all dark and silent. The door next to the bar led to the kitchen. He didn't see anyone back there.

Then he heard a woman's thick Long Island accent. "What the hell? It's not even eleven. We're not open yet."

Ott looked up to see a tall, athletic-looking woman with frizzy black hair behind the bar, dressed all in black.

Ott stated, "Sorry, I was hungry."

"Jesus Christ, eat around noon like everyone else," she muttered.

Ott didn't like the verbal abuse. Especially when he had done nothing to deserve it. He calculated the odds of other workers showing up if he took action right now against the woman yelling at him to leave.

He felt for the knife in his front pocket. He pictured what he would do to her given enough time. It made him feel excited instead of annoyed. *Why wait?*

The woman continued to work behind the bar. She didn't look up again.

He slipped on his rubber surgical gloves and circled the area, measuring his angle of attack. He inched closer, blade extended. The bartender still had her head down, slicing a small mountain of lemons and limes. She'd never see him strike.

Suddenly Ott heard the noise of the front door opening, and a man's voice called out to the bartender. "Boss told me to come in early, help you prep. Tell me you're glad to see me!"

Ott wasn't glad. He quickly folded and stowed the Gerber knife, ducked his head, turned, and walked out the way he'd come in.

Ott decided he would follow her home later and make her his grand statement before he left New York. He wouldn't even bother with reconnaissance. If she lived with anyone else, they could be part of his farewell masterpiece too. He was already picturing it in his mind. Walls smeared with blood. Her body laid out in the middle of the living room.

New York really was going to be a hard place to leave.

CHAPTER 83

MY HEART WAS thumping as I jumped into my car and raced back up Broadway. Despite state and local ordinances, I had my cell phone in hand. Out of habit, I almost dialed Brett Hollis. Instead, I tried Harry Grissom. There was no answer. For all I knew, he was down at One Police Plaza, explaining how I'd left John Macy alone in the office. Then I tried Emily Parker. I got her voicemail.

As soon as I got to my desk, my next call was to Alvin Carter in the Atlanta Police Department.

As soon as he answered, I blurted, "This is Michael Bennett with the NYPD. I think I might be onto something. Have you ever heard of a company called Computelex?"

"Nope. Not that I recall."

"Can you check with the employers of the victims down there to see if anyone from that company ever visited their offices?"

"What do you got?"

"Two victims, each worked at different businesses in separate industries. Both businesses had someone from this company Computelex on-site, working on their computers."

There was a moment's pause. "Your theory is that the killer works for this computer company?"

"I know it's a long shot, but the timelines match up. I'm following up on whether the fact that a Computelex employee visited the office of both victims is statistically unlikely. If it was a big company like Microsoft, maybe. But I've never heard of this Computelex."

"I'm on it."

I then made the same call to San Francisco PD.

I had checked further with Manhattan Family Insurance, where Elaine Anastas had interned, and the medical supply company that had employed Chloe Tumber. The best they could tell me about the Computelex representative was that he was a white male. Neither company was even sure of his name. Someone from the insurance company thought it might be David. No one at either company saw him interact with the victims.

I heard a voice and glanced up from my computer screen to see John Macy standing at my desk with another man I didn't recognize.

Macy said, "I guess you thought it was pretty funny to leave me here in the office."

I went back to my computer. "Not now, Macy. I'm busy." I tuned him out.

"I don't think you're that busy. In fact, I know you're not. This is Detective William Funcher."

I kept my head directly in front of the monitor as I said, "Nice to meet you, Detective Funcher."

Macy said, "He's your replacement. You're no longer on the serial killer case." Finally I looked up at the men. Funcher looked uncomfortable. Macy was beaming. This was what he'd been waiting for. And he wanted to add a little drama to it. I hated to disappoint him.

"Where do you work now, Funcher?"

"The One-Eleven."

"Where's that, Queens?"

"Yeah, 215th Street."

"You work in homicide?"

"General assignment."

"And how do you know Mr. Macy?"

The fact that I didn't get an answer right away told me this wasn't a case of a competent detective rising to the top. Funcher was just the first guy Macy could find who'd agreed to come up here.

I wrote down the information from my computer screen about Computelex. They were based in Omaha, Nebraska, but claimed to cover the whole country. This might be the right lead.

I looked up again at the two men standing in front of my desk. "Fortunately, I don't work for you, Macy. I work for a guy named Harry Grissom. And if he walks in here and tells me I'm replaced, I will give everything I have to Detective Funcher. Until then, like I said, I am really busy."

That's when Macy made a major error. He touched me without permission.

CHAPTER 84

AS SOON AS I felt John Macy's hands on my shoulders, something in me snapped. It may seem minor, but what he did is technically an assault. That's what I kept in my head as I reacted. I could picture it in a report. *I was in fear for my safety after he assaulted me.* That sounded good. I was going to go with that.

I really don't know if it was instinct or machismo that made me spring out of the chair and turn to face Macy. I could've told him to cut it out and kept working. Instead, I was now face-to-face with the mayor's aide.

I snarled, "Keep your damn hands off me."

Macy wasn't about to back down either. "You know what I can do to your career? You're nothing but a minor cog in city government."

"For a minor cog, you seem to spend a lot of time keeping me from turning with all the other cogs."

"I don't like your attitude one bit. You have no respect for your superiors."

That caught me by surprise. I'll admit I'm a smart-ass. I'll admit I can't control my mouth. But I have a great deal of respect for my superiors. Any man or woman who worked their way up the ladder at the NYPD deserved respect.

I said, "I respect my lieutenant. I respect our captain. I respect the commissioner of the NYPD."

Macy said, "But not me?"

"You're not my superior."

"I'm the commissioner's superior." Macy looked like he was losing it. His voice was becoming a little shrill. His eyes were twice as big as normal. And he was sputtering. Any time a politician is at a loss for words, watch out.

That's why it didn't surprise me too much when he grabbed my shirt with both hands. He pulled me close to him like a school-yard bully and raised his voice. "You hear me, Bennett? I—"

That's when I decided to react. Maybe *retaliate* is the better word. But I knew I had to do it subtly.

I'm not saying I set up the mayor's aide. I will say that as a cop, I'm aware of my surroundings at all times. At least I try to be. I had the chair that was right next to me hooked with my right foot. It was pretty close to Macy. All I did was nudge it. Okay, a little more than a nudge. It hit him directly in the groin. That's why he stopped mid-sentence.

Macy released his grip on my shirt and stumbled back a few feet until he bumped into the leather office chair and flopped into it like a bag of old potatoes. Clearly his main concern was the excruciating pain radiating from his testicles. Every man knows the feeling.

I casually turned my attention to the cop, Funcher. "How'd you really end up in this embarrassing and awkward position?"

He slowly backed away from me and raised his hands so I could see he wanted nothing to do with me or this situation.

Funcher said, "I know Macy socially, through my wife. In my circles, he has a reputation for being loose-lipped, but he was all business this time. He told my sergeant the mayor's office needed me, so I agreed to meet him here this morning."

"So you're not looking to snake this case?"

"No way."

"Then we're good." I completely ignored both men and went back to work.

After about thirty seconds, Funcher turned to leave.

I called after him. "Wait." When he turned to look at me, I said, "Take your date with you." I tilted my head at Macy.

Funcher said, "No can do. I'm going back to the One-Eleven. He's not authorized to ride in an NYPD vehicle." The detective turned and walked away without another word.

I liked Funcher. To the point. No fuss. And smart enough to realize when he was in over his head.

Harry walked into the office, passing Funcher on his way out. My lieutenant strolled over to my desk and asked, "Who was that?"

"He dropped Macy off here."

He and I both looked over at Macy, who appeared to be recovering from the blow to the testicles. Harry dropped his voice, "Jesus, what's that ass want now?"

I shrugged and said, "I guess he just wanted to hang out."

We both gave the motionless mayor's aide another glance, then I said to Harry, "Let's talk."

As soon as we were out of Macy's earshot, I said, "I need to fill you in on a computer company that may be important to the case."

CHAPTER 85

I HAD NEVER done so much investigative work from my desk. By the afternoon, I had compiled all the information on Computelex I could find from the internet. I even had the phone number of the head of human resources, one Lynn McKague. The photo on the company website showed an attractive, friendly-looking woman with a broad smile.

I dialed, and as the phone rang, I said a silent prayer that she'd answer. I needed to actually talk to her. I didn't want to risk leaving a message. For all I knew, the man in question could be Computelex's employee of the year, or she could even be his girlfriend.

A bright, friendly voice answered the phone with "HR, this is Lynn."

"Lynn McKague?"

"That's right. Who's this?"

I gave her my full, formal title.

"Hello, *Detective*," she said cautiously.

"Ms. McKague, I need a few minutes of your time."

"Before I answer any questions," she said, "you're calling about company business, not about me personally, correct?"

"That's correct."

"I'm sorry, but unless you've got a subpoena, company policy forbids me from continuing this conversation. The privacy of our clients is important to our business model."

"This isn't about one of your clients. It's about an employee."

"I wish I could help, but I'm afraid the same rule applies."

I had to take a moment to consider my next course of action. I said, "Can you confirm an individual's employment status?"

"If you have a name, I can verify that employee's work history. That I can do."

"Is there a white male Computelex employee currently working in the New York area?" I rolled the dice, hoping I wouldn't spook her—or the man I was looking for. "It's important that I speak to this person about a lead on a string of homicides."

"Is he a witness? I can send him a message to contact you."

"No, I would ask you please *not* to say anything to him."

"So he's *not* a witness. This sounds more serious." It was half statement, half question.

I didn't respond.

There was a long silence on her end.

I finally said, "Ms. McKague? Did I lose you?"

"No, you didn't lose me. I was reviewing some records." The HR manager hesitated again. Then she stammered, "What ki-kind of questions do you need answered?"

I almost leapt up from my chair and cheered. Instead, I focused and said, "We understand that a man in your employ travels on contract work. I'm going to give you some dates and locations. A name would help a great deal. Barring that, a yes or no on whether at those times this employee was working in those cities."

Lynn McKague spoke slowly. "Yes, I am able to merely confirm information you have already."

I gave her the dates of the Atlanta and San Francisco homicides. I could hear her fingers tapping at her keyboard. I waited while she checked the information.

When she came back on the line, there was a slight tremor in her voice. "Yes, one employee was also in Atlanta and San Francisco during the dates you gave me. He has worked for us for a number of years." After an awkward pause, she asked, "What's this about?"

I could've given her some snarky reply like *I'm not allowed to tell you without a subpoena.* But this case was too important to screw around.

"And when did he arrive in New York City?"

"He's been there for slightly over six weeks." Well within the range of the homicides here. I could almost hear Lynn McKague mentally debating her next admission. "His name is Daniel Ott."

Daniel Ott. This was our man. I was sure of it. "One last question, Ms. McKague. Would you be willing to share with me the name of the hotel where Mr. Ott is staying in New York City?"

After only a brief pause, she gave me the name and address of a chain hotel in the Flatiron District.

She also gave me Daniel Ott's cell phone number.

"Ms. McKague," I said, "thank you for your help."

I meant it.

CHAPTER 86

THE INSTANT I ended the call to Omaha, my phone rang. Pam Lundsford from San Francisco PD was on the line.

She started right off with "These cases weren't mine. The original detective, Sean Lynch, has retired since then. This case aged him. He left the force, but he's never given up on it. His theory was that the killer left town. Maybe he was right."

I agreed. It's what he did while he was *in* town that I needed to pin down.

Detective Lundsford said, "I saw your homicides on CNN. Bad break that the killer you caught was a copycat. I hope this doesn't kill your lead on the main suspect."

"I have some new information there," I assured her.

"Good, because I contacted the victims' employers like you asked. No link to Computelex. I checked it four different ways and made sure the representative from the employer knew exactly what I was asking."

Not the answer I was expecting. I explained that Computelex had just confirmed our killer's presence in San Francisco at the time of both murders.

"I have an idea," Detective Lundsford said. "Can I bring Lynch in? He might have another angle."

"Sure. Either it's going to be over soon or this lead won't mean anything."

After I hung up the phone, it rang again. Detective Alvin Carter from Atlanta calling. I answered it immediately. "You got good news for me, Alvin? I got confirmation from Computelex that a Daniel Ott was working in Atlanta on the dates of all five homicides, but I need more."

Carter said, "Well…"

He was about to drop something on me. Most detectives can't pass up a chance for a little dramatic pause.

Carter continued, "The victim who was murdered at a realtor's office, Holly Jones? This was my case."

I said, "I sense you're about to impress me with some spectacular police work."

"You have no idea."

"Go ahead. Hit me with it."

Alvin Carter said, "I canvassed the area after the homicide. Went a couple of blocks in each direction. One of the companies about a block away delivered wholesale flowers to florists and grocery stores all over Georgia. A really big operation."

"And?"

"I called them. They *did* contract Computelex to combine their delivery van radios, telephone, and computer activity. It turns out the Computelex tech was there at the same time the killing spree was going on in this area."

There was a long silence between us on the telephone as I let that information sink in.

I said, "Did you get a description of the tech?"

"Average-looking white guy. That was the best they could come up with. His name was Daniel Ott. He had to sign in every day for insurance reasons. No one at the company has given him a single thought since he left. He made almost no impact on them."

I said, "I owe you a beer."

"Catch this asshole and I'll buy *you* a keg."

"You're on," I said.

Now, this was how detectives were supposed to operate.

As soon as I hung up, I called out, "Harry!"

CHAPTER 87

DANIEL OTT GOT lucky and saw the grumpy barmaid leaving The Queen's Castle not long after lunch. It was days like this, when he found someone truly deserving of his attention, that he was glad he was so careful. As long as he could maintain his cool, he knew he could do this indefinitely.

He followed her for a few blocks, then saw her go into an apartment building. A few minutes later, someone opened the blinds in the corner apartment on the third floor. Ott smiled. He calculated how much time he wanted to spend with this barmaid. He'd already decided that if anyone else was home, he'd take them down with her.

He reached down and touched the work pouch on his belt. It had a knife, some zip ties, and a pair of gloves. He also had a seven-inch steel rod. He had wondered what it would be like to drive the rod through someone's temple. Or maybe hold it over her chest and let her contemplate what was about to happen. Power surged through him when he was deciding how someone might die.

He pictured this woman on the floor of her apartment, duct tape wrapped around her mouth. Ott could sit on top of her as long as he wanted before he attacked her eye. Before he taunted the police by mixing her blood with the blood from a previous victim. He couldn't remember anyone he'd looked forward to dealing with more than this barmaid. It was as much for her behavior and attitude as it was about his leaving a legacy here in New York.

If that happened with the help of a foolish copycat, so be it. CNN was already talking about him. He couldn't imagine the coverage when yet another body landed in the morgue. By then he would be back in Omaha, recharging before he went out into the world again.

His phone rang in his pocket. He casually picked it up without taking his eyes off the apartment. Even as he heard his younger daughter's voice say, "Hello, Daddy!" he never stopped staring at the apartment.

He said, "Hello, my angel."

"When are you coming home, Daddy?"

He could hear his wife prompting his daughter. He said, "Soon, my angel, soon."

"Are you almost done in York City?"

Ott heard his wife correct her.

The little girl repeated, "Are you almost done in New York City?"

"Yes, little angel. I only have one more job to complete." He smiled.

CHAPTER 88

IT DIDN'T TAKE me long to schedule a team meeting in the Gramercy Park area at the Thirteenth Precinct, the closest precinct to the hotel where Daniel Ott was staying.

All the homicide detectives with cases related to this killer were here: Terri Hernandez, looking like an athletic college student even with her heavy ballistic vest; Javier Tunez, reviewing case details on his phone; Dan Jackson, a mountain in his tactical gear; Raina Rayesh, focused and going through notes.

And all of us were wearing our blue NYPD raid jackets. We detectives were going by the book today.

We also had a uniformed sergeant and five uniformed patrol officers. This was a newer tactic we'd used in the last few years. People got so concerned about the chance of someone impersonating a detective, having a uniformed officer with us often helped. Harry Grissom had arranged for that. The big sergeant was named Mike Sadecki. He looked like he shaved with a machete. I was glad to have him with us.

"We're not here to do anything fancy. Some of us will stay outside in case he runs. We'll all stay on channel 3 on our radios," Harry explained. "We got no warrant. We just want to get eyes on this guy. Talk to him for a few minutes without worrying about dealing with the district attorney or anything like that. If we got a warrant, we couldn't talk to him, because it's assumed he's represented. That's just stupid local DA policy."

Raina Rayesh asked, "How sure are you about this guy?"

I answered that. "If he's not our suspect, there are a lot of coincidences. His work schedule puts him in three different cities during three corresponding murder sprees." I distributed printouts of his driver's license. "He's about five foot ten, very average-looking. No one ever seems to notice him."

Twenty minutes later, we had developed a simple but effective plan: Harry, Raina, and I would walk into the hotel lobby with Sergeant Sadecki.

The hotel was six stories tall and tucked between two fifteen-story buildings, its exterior so bright and cheerful that it looked out of place in the city. This wasn't a Ritz-Carlton or even a Marriott. This was the kind of place a family traveling on a budget stayed—or where a company put up a worker on extended assignment.

There were two clerks behind the counter but no one else in the plain, practical lobby. I walked toward a middle-aged woman with neatly tied-back brown hair who looked to be the senior clerk, but she turned away and disappeared into a room behind the front desk. That left a young, hipster-looking dude with mismatched earrings and hair that looked like it hadn't been combed in a couple of days.

The young man looked up at the uniformed sergeant and me. We stepped all the way to the counter so we could look over into the space behind it.

The clerk was clearly surprised. And not terribly happy to see us police officers inside the hotel. "What do you guys need?"

I smiled and stayed polite. "Do you have a Daniel Ott registered here?"

"Can't tell you. Can't tell the cops anything without a warrant."

The sergeant used a fatherly tone when he said, "Son, this is really important. We're just asking if he's here."

"And I'm just telling you, I can't say anything without a warrant."

"Can't or won't?"

"Both."

I asked, "Is your supervisor here?"

"Nope. I'm the assistant manager. And I'm telling you to get a warrant. I'm also about to tell you to leave the hotel unless you have one." He worked hard at leveling an intimidating stare at Sadecki.

I put a hand on the sergeant's shoulder. Sadecki was used to dealing with this attitude toward the police. But he clearly had no patience for it.

I said with a smile, "We'll call your corporate office and wait in the lobby here."

"You can't wait in the lobby."

As we turned, Sergeant Sadecki said, "Go ahead, call the cops on us."

CHAPTER 89

I STOOD WITH Sergeant Sadecki and Detective Raina Rayesh in the corner of the empty lobby farthest from the desk clerk.

I had an idea.

I called Terri Hernandez on the radio. "We're having a problem with the clerk. Can you turn your raid coat inside out, then come through the lobby and go up the stairs? Just wait there for me to call you. Don't take any action or do anything."

All she said was "Give me thirty seconds."

That's why I like working with my friends. They never give me excuses.

A minute later, I had the big sergeant block the clerk's view of me while I pulled out my cell phone and called the hotel. The clerk picked up on the first ring. As soon as he said his standard welcome, I kept my voice very low and raspy.

I said, "Dude, I'm glad you answered. This is Daniel Ott. Cops might be looking for me." I glanced over my shoulder.

The clerk was working hard to keep a neutral face. All he said was "Okay."

I continued on as Daniel Ott. "Can you get to my room right now?"

"Not this second."

"I got a thousand bucks if you can come up and help me for less than a minute."

"Yes, sir, I'll be right up."

I smiled at the way the clerk tried to keep his tone professional and efficient.

Just then, Terri walked past us. She turned and took the stairway like she'd been staying at the hotel for weeks. No one gave her a second look.

The clerk called for the woman from the back room and asked her to watch the front desk. He made a point of saying loudly, so we all could hear him, "And don't tell the cops anything. They don't have a warrant."

I watched the clerk get into the elevator. When it stopped on the third floor, I called Terri quickly to tell her what floor to check.

"I'll swing by," she said. "Call you back in a minute."

Less than a minute later, my phone rang. Terri said, "Ott's there, in room 319, on the west side of the building. The clerk was talking to him as I walked past. All I saw was a white male in a short-sleeved white shirt and blue pants. Almost like uniform pants. Very average-looking."

Concise yet thorough. As good a report as I had ever heard. Sounded like our guy.

Today was the day we'd finally meet. I was sure of it.

CHAPTER 90

THROUGH RUNNING WATER, Daniel Ott heard the knock on his door. He was at the sink, sanitizing the tool he had used to kill the barmaid. His last New York City kill.

Ott looked through the peephole and immediately recognized the scraggly hotel clerk. He twisted his head and could see there was no one standing next to the man. He opened the door slowly.

Ott stared at the young man but got no response. Finally, he said, "Yes?"

The clerk said, "You just called the front desk and said the cops were looking for you. I couldn't answer you because they were standing nearby. I played them like fools."

Ott assessed the clerk's bad posture and dirty fingernails. He doubted the young man had played anyone for a fool.

Just then an attractive woman with dark hair walked past in

the hallway. Her eyes cut into the room for just a moment. Ott immediately pegged her for a cop. Detective Michael Bennett couldn't be far behind.

Ott stepped over to the table where his work pouch sat. He pulled on a fresh pair of rubber gloves, replaced the freshly washed tool, picked up the kit, and clipped it onto his belt.

"The cops are downstairs in the lobby right now?" he asked.

The clerk looked confused. "Yes. Isn't that why you called me?"

Ott could put the pieces of this puzzle together. He knew they had tricked this dull-witted clerk, and he knew he had to get moving right now.

The clerk said, "You said there'd be a thousand bucks in it for me if I helped you."

"You haven't figured out that wasn't me on the phone? They were just trying to trick you into giving away my room number." Ott almost felt bad for the clerk. The young man's look of confusion turned to disappointment.

Ott pulled out his wallet. He had withdrawn some extra cash in preparation for his trip home. He handed a fistful of twenties and tens to the clerk. "I don't know how much is there, but I'll try to get you some more. I need you to do something that will help me out and piss off the cops at the same time."

The clerk smiled. "All right!"

"Is the woman who passed us still in the hallway?"

The clerk looked in each direction. "I don't see anyone."

Ott stepped into the hallway and shut the door silently. He whispered as they walked to the stairwell, "Run down the stairs and shout, *He's out on the fire escape, climbing to the roof!* Make sure the cops hear you," Ott stressed to the clerk.

"Then what do I do?"

"Run out the front door. Don't stop for anything."

"How will I get the rest of the money from you?"

Ott was surprised the clerk had thought that far ahead. "I'll leave it in an envelope at the front desk later."

The clerk said, "What do the cops want you for?"

Ott paused, then said, "I burned down an ICE building."

"Cool."

"Do what I said and we'll both be heroes."

Ott sent the clerk scurrying down the main stairs. He looked in every direction and saw no sign of the woman from earlier.

Ott headed for the rear stairway. The door was locked, but it took only a couple of twists with the screwdriver to pop it open.

He hoped his hasty plan would work.

CHAPTER 91

I WAS STARTLED by a shout. I looked up at the wide staircase and saw the hipster clerk rushing down. It took a moment to realize what he was saying.

The scrawny clerk yelled, "He's on the fire escape! He's climbing to the roof!"

Sergeant Sadecki said, "What?"

When the clerk reached the bottom of the stairs, he turned and ran right out the front door of the hotel.

Instantly, I called Terri on her cell phone. "The clerk just ran out of here shouting that Ott is on the fire escape climbing to the roof."

Terri said, "Stand by one sec." She came back on the phone and said, "The door to 319 is closed and locked."

"Can you see the fire escape from anywhere?"

Another few seconds later and Terri said, "I can see most of it from a window at the end of the corridor. I don't see anyone on it from this vantage point."

I said, "Stay on the door in case it's a trick. Listen on the radio." I wasted no time in turning to the sergeant. "Alert your guys outside. Call in some more help. And while you're at it, call Grissom. Ott might be anywhere by now."

I raced up the stairs as the others started to fan out and search for our suspect.

I found Terri Hernandez in front of 319. I pulled my gun, and she did the same. Without a word, I turned and kicked the door to 319. With a loud crack, it snapped open and slammed into the wall.

We entered the two-room suite with our guns pointed in front of us. I swung to my left to make sure the bathroom was empty. Terri kept moving forward into the small living room. She waited for me to catch up as we moved into the bedroom.

Terri cleared the second bathroom.

I did a quick sweep under the bed and in the closet. Nothing. The windows were all closed and locked from the inside.

I tried to think where Ott might have gone.

I got on the radio. "The room's empty. It doesn't look like he got on the fire escape. There are at least two levels under-ground. Mostly for maintenance and storage. Has anyone seen anything there?"

The uniformed sergeant came on and said they had covered the entire outside and he had someone searching the roof.

Detective Raina Rayesh came on the radio and said, "The other clerk tells me Ott checked in six weeks and three days ago. She gave me a set of passkeys so we don't have to kick in any doors."

Terri Hernandez mumbled, "Too late."

Terri and I met the cops from the roof and we searched each floor, stairwell, and elevator carefully. We found nothing.

More cops arrived, including my lieutenant, but we still had no idea where Daniel Ott had disappeared to. Harry Grissom put his arm around my shoulders, knowing how I must feel.

He said, "This is a win. We know who this guy is now. What he looks like. For once we can use the media to our advantage."

CHAPTER 92

I SAT WITH Harry Grissom in the hotel lobby as for the second time in days we crafted a news release revealing the identifying details of a serial killer.

By the time we'd announced Jeffrey Cedar's crimes, he was already dead.

This was a far more sensitive situation. We would be getting a murderous fugitive's name and picture out into the public in the midst of an active hunt for him. Plus, there was an incoming report of a fresh homicide, done at an apartment in Queens, that fit Ott's profile. The public needed to understand that anyone who got in his way could be in danger. Or, for different reasons, anyone who had helped him.

Raina Rayesh had questioned the male clerk when he returned to the hotel. Under a little pressure, he confessed that he'd helped Ott escape. He said he did it for money and admitted that he'd come back to look for the balance of his payout.

When Raina told him his actions amounted to aiding and abetting a fugitive, which made him an accessory to Ott's crimes, the clerk tried to walk it all back, saying he thought Ott was only involved in some kind of antifa bullshit, not the murders that had been all over the news.

As she cuffed him, Raina had said, "Tell it to your lawyer."

We never did need to call on the retired Detective Lynch from SFPD, but Harry and I did have to prepare for a talk with the bigwigs at One Police Plaza. But first, while Harry finished the details on the press release, I wanted to take another look around the hotel.

Raina gave me the ring of passkeys, and I went down a level to a dark storage area. The same key opened all the locked maintenance doors. Behind one of the doors was the maintenance stairwell. It went down another level.

I couldn't be sure if someone had searched here, so I took the stairs down. It was about as I'd expected: dark and musty, with an unused workbench covered with tools sitting in the corner. Seemed like the kind of place a killer on the run might hide out. Especially one who used tools only as weapons.

I thought about calling Terri Hernandez to come down and give me a hand, but I realized I could see the entire level. Especially now that it was becoming clear that Ott had somehow given us the slip, I didn't need any help. I took a few minutes to look in the corners and under a couple of cabinets, but there was nowhere to hide here, and no street exit. The only way in or out of this room was via the maintenance stairwell or the elevator.

As I turned back to the stairwell, I noticed a familiar struc-
ture. One of those big, wall-mounted circuit boxes. Maybe they
were called junction boxes.

Where had I seen one of these before?

I hesitated, looking at the box.

CHAPTER 93

OTT COULDN'T SEE his watch, but by counting his breaths, he knew he'd spent at least thirty minutes crammed inside a junction box on the bottom floor of his extended-stay hotel. This one hadn't been nearly as hard to get into as the one at the library. But between the conduit and wires streaming through the box, it was just as uncomfortable.

The question was, how long would the cops search? His escape plan hinged on the cops thinking he had left the area. Enough time had probably passed to make them believe it.

Noises buzzed through the junction box. He heard a couple of air conditioners cycling. He also heard the distant sound of a toilet flushing. And then, for the past few minutes, silence.

He was preparing to open the door and slide out of the box when he heard a noise so close that it could only have been made by someone looking for him. But it couldn't be.

The quick glimpse he'd gotten of the room had told him it was rarely used.

He thought about what he had on him. Tools, his wallet, his burner phone, and his personal phone. Not that he could use the personal phone again. Ever. Or his credit cards. He hadn't even thought about never seeing his daughters or wife again. But those were the facts laid out in front of him.

Once he escaped from this hotel, he'd have to leave his whole life as Daniel Ott behind.

Ott shifted his weight. He stayed in place for a moment, listening. Then he raised his left arm enough to move the sliding lock and open the door to the junction box.

He let it swing wide. In the glow from the single light on in the corner, the room appeared to be empty. He sat there for a moment, listening. Then he stretched his legs out and let them drop over the side of the box, giving himself a moment to let the blood return to his limbs. Finally, Ott slid out of the box and landed quietly on the rough concrete floor.

He had to smile. The cops may have figured out who he was and where he was staying, but they had not caught him. He was still smarter than them.

Ott turned to close the door to the junction box. He didn't want anyone getting any ideas about how he had escaped. He might use a similar hiding place again.

As he turned from the box, Ott was startled to see a tall man casually leaning against the door to the stairwell. It took a moment, but he recognized him as Detective Michael Bennett.

"Nice try, Ott," Bennett said, "but you already used the same trick at the library. I'm slow, but I still pick up on patterns given enough chances."

Ott's eyes darted around the room, and he reached for a tool from his pouch.

Bennett didn't change his tone. "Don't even think about it." He moved his right hand and showed Ott he was holding a pistol. "And I already sounded the alarm. You're not getting away from NYPD this time."

Ott raised his hands slowly.

CHAPTER 94

I ARRESTED DANIEL OTT without incident.

Arrested without incident. That's always the best line in a report.

With Harry Grissom's help, we soon had Ott ensconced in an interview room at the Thirteenth Precinct. It might've been the fastest I ever got a murder suspect from the field to a full-blown interview.

The room was wired for sound and video, but I wasn't going to take any chances. He was a tech guy, probably studied engineering. That meant he would be working the room, looking for an escape hatch. Not this time.

I sat behind a cheap wood-veneer table on an uncomfortable plastic chair facing Daniel Ott, who was struggling to get used to the constraint of having his hands cuffed behind his back. He kept knocking the metal against the back of his plastic chair.

I pulled out my notebook and my tape recorder.

There was also an old-style two-way mirror. We couldn't see anything in the outer room, but I could imagine how many people were crammed in there to hear this interview of a killer who had bested law enforcement for nearly a year, though his streak could've been even longer.

I had already gotten a few calls, with increasing frequency, from Emily Parker at the FBI. She probably wanted to tip me off that the FBI was about to horn in. Typical. She'd been too busy to access FBI resources when I needed them, and now that I'd found our suspect without her help, I was too busy to talk.

It's unusual to interview a suspect solo. Partners practice the substance and order of their questions, who will do the asking and who will take notes. This was not a usual situation. Thank God I had a boss who had faith in me. He realized I'd be better off on my own.

I read Ott his rights and made sure he understood each of them. I asked him the usual questions, like name, age, and marital status. He didn't seem to hold back any information. He told me about his wife and two daughters in Omaha. Then he surprised me by saying, "I read that you have ten kids. How does that work?"

This guy was a level beyond most criminals. He was the first suspect ever to confess that he'd researched me, and I was completely thrown when he started questioning *me* in the middle of a police interview. Usually the person whose hands aren't cuffed is the one asking the questions.

I decided to answer him, thought it was a step in the right direction for building rapport. "It usually works pretty well," I said, "but organizing ten kids can be a challenge."

There was nothing threatening about his physical appearance.

He was a pleasant-looking, clean, reasonably well-dressed man. Most people wouldn't have a problem talking to him.

I did. I was the father of six daughters, and he'd killed more women than I had in my entire family.

He seemed so normal, or *The man I knew could never murder people,* I could already imagine Ott's neighbors saying when the media descended upon them.

I asked, "You need anything? Something to eat? A drink?" Suspects were quick to claim mistreatment, and I wasn't about to lose this crucial statement on that account.

Ott looked me right in the eye and said, "I'm not hungry. And your process is inefficient. I can save us all some time."

"How's that? From the moment you committed your first murder you were on stolen time. You stole years of your victims' lives that they and their loved ones will never get back."

"That's one way of looking at my actions, Detective Bennett," Ott said. "I see them differently."

We were approaching a stalemate, so I changed tack.

"How do you choose your victims?" I asked.

"American women with their attitudes and smart mouths set me off," he said. "I heard an intern at an insurance office brag that she was studying communications in college so she'd never have to be a lonely telephone tech. Can you believe that? I am a grown man who provides for his family and that little bitch was looking down her nose at me."

He was talking about Elaine Anastas.

"That's why you killed her, and then wrote that threatening letter, 'To the Women of New York'?"

"I was teaching them a lesson. I wrote that I would kill the ones who didn't respect me, and I always do exactly what I say,"

Ott sneered. "I've been killing women for ten years, Detective Bennett, longer than that partner of yours has been on the force. A significant portion of your own career."

I can sit quietly through the most horrifying stories, nodding along with what feels like perverse encouragement. Lots of *I see* or *Wow* as a suspect continues detailing incriminating actions, when all along I really want to scream *You sick asshole.*

But in all my years interviewing suspects, this was the first time I had ever been left absolutely speechless.

I forced myself to continue the interview.

"Do I understand you correctly?" I said. "Are you making a confession?"

"I confess to committing the capital offense of first-degree murder. *Many* times over."

"Mr. Ott, I've advised you of your rights," I said. "Are you sure you want to continue?"

"Oh, I'm just getting started," Ott said. "You have no idea what I've done, what I planned to be doing for the rest of my life, until you came along. You, who didn't even understand the messages I left."

I ignored his taunt. "Why don't you start by telling me about the homicides here in New York. Then we'll review Atlanta and San Francisco, where your presence was verified during all of the related murders in those cities."

"That's how you found me, isn't it?" Ott asked. "Timed the murders to the schedule of my contract work?"

I knew better than to confirm any information. "There were a lot of factors that went into your arrest."

Ott ignored my non-answer to his question and continued. "And then you saw me at the library. That was my big mistake.

I got so used to most people looking right through me that at a crucial time I forgot a detective might be watching. You got my attention that day as a worthy opponent," Ott said. "I tried and failed to derail your investigation. You won. And now I won't hold anything back. I promise."

I sat there, astonished, as Daniel Ott began listing the murders he'd committed in New York City.

"When I first arrived in New York," he said, "I went exploring, looking for interesting neighborhoods and people I wanted to spend time with."

"That's your way of saying you wanted to kill them, isn't it?" I asked.

He nodded, then said, "I found a woman in the Bronx, and one in Brooklyn. I don't even know their names, only that they had loud American mouths on them."

Ott made no effort to hide his obsession with forcing women to obey rules and show respect. I shuddered to think how he treated his wife and daughters.

"It was easier to get to know the women in Manhattan," Ott said. "I met them on the job. One was a law student moonlighting in a medical supply office. And I told you about that disrespectful intern already."

"She had a name," I said. "Elaine. Her mother and friends called her Laney."

CHAPTER 95

TACTICALLY, IT WASN'T the smartest idea to loosen Daniel Ott's handcuffs and move them to the front, but I had to reward him for being so forthright.

Though Ott, by his own admission, had made some mistakes, I knew he was skilled and he was smart. Scary smart. He'd evaded us a number of times. I didn't want to find out he was some kind of martial arts genius or an assassin who could take a straw and cram it up your nose into your brain. Or maybe I'd just watched too many Jason Bourne movies.

"Tell me about the librarian," I said, focusing on one of the recent murders I was not absolutely sure he'd committed. I wanted confirmation one way or the other. "That's where your pattern seems to have suddenly shifted."

"I didn't want to kill the librarian," Ott said, "and I didn't enjoy it the way I did spending time with the others. When she confronted me in the computer room, she saw my face, and I couldn't risk her recognizing me."

"That doesn't explain why you killed the young man," I said.

"He was there." Ott shrugged. "I tried to do a quick job in front of the apartment building since there were people nearby, so I slashed her across her throat and intended to keep walking. Then that guy came out of the building at the wrong time and saw her dead body. I had to kill him too. I had no choice."

There's always a choice, I wanted to say, but someone like Ott would never understand.

"And the bartender from The Queen's Castle?" I asked, referring to the incident report I had been handed as I entered the interview room.

"My latest victim," Ott said with a fearsome smile. "How I did enjoy her, once she stopped talking."

This story was getting sicker and sicker, but I had mostly known the answers to the questions I had been asking Ott. I was about to forge into unknown territory.

"What about the murder on Staten Island?"

"Staten Island?" he said. "I've never even been there."

"You had nothing to do with the stabbing of Marilyn Shaw in her apartment?" I said, showing Ott a picture of the murder victim.

He leaned back like we were old friends having a beer after work. "That must've been the one I read about in the paper. I have enjoyed reading about myself, but you know as well as I do that the media is wrong most of the time. It should have been obvious I wasn't the Staten Island killer."

I took my time writing some notes. I needed to think about this. I wanted him to think about it too.

I asked him about the SoHo homicide, which was another one he hadn't confessed to. "What about Lila Stein in SoHo?" Again, I displayed a photo of the victim.

He shook his head. "Not me."

I looked at Ott, trying to get a feel for him. Here was a guy who had freely admitted to committing half a dozen murders in the city. Plus more across the country that he'd done throughout the past decade. I had to dig deeper.

"In your letter to the New York *Daily News*," I said, "you wrote, 'Think of the one who has killed the most. I am better than him.' Who is that?"

"The person who killed those two women was trying to copy me," Ott said. "Everyone should copy the master, the one who has killed the most. The Butcher of Rostov. The Red Ripper. I learned his ways when I was a young man, working for my first employer."

Ott's confession had been flowing, then suddenly he'd turned cryptic. My mind flashed on the prolific serial killers Ott had been tracking. *Little. Bundy. Chikatilo.*

I took an educated guess. "Andrei Chikatilo."

Ott looked surprised and pleased. "You know the master's name."

But there was more I had to know.

"You took the blood of your victims and mixed it with blood at fresh crime scenes," I said. "You haven't been home for more than six weeks. Where is the blood of your New York victims?"

"The blood vials I collected here are in sealed plastic bags inside a can falsely labeled shaving cream. You can find it in my hotel room. The others are in a safe in my home office. I wouldn't want my girls getting into them."

I couldn't resist asking, "Why do you mutilate the women's left eyes?"

"That's simple. I stand over them, and they're completely in my control. The last sight they see is my face."

Internally, I was reeling with horror, but I couldn't stop the interview.

"Did you push a woman in front of a bus near our office?"

"By the elevated train?"

I nodded, already knowing the response.

"I *meant* to shove the detective with the broken nose. He tried to be a hero and lost."

I had to move off the subject before I got too angry and did something stupid. I simmered for a minute. I was too wound up that Ott had made Hollis his target. That he had known about my kids, about Mary Catherine and our wedding. I couldn't focus.

But there was one more question I had to ask. "Why did you sign your letter 'Bobby Fisher'?"

Before Ott could answer, I heard voices outside the door. Loud voices. Arguing.

CHAPTER 96

THE SOUNDS OUTSIDE the interview room brought even Daniel Ott up short.

Someone bumped against the door. This was more than an argument. This was a scuffle. Then I heard Harry Grissom's voice. He was regaining order.

I stood up and gestured for Ott to stay seated. I walked across the small interview room and popped open the door. I stuck my head out into the hallway with the idea of shouting, *Keep it down!*

Instead, I was shocked into silence at the sight of Harry and a precinct captain named Jefferson squaring off with several extremely well-dressed people, including Robert Lincoln, the assistant special agent in charge of the New York FBI office.

How did they even know we made an arrest? Are they trying to physically steal our suspect?

What I said was "Hey, what's going on?" My voice sounded remarkably calm, especially considering my confusion.

Emily Parker stepped through the pack of people. She looked at Harry as if she was trying to calm down an angry lion. Then she turned to me. "We have a federal warrant for your suspect, Daniel Ott."

I stepped out into the hall and shut the interview room door behind me. "You worked a separate case on him? Without even talking to me?"

"Mike, it's not what you think."

It was Harry Grissom who spoke next. "*I* think it's bullshit. This is just some kind of stupid FBI ploy. They're claiming this mope is a spy."

I twisted my face as I looked at Emily.

She nodded.

A spy? That's why Emily had been stalling the help she'd promised me. She was after a bigger prize.

The world seemed to be spinning too quickly. I'd had my run-ins with the FBI over the years. I'd cracked a lot of jokes about the federal agency. Never in my wildest dreams had I thought they were capable of taking control of a suspect who was in the midst of confessing to multiple homicides. The only real question I had was if they had fabricated an excuse to steal my suspect, or if they'd specifically withheld information and waited for the right time to screw up my case.

It was Robert Lincoln who took advantage of my shock. He stepped forward and slipped into the interrogation room so smoothly, I barely even noticed him sliding past me.

I stepped back into the room as well. Ott didn't acknowledge anything unusual going on.

Lincoln looked at him and said, "You're Daniel Ott, correct?"

He nodded.

"I'm Robert Lincoln with the FBI. You're in the custody of the NYPD, but I have a federal warrant. It has nothing to do with the homicides Detective Bennett has been questioning you about."

Ott said quietly, "I've been expecting you. My previous employer must have sent you."

"And who would that be?"

"The Russian government."

I stepped between him and the FBI ASAC. I turned to the FBI ASAC and said, "What the hell are you talking about? What's your warrant for?"

The athletic, well-dressed man smiled. "Espionage. He came to the US about twelve years ago working for the Russian government. They lost track of him almost a decade ago. And so did we. But now we finally have him."

"You mean, *I* have him."

"Not any longer."

CHAPTER 97

THE LITTLE INTERVIEW room was crowded with NYPD brass and FBI agents. Ott continued to sit quietly on the plastic chair with his handcuffed hands folded in his lap. Two FBI agents stood on either side of Ott like someone from the NYPD might try to grab him and run.

Ott wasn't Jason Bourne. And he wasn't Andrei Chikatilo. But he *was* dangerous.

I was smart enough to let Harry Grissom do most of the talking. The way he snatched the warrant out of Robert Lincoln's hands told me just how pissed off he really was.

Harry turned to the FBI ASAC and said, "Where's the affidavit for the warrant?"

"It's sealed. National security. You don't need to see it anyway. All you need to know is that it's a legitimate warrant that says the FBI is taking custody of Daniel Ott. Are you disputing that?" Lincoln was sharp and not about to wilt under the searing glare of my lieutenant.

Emily Parker quietly tugged on my elbow and moved me out into the slightly less crowded hallway. She said, "This is no joke, Mike. The case is legit. Daniel Ott came here as a spy under the assigned American identity David Hastings. He was told to marry and raise an American family, but about ten years ago he met a Polish woman and used her contacts to change his identity. Then he disappeared."

"Is serial killing part of his assignment?"

"He is a trained assassin, but we've learned that as a young man, he developed an interest in the Russian serial killer Andrei Chikatilo that escalated into an obsession when Chikatilo was executed in 1994. He was never known to have acted on it. We now know that was false information."

"How'd you pick up on the fact that Daniel Ott used to be David Hastings?"

"We suspected it from a DNA hit from a cold case in Omaha. Then we heard from a source in the NYPD that you'd made an arrest, and the source also sent us a copy of Ott's fingerprints from here at the precinct. All we had to do was fill in the last part of the affidavit and here we are."

"So this isn't just some cheap ploy by your asshole boss?"

"He's been circling for days, waiting for you to make the solve. Several of us wanted him to wait until after you finished your interviews and Ott was booked into Rikers Island. Lincoln did want you to get credit for that."

I wanted to believe my old friend, but Lincoln never wanted to share credit, especially with me. I stepped back into the room. An agent I didn't recognize spoke to Ott in what sounded like Russian. Ott answered him. Also in what I assumed was Russian.

As two FBI agents helped Ott to his feet, Harry Grissom leaned in close to me and said, "At least he's not getting back on the street. It hurts to lose a suspect this way, but we did everything we could."

"I know, Harry. All I wanted to do was stop the killings. I'm getting used to the FBI taking credit for shit." Then I smiled.

Harry gave me a concerned look and said, "You're not having some kind of seizure, are you?"

"No, Harry. Ott is going to prison, and I'm getting married. Moving on."

Ott turned to me as he was led to the door. "I'm glad you'll get to see your daughters grow up, Detective Bennett. That's what I'll miss the most."

CHAPTER 98

I MANAGED TO time my homecoming to the news of the arrest hitting the airwaves. It was a sweet moment. Mary Catherine greeted me with a big hug and a kiss on the lips. The kids joined in with cheers and high fives all around.

Stopping these murders was an important accomplishment, but I was having a seriously hard time wrapping my head around the shadow case—in which Daniel Ott was not only a killer but a killer spy.

It was an unbelievable story. My wife-to-be was the second person I told. First honors belonged to my NYPD partner.

I had stopped in to visit Hollis on my way home. Even from his hospital bed, with half his body in a cast, he'd still managed a pretty good string of obscenities describing his outrage over the FBI stealing our case.

Our professional bonding ended the moment Brett Hollis's

mother entered the room, however, and motioned me out into the hallway with her.

Mrs. Hollis said, "Are you trying to stir him up? I'm running out for a sandwich. Don't be here when I get back."

I had to ask. "Have I done something to offend you?"

She clearly had an answer at the ready, but paused, almost as if for dramatic effect. "You allowed him to believe that he could be like you, and that delusion nearly got him killed. I have no use for the NYPD. Or for you."

"Your son is a fine detective, a credit to the force," I said.

"But he will never be 'Michael Bennett.' If he keeps trying for the impossible, it will cost him his life."

She was dead serious. I had to wonder if there was any truth to what she was saying. *Had* I put Hollis in danger? Or was Ott to blame?

As I stepped back into the room, I found Hollis sitting up in bed, reading a book about serial killers. Of course.

"I see you're studying for our next case, but I can say with authority our serial killer case is closed," I said. "You made a lot of the important breakthroughs. You should be proud."

"I just followed your lead," he said. But then his bright smile faded.

Hollis had responded well to praise in the past but now seemed distracted. He hadn't really been listening to what I was saying because he had been waiting to tell me something.

He stopped to gather himself, as if rehearsing his next words in his mind before speaking them. "I wasn't reading that book for our next case. In fact, there won't be another case. Not with us working as partners. Not any case." He stopped short, choked up, and stifled a sob.

What the hell is Hollis talking about?

"What are you saying?" I asked. "What's wrong?"

He raised a hand, and my gaze followed, settling on the stack of papers resting on his night stand.

"What's that? Workers' comp paperwork?"

Hollis shook his head. "That's what I've been trying to tell you," he said, pausing to run a tissue across his face. "I've been examined by two different department doctors. They want me to go out on disability." His voice had trailed off, like that of a beaten man.

It was the first I'd heard of this career-ending medical directive. I stood in silence, shocked.

"What are the doctors' main concerns?" I finally asked.

Hollis said, "It has to do with liability. The injuries I sustained from the impact of the bus were too pervasive, and too damaging to withstand the physical stress of detective work."

He blew his nose, then looked me in the eye. "I'm going to physical therapy starting next week. I'll see how that goes." He tried to sit up straighter. "There's a chance I could come back. They say they'll have to monitor me closely, especially my legs and hips. My mom is all about me leaving the NYPD and trying another line of work."

This young man was truly torn. The pressure from his mom wasn't making it any easier on him. But maybe there was some truth to what she was saying. Maybe, without even realizing it, I'd put pressure on him. By believing in him, I'd emboldened him to do too much too soon. On the other hand, it was because of his courageous actions that Kelly Konick was still alive and a dangerous killer was off the streets.

I studied the bruises around his face. Finally, I said, "What do *you* want to do?"

"I want to be a cop." His voice had some power in it now.

"Why?"

"I want to make a difference. To help people."

I nodded. "Those are the right reasons to be a cop. Most people have never felt the desire to work in our profession, which makes that feeling, that drive, impossible to understand. Police work has been such an important part of my life, but I realized something as I got older."

"What?"

"There are *other* important things in life. There are *other* ways to help people. You need to decide where to dedicate your talents."

"What I want to do is come back to work. Do you think I'd be able to come back to our squad?" He sounded like a kid asking permission to go out on a Saturday night.

I smiled. "I guarantee you'd be welcomed back as a star."

For the first time since I'd arrived, he looked hopeful.

This man had earned the right to be called my partner.

CHAPTER 99

MARY CATHERINE HAD the best idea for working it all out, just as she always did.

My late wife, Maeve, had been the one to introduce us, in a way. Maeve had been the one who'd hired Mary Catherine, sight unseen, from Ireland. Mary Catherine had shown up on my doorstep just when I needed her. I knew this was no coincidence. Maeve had planned out a happy life for me even while she was dying of cancer. Maeve had done it all. That was the way she was. Unselfish.

And so was Mary Catherine. She could read the strain on my face, about Hollis, about Ott, about everything except my family.

"You need a good bike ride," she said, ordering me to change. Shawna and Chrissy spoke up, then Eddie, Trent, and Jane. Five of ten kids wanted to come with us.

Mary Catherine said, "Anyone who can keep up is welcome to come along."

I knew that was the kind of challenge she and I would both regret.

We started out slowly—after I first had to pump up a couple of tires in the basement, and everyone had to find and put on their approved bike helmets—carefully working our way toward the bike paths in Riverside Park.

Once we got in the park, Shawna turned and grinned. She said, "Mary Catherine, you can come with us." She paused for best possible dramatic effect, then added, "If you can keep up."

That's how I remember the massive bike race starting. I pedaled until I thought my legs would drop off. My lungs burned and my vision might have blurred a little bit. And I still could not catch my fiancée. No one could. She had the form and grace of a professional cyclist.

I could say the race lasted for days and people died from exhaustion. But that wouldn't do it justice. The way Mary Catherine rode down those young people and then raced ahead of all of us, she was putting on a show.

She had a competitive streak and had somehow effectively hidden it from us until now. Or maybe we had just refused to see it. The kids would never look at her quite the same way again. Neither would I.

By the time I caught up to her near a water fountain that we used as a meeting point, she was sitting on a park bench with her helmet off like she'd been waiting for us for hours. All I could do was laugh—once I could breathe again, that is.

The kids stared at Mary Catherine like she had jumped off the pages of a Marvel comic book.

I sat down next to her as the kids got water and greeted a couple of their friends who had been playing in the park.

I said, "I like to see you smile after slapping down the kids and me."

"That *was* fun," she agreed. "But it's not why I'm smiling so much."

"Oh, yeah? Why *are* you smiling so much, then?"

"Our wedding is only a few days away. This Saturday, you'll be my husband."

I reached over and took her beautiful face in my hands and kissed her. She kissed me back. It almost made me forget we were in public. That is, until the kids crowded around us.

Trent said, "Why don't you guys get a room?"

Jane said, "Did I act that way around Allan?"

Trent and Eddie nodded at the same time.

All Jane could say was "Ouch. I'll keep that in mind in the future."

Then we all folded into a laughing, hugging ball of crazy New Yorkers.

CHAPTER 100

ON OUR WAY home, I said a silent prayer, thanking God for the wonderful life I had. And for my bright, healthy kids and my smart, beautiful fiancée. I was in a particularly grateful mood.

Then came Fiona and her seventh-grade math homework. It never got any easier, no matter how many times I helped each of the kids in succession.

Fiona hadn't put out a general call for assistance. Only her dad's help would do, and I couldn't ignore it. But holy cow. I'd been pretty good at math in school. The same school that Fiona went to now. How could I look at this page and not understand a single instruction?

After about fifteen minutes of reading the problems and searching through her book for an example I understood, I had to look at Fiona and say, "We need more help. Ask Eddie."

From my seat at the dining room table, I called to Mary

Catherine in the kitchen. Her reply was short and to the point. "I can't spare Eddie. You're the one with a college degree."

I said, "A degree in philosophy doesn't prepare you for seventh-grade math."

"Does it prepare you for anything?"

"'I am the wisest man alive, for I know one thing, and that is that I know nothing,'" I quoted. "Socrates."

Mary Catherine said, "You were already proving your point. You didn't have to back it up with a quote."

Brian casually strolled over to the dining room table. He looked at the book and checked some information on an earlier page. Then he explained to Fiona how to do the problems. Correctly. Amazing.

When Brian was finished, Fiona looked at me and said, "Thanks, Dad."

"What'd I do?"

Fiona smiled. "You adopted a smart kid like Brian."

I let out a laugh. "I guess that *was* a good move."

Brian's smile compounded my good mood. If things are going well with the kids, nothing else really matters.

Mary Catherine called out a good-bye. She was taking the girls for a dress fitting that would last a few hours. The younger boys were all in their rooms, working on some school project. That left just Brian and me.

He was in the living room, reading a *Men's Health* magazine. I flopped down on the other end of the couch where he was sitting.

"How's it going?" I asked.

He grunted. It wasn't hostile or disrespectful. Just efficient. Then he said, "How's it going with you?"

"Honestly," I told him, "I don't really know. I'm just glad to be home."

I decided I needed an answer to the question that had been bothering Mary Catherine and me for so long. I turned to my oldest son and said, "Where do you go all day?"

Brian closed the magazine and gave me a weak smile.

I said, "You can tell me, off the record if you want." After an uncomfortable silence, I added, "I know about the bank withdrawals. I'm not trying to be nosy. I want the best for you. I'm here to help. Any way I can." I hoped my voice wasn't betraying the fear and desperation I was feeling. I really couldn't imagine what Brian might say right now. And suddenly it occurred to me that it could be worse than anything I could dream of.

Brian sighed. He started slowly. "It was going to be a wedding gift."

"Brian, we don't need—"

He held up his hand. "No, Dad, it's not like that."

Now he had my full attention.

Brian said, "Remember when I said I was looking into air-conditioning repair?"

I didn't. I probably heard him tell me and then put it down to one of those ideas kids talk about but never act on.

Brian said, "I didn't make much of a plan at first, but then I signed up to finish my certification. I'll be done in about three weeks. I've already got a job with a company that services office buildings in Manhattan."

I had a lot of questions, but this was my son's story to tell. I let him talk.

Brian said, "I heard people saying how trade school was better than college, so I looked at a few different trades, and air-conditioning repair seems to make the most sense. And I like it."

If Brian expected me to give him a speech, he was wrong. All I did was turn and hug this young man who'd made me so proud.

As I sat there holding my son, I felt my eyes start to water. Then Brian started to cry. I finally felt like I had my son home again.

CHAPTER 101

THE NEXT DAY, I found myself standing in a crowd outside One Police Plaza. Harry Grissom had called me to tell me about the news conference. He said I didn't have to be there. He also said if I did come, it would last only an hour at most. Though I didn't see how that was likely once I heard the mayor start with "Once again our city is safe."

I tuned him out, sorry I'd wasted my morning coming down here. Then I turned to my right and saw John Macy standing near me, sharply dressed in a dark suit with a red tie.

He faced me and said, "Detective, nice to see you. Too bad you couldn't keep hold of your prisoner."

"Too bad you couldn't keep hold of confidential information," I countered. "Your buddy Funcher dropped a hint that you have a tendency to overshare during happy hour. I asked around, and sure enough, the late Jeffrey Cedar was on the outer edge of your circle.

You were the one who let slip to a copycat serial killer the detail about Ott's signature of stabbing his victims in the eye. The detail we were withholding from the press. But you didn't tell Cedar which eye. Ott is right-handed. And Cedar was left-handed. Which explains why Ott went for the left eye and Cedar for the right."

As I turned away from him in disgust, I added, "How're your balls feeling? The mayor is about to put them in a sling." Harry Grissom had stepped up on the other side of me. Macy had a lot of questions to answer, and he wouldn't be going anywhere until he did.

We listened as the mayor, the NYPD commissioner, and Robert Lincoln, assistant special agent in charge of the FBI in New York, all made comments about the arrest of Daniel Ott. There was no mention of him being a spy.

Harry Grissom leaned toward me and said, "Macy has been reassigned. He now reviews business licensing for anything that doesn't relate to food or beverage."

"Sounds like a slice of heaven."

Harry chuckled. "I've still got friends who don't put up with people screwing with the NYPD. But there is a catch."

"I don't like the sound of that. What sort of catch?"

Harry said, "There was no copycat killer. Receptionist Olivia Green was lying—not about Jeffrey Cedar but in her dealings with the IRS. In exchange for amnesty, she'll say Cedar panicked after having a domestic dispute with his wife and died avoiding arrest. Daniel Ott takes the blame for all the murders. The mayor's office prefers to calm public fears about two different killers loose in the city."

"But none of it's true."

"Neither is Santa Claus, but people still believe," Grissom said. "See you at the wedding."

CHAPTER 102

MY WEDDING DAY arrived. I sat in a small room just off the altar of Holy Name. Mary Catherine and I were putting the kids to good use today. Brian was my best man. Trent, Eddie, and Ricky were the groomsmen and ushers. Juliana was the maid of honor. Jane, Bridget, and Fiona were bridesmaids. Shawna and Chrissy were the flower girl and ring bearer respectively. My grandfather, Seamus, would be the one to marry us.

Following tradition, I had not seen or spoken to Mary Catherine today. She and the girls had spent the night in a hotel. It was as close to a bachelorette party as Mary Catherine wanted.

The boys and I had had a pretty good bachelor party too. We'd continued the video game marathon that had been interrupted in the line of duty, and we also managed to eat six pizzas, drink eight liters of soda, and destroy a pile of chicken wings.

At the moment, Brian sat with me, and the other boys rotated to my side as their ushering duties allowed. They all looked extremely sharp in their tuxedos.

Sister Sheilah popped her head into the little room where we waited. She was in full habit but looked different somehow. Then I realized she was wearing makeup. Not a ton, but enough to change her look dramatically.

Sister Sheilah said, "It's showtime. Your boys have seated all the guests, and your grandfather told me to get you moving."

Brian and I stood together. He took a moment to straighten my tie and brush a microscopic piece of lint off my shoulder.

Then Sister Sheilah stepped forward. As a child, I'd been her student, and she'd also taught all ten of my children. In her eyes, I'd never grown up. Sheilah looked at me, giggled, and pinched me on the cheek, repeating the words she'd been saying for months: "I can't believe our little Michael Bennett is getting married."

Today, it was finally true.

She kissed me on the forehead, and I received her blessing.

Brian and I took our positions at the front of the church. It was all I could do not to cry at the sight of my sons escorting their sisters down the aisle to take their places near the altar.

Chrissy followed, holding our rings, and Shawna dropped rose petals on the way to join us at the front of the church. This was a family event. Only Maeve was absent. I felt her looking down on me and smiling at the happiness she'd brought me and the kids by sending Mary Catherine.

The crowd was a sea of familiar faces. Harry Grissom sat next to Terri Hernandez. All the priests and nuns from the church intermingled with dozens of friends.

A movement flashed in the back corner of the church, and I craned my neck to see. It was Brett Hollis, sitting in a wheelchair, raising his arm in something between a wave and a salute. I was honored by his presence, even more so that he was accompanied by detectives from our squad—not his mother.

It was tough to keep the stupid grin off my face. Everything was great.

Then it got better. Almost to the point of fantasy.

The organist played the opening chords to the "Bridal Chorus"—"Here Comes the Bride." Mary Catherine, dressed all in white, took her cue, appearing to float along the rose petals Shawna had tossed onto the carpeted aisle.

The veil covered her face, but I could tell she was beaming with joy. She touched hands with several people in the pews as she continued her graceful glide toward me.

She was so gorgeous, I barely noticed my grandfather walking her down the aisle. He looked sharp too. Dressed in his best vestments, he stood tall and walked with a determined pace, planting each foot carefully.

I felt the lump in my throat grow as a few tears started to leak out of my eyes and my hands trembled.

Then Mary Catherine stopped, joining me at the altar, and taking hold of both of my hands. The effect was instantaneous, as calming as a shot of a tranquilizer.

Things rolled quickly from there. I know my grandfather conducted the service, but I cannot recall a word of it. I don't even remember reading the vows I had written and that Juliana and Jane had approved.

All that I remember—all that I will remember until I'm an old man—is lifting Mary Catherine's veil and melting when I saw her beautiful porcelain face, yet with a pale spray of freckles, like any good Irish girl should have.

We kissed. Our first kiss as husband and wife. And then we were enveloped by a sea of children and an elderly priest. We stood in front of all of our friends, hugging like we'd never let go.

It was probably the best moment of my entire life.

Have You Read Them All?

STEP ON A CRACK
(with Michael Ledwidge)

The most powerful people in the world have gathered for a
funeral in New York City. They don't know it's a trap devised
by a ruthless mastermind, and it's up to Michael Bennett to
save every last hostage.

RUN FOR YOUR LIFE
(with Michael Ledwidge)

The Teacher is giving New York a lesson it will never forget,
slaughtering the powerful and the arrogant. Michael Bennett
discovers a vital pattern, but has only a few hours to save
the city.

WORST CASE
(with Michael Ledwidge)

Children from wealthy families are being abducted. But the
captor isn't demanding money. He's quizzing his hostages on
the price others pay for their luxurious lives, and one wrong
answer is fatal.

TICK TOCK
(with Michael Ledwidge)

New York is in chaos as a rash of horrifying copycat crimes
tears through the city. Michael Bennett investigates, but
not even he could predict the earth-shattering enormity
of this killer's plan.

I, MICHAEL BENNETT
(with Michael Ledwidge)

Bennett arrests infamous South American crime lord Manuel Perrine. From jail, Perrine vows to rain terror down upon New York City – and to get revenge on Michael Bennett.

GONE
(with Michael Ledwidge)

Perrine is back and deadlier than ever. Bennett must make an impossible decision: stay and protect his family, or hunt down the man who is their biggest threat.

BURN
(with Michael Ledwidge)

A group of well-dressed men enter a condemned building. Later, a charred body is found. Michael Bennett is about to enter a secret underground world of terrifying depravity.

ALERT
(with Michael Ledwidge)

Two devastating catastrophes hit New York in quick succession, putting everyone on edge. Bennett is given the near impossible task of hunting down the shadowy terror group responsible.

BULLSEYE
(with Michael Ledwidge)

As the most powerful men on earth gather for a meeting of the UN, Bennett receives shocking intelligence that there will be an assassination attempt on the US president.
Are the Russian government behind the plot?

HAUNTED
(with James O. Born)
Michael Bennett is ready for a vacation after a series of crises push him, and his family, to the brink. But when he gets pulled into a shocking case, Bennett is fighting to protect a town, the law, and the family that he loves.

AMBUSH
(with James O. Born)
When an anonymous tip proves to be a trap, Michael Bennett believes he personally is being targetted. And not just him, but his family too.

BLINDSIDE
(with James O. Born)
The mayor of New York has a daughter who's missing. Detective Michael Bennett has a son who's in prison. Can one father help the other?

ABOUT THE AUTHORS

JAMES PATTERSON is one of the best-known and biggest-selling writers of all time. His books have sold in excess of 385 million copies worldwide. He is the author of some of the most popular series of the past two decades – the Alex Cross, Women's Murder Club, Detective Michael Bennett and Private novels – and he has written many other number one bestsellers including non-fiction and stand-alone thrillers.

James is passionate about encouraging children to read. Inspired by his own son who was a reluctant reader, he also writes a range of books for young readers including the Middle School, Treasure Hunters, Dog Diaries and Max Einstein series. James has donated millions in grants to independent bookshops and has been the most borrowed author in UK libraries for the past thirteen years in a row. He lives in Florida with his family.

JAMES O. BORN is an award-winning crime and science-fiction novelist as well as a career law-enforcement agent. A native Floridian, he still lives in the Sunshine State.

THE PRESIDENT'S DAUGHTER

BY

BILL CLINTON

— AND —

JAMES PATTERSON

Lake Marie, New Hampshire

AN HOUR OR SO after my daughter, Mel, leaves, I've showered, had my second cup of coffee, and read the newspapers—just skimming them, really, for it's a sad state of affairs when you eventually realize just how wrong journalists can be in covering stories. With a handsaw and a set of pruning shears, I head off to the south side of our property.

It's a special place, even though my wife, Samantha, has spent less than a month here in all her visits. Most of the land in the area is conservation land, never to be built upon, and of the people who do live here, almost all follow the old New Hampshire tradition of never bothering their neighbors or gossiping about them to visitors or news reporters.

Out on the lake is a white Boston Whaler with two men supposedly fishing, although they are Secret Service. Last year the *Union Leader* newspaper did a little piece about the agents stationed aboard the boat—calling them the unluckiest fishermen in the state—but since then, they've been pretty much left alone.

As I'm chopping, cutting, and piling brush, I think back to two famed fellow POTUS brush cutters—Ronald Reagan and George W. Bush—and how their exertions never quite made sense to a lot of people. They thought, *Hey, you've been at the pinnacle of fame and power, why go out and get your hands dirty?*

I saw at a stubborn pine sapling that's near an old stone wall on the property, and think, *Because it helps. It keeps your mind occupied, your thoughts busy, so you don't continually flash back to memories of your presidential term.*

The long and fruitless meetings with congressional leaders from both sides of the aisle, talking with them, arguing with them, and sometimes pleading with them, at one point saying, "Damn it, we're all Americans here—isn't there anything we can work on to move our country forward?"

And constantly getting the same smug, superior answers. "Don't blame us, Mr. President. Blame *them.*"

The late nights in the Oval Office, signing letters of condolence to the families of the best of us, men and women who had died for the idea of America, not the squabbling and revenge-minded nation we have become. And three times running across the names of men I knew and fought with, back when I was younger, fitter, and with the teams.

And other late nights as well, reviewing what was called—in typical innocuous, bureaucratic fashion—the Disposition Matrix database, prepared by the National Counterterrorism Center, but was really known as the "kill list." Months of work, research, surveillance, and intelligence intercepts resulting in a list of known terrorists who were a clear and present danger to the United States. And there I was, sitting by myself, and like a Roman emperor of old, I put a check mark next to those I decided were going to be killed in the next few days.

The sapling finally comes down.

Mission accomplished.

I look up and see something odd flying in the distance.

I stop, shade my eyes. Since moving here, I've gotten used to the different kinds of birds moving in and around Lake Marie, including the loons, whose night calls sound like someone's being throttled, but I don't recognize what's flying over there now.

I watch for a few seconds, and then it disappears behind the far tree line.

And I get back to work, something suddenly bothering me, something I can't quite figure out.

BASE OF THE
HUNTSMEN TRAIL

Mount Rollins, New Hampshire

IN THE FRONT SEAT of a black Cadillac Escalade, the older man rubs at his clean-shaven chin and looks at the video display from the laptop set up on top of the center console. Sitting next to him in the passenger seat, the younger man has a rectangular control system in his hand, with two small joysticks and other switches. He is controlling a drone with a video system, and they've just watched the home of former president Matthew Keating disappear from view.

It pleases the older man to see the West's famed drone technology turned against them. For years he's done the same thing with their wireless networks and cell phones, triggering devices and creating the bombs that shattered so many bodies and sowed so much terror.

And the Internet—which promised so much when it came out to bind the world as one—ended up turning into a well-used and safe communications network for him and his warriors.

The Cadillac they're sitting in was stolen this morning from a young couple and their infant in northern Vermont, after the two men abandoned their stolen pickup truck. There's still a bit of blood spatter and brain matter on the dashboard in front of them. An empty baby's seat is in the rear, along with a flowered cloth bag stuffed with toys and other childish things.

"Next?" the older man asks.

"We find the girl," he says. "It shouldn't take long."

"Do it," the older man says, watching with quiet envy and fascination as the younger man manipulates the controls of the complex machine while the drone's camera-made images appear on the computer screen.

"There. There she is."

From a bird's-eye view, he thinks, staring at the screen. A red sedan moves along the narrow paved roads.

He says, "And you are sure that the Americans, that they are not tracking you?"

"Impossible," the younger man next to him says in confidence. "There are thousands of such drones at play across this country right now. The officials who control the airspace, they have rules about where drones can go, and how high and low they can go, but most people ignore the rules."

"But their Secret Service—"

"Once President Matthew Keating left office, his daughter was no longer due the Secret Service protection. It's the law, if you can believe it. Under special circumstances, it can be requested, but no, not with her. The daughter wants to be on her own, going to school, without armed guards near her."

He murmurs, "A brave girl, then."

"And foolish," comes the reply.

And a stupid father, he thinks, to let his daughter roam at will like this, with no guards, no security.

The camera in the air follows the vehicle with no difficulty, and the older man shakes his head, again looking around him at the rich land and forests. Such an impossibly plentiful and gifted country, but why in Allah's name do they persist in meddling and interfering and being colonialists around the world?

A flash of anger sears through him.

If only they would stay home, how many innocents would still be alive?

"There," his companion says. "As I earlier learned…they are stopping here. At the beginning of the trail called Sherman's Path."

The vehicle on screen pulls into a dirt lot still visible from the air. Again, the older man is stunned at how easy it was to find the girl's schedule by looking at websites and bulletin boards from her college, from something called the Dartmouth Outing Club. Less than an hour's work and research has brought him here, looking down at her, like some blessed, all-seeing spirit.

He stares at the screen once more. Other vehicles are parked in the lot, and the girl and the boy get out. Both retrieve knapsacks from the rear of the vehicle. There's an embrace, a kiss, and then they walk away from the vehicles and disappear into the woods.

"Satisfied?" his companion asks.

For years, he thinks in satisfaction, the West has used these drones to rain down hellfire upon his friends, his fighters, and, yes, his family and other families. Fat and comfortable men (and women!) sipping their sugary drinks in comfortable chairs in safety, killing from thousands of kilometers away, seeing the silent explosions but not once hearing them, or hearing the shrieking and crying of the wounded and dying, and then driving home without a care in the world.

Now, it's his turn.

His turn to look from the sky.

Like a falcon on the hunt, he thinks.

Patiently and quietly waiting to strike.

SHERMAN'S PATH

Mount Rollins, New Hampshire

IT'S A CLEAR, cool, and gorgeous day on Sherman's Path, and Mel Keating is enjoying this climb up to Mount Rollins, where she and her boyfriend, Nick Kenyon, will spend the night with other members of the Dartmouth Outing Club at a small hut the club owns near the summit. She stops for a moment on a granite outcropping and puts her thumbs through her knapsack's straps.

Nick emerges from the trail and surrounding scrub brush, smiling, face a bit sweaty, bright blue knapsack on his back, and he takes her extended hand as he reaches her. "Damn nice view, Mel," he says.

She kisses him. "I've got a better view ahead."

"Where?"

"Just you wait."

She lets go of his hand and gazes at the rolling peaks of the White Mountains and the deep green of the forests, and notices the way some of the trees look a darker shade of green from the overhead clouds gently scudding by. Out beyond the trees is the Connecticut River and the mountains of Vermont.

Mel takes a deep, cleansing breath.

Just her and Nick and nobody else.

She lowers her glasses, and everything instantly turns to muddled shapes of green and blue. Nothing to see, nothing to spot. She remembers the boring times at state dinners back at the White House, when she'd be sitting with Mom and Dad, and she'd lower her glasses so all she could see were colored blobs. That made the time pass, when she really didn't want to be there, didn't really want to see all those well-dressed men and women pretending to like Dad and be his friend so they could get something in return.

Mel slides the glasses back up, and everything comes into view.

That's what she likes.

Being ignored and seeing only what she wants to see.

Nick reaches between the knapsack and rubs her neck. "What are you looking at?"

"Nothing."

"Oh, that doesn't sound good."

Mel laughs. "Silly man, it's the best! No staff, no news reporters, no cameras, no television correspondents, no Secret Service agents standing like dark-suited statues in the corner. Nobody! Just you and me."

"Sounds lonely," Nick says.

She slaps his butt. "Don't you get it? There's nobody keeping an eye on me, and I'm loving every second of it. Come along, let's get moving."

Some minutes later, Nick is sitting at the edge of a small mountain-side pool, ringed with boulders and saplings and shrubs, letting his feet soak, enjoying the sun on his back, thinking of how damn lucky he is.

He had been shy at first when meeting Mel last semester in an African history seminar—everyone on the Dartmouth campus knew who she was, so that was no secret—and he had no interest in trying to even talk to her until Mel started getting crap thrown at her one day in class. She had said something about the importance of microloans in Africa, and a few loudmouths started hammering her about being ignorant of the real world, being privileged, and not having an authentic life.

When the loudmouths took a moment to catch their respective breaths, Nick surprised himself by saying, "I grew up in a third-floor apartment in Southie. My Dad was a lineman for the electric company, my Mom worked cleaning other people's homes and clipped coupons to go grocery shopping, and man, I'd trade that authentic life for privilege any day of the week."

A bunch of the students laughed. Mel caught his eye with a smile and he asked her after class to get a coffee or something at Lou's Bakery, and that's how it started.

Him, a scholarship student, dating the daughter of President Matt Keating.

What a world.

What a life.

Sitting on a moss-colored boulder, Mel nudges him and says, "How's your feet?"

"Feeling cold and fine."

"Then let's do the whole thing," she says, standing up, tugging off her gray Dartmouth sweatshirt. "Feel like a swim?"

He smiles. "Mel…someone could see us!"

She smiles right back, wearing just a tan sports bra under

the sweatshirt, as she starts lowering her shorts. "Here? In the middle of a national forest? Lighten up, sweetie. Nobody's around for miles."

After she strips, Mel yelps out as she jumps into the pool, keeping her head and glasses above water. The water is cold and sharp. Poor Nick takes his time, wading in, shifting his weight as he tries to keep his footing on the slippery rocks, and he yowls like a hurt puppy when the cold mountain water reaches just below his waist.

The pond is small, and Mel reaches the other side with three strong strokes, and she swims back, the cold water now bracing, making her heart race, everything tingling. She tilts her head back, looking up past the tall pines and seeing the bright, bare blue patch of sky. Nothing. Nobody watching her, following her, recording her.

Bliss.

Another yelp from Nick, and she turns her head to him. Nick had wanted to go Navy ROTC, but a bad set of lungs prevented him from doing so, and even though she knows Dad wishes he'd get a haircut, his Southie background and interest in the Navy scored Nick in the plus side of the boyfriend column with Dad.

Nick lowers himself farther into the water, until it reaches his strong shoulders. "Did you see the sign-up list for the overnight at the cabin?" he asks. "Sorry to say, Cam Carlucci is coming."

"I know," she says, treading water, leaning back, letting her hair soak, looking up at the sharp blue and empty sky.

"You know he's going to want you to—"

Mel looks back at Nick. "Yeah. He and his buds want to go to the Seabrook nuclear plant this Labor Day weekend, occupy it, and shut it down."

Poor Nick's lips seem to be turning blue. "They sure want you there."

In a mocking tone, Mel imitates Cam and says, "'Oh, Mel, you can make such an impact if you get arrested. Think of the headlines. Think of your influence.' To hell with him. They don't want me there as me. They want a puppet they can prop up to get coverage."

Nick laughs. "You going to tell him that tonight?"

"Nah," she says. "He's not worth it. I'll tell him I have plans for Labor Day weekend instead."

Her boyfriend looks puzzled. "You do?"

She swims to him and gives him a kiss, hands on his shoulders. "Dopey boy, yes, with you."

His hands move through the water to her waist, and she's enjoying the touch—just as she hears voices and looks up.

For the first time in a long time she's frightened.

LAKE MARIE

New Hampshire

AFTER GETTING OUT of the shower for the second time today (the first after taking a spectacular tumble in a muddy patch of dirt) and drying off, I idly play the which-body-scar-goes-to-which-op when my iPhone rings. I wrap a towel around me, picking up the phone, knowing only about twenty people in the world have this number. Occasionally, though, a call comes in from "John" in Mumbai pretending to be a Microsoft employee in Redmond, Washington. I've been tempted to tell John who he's really talking to, but I've resisted the urge.

This time, however, the number is blocked, and puzzled, I answer the phone.

"Keating," I say.

A strong woman's voice comes through. "Mr. President? This is Sarah Palumbo, calling from the NSC."

The name quickly pops up in my mind. Sarah's been the deputy national security advisor for the National Security

Council since my term, and she should have gotten the director's position when Melissa Powell retired to go back to academia. But someone to whom President Barnes owed a favor got the position. A former Army brigadier general and deputy director at the CIA, Sarah knows her stuff, from the annual output of Russian oilfields to the status of Colombian cartel smuggling submarines.

"Sarah, good to hear from you," I say, still dripping some water onto the bathroom's tile floor. "How're your mom and dad doing? Enjoying the snowbird life in Florida?"

Sarah and her family grew up in Buffalo, where lake effect winter storms can dump up to four feet of snow in an afternoon. She chuckles and says, "They're loving every warm second of it. Sir, do you have a moment?"

"My day is full of moments," I reply. "What's going on?"

"Sir...," and the tone of her voice instantly changes, worrying me. "Sir, this is unofficial, but I wanted to let you know what I learned this morning. Sometimes the bureaucracy takes too long to respond to emerging developments, and I don't want that to happen here. It's too important."

I say, "Go on."

She says, "I was sitting in for the director at today's threat-assessment meeting, going over the President's Daily Brief and other interagency reports."

With those words of jargon, I'm instantly transported back to being POTUS, and I'm not sure I like it.

"What's going on, Sarah?"

The briefest of pauses. "Sir, we've noticed an uptick in chatter from various terrorist cells in the Mideast, Europe, and Canada. Nothing we can specifically attach a name or a date to, but something is on the horizon, something bad, something that will generate a lot of attention."

Shit, I think. "All right," I say. "Terrorists are keying themselves up to strike. Why are you calling me? Who are they after?"

"Mr. President," she says, "they're coming after you."

'CLINTON'S INSIDER SECRETS AND PATTERSON'S STORYTELLING GENIUS MAKE THIS THE POLITICAL THRILLER OF THE DECADE'

LEE CHILD

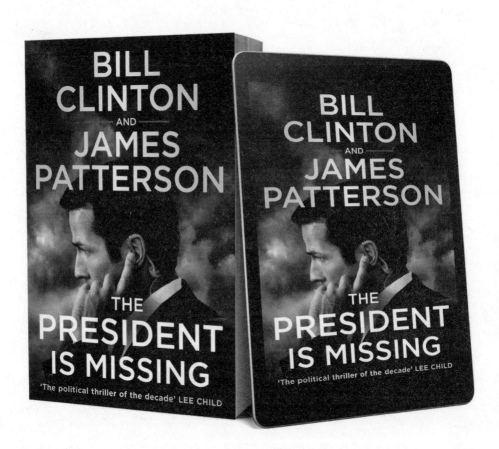

'Difficult to put down'
Daily Express

'Satisfying and surprising'
Guardian

'A quick, slick, gripping read'
The Times

'A high-octane collaboration . . . addictive'
Daily Telegraph

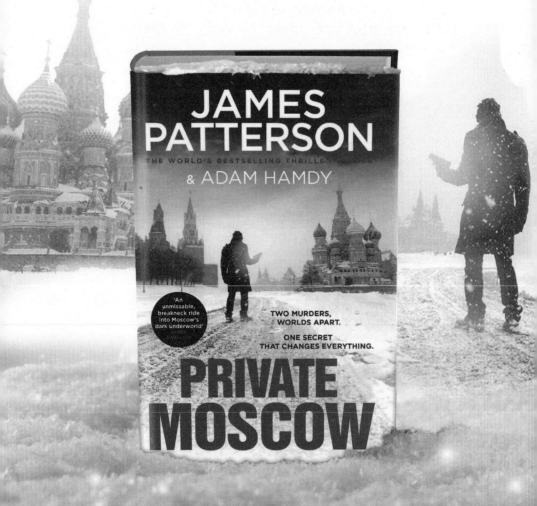

'An unmissable, breakneck ride into Moscow's dark underworld'
JAMES SWALLOW

'Great action sequences ... breathtaking twists and turns'
ANTHONY HOROWITZ

'Exhilarating, high-stakes action'
LESLEY KARA

JAMES PATTERSON

THE WORLD'S BESTSELLING THRILLER WRITER

& ADAM HAMDY

'An unmissable, breakneck ride into Moscow's dark underworld'
JAMES SWALLOW

TWO MURDERS, WORLDS APART.

ONE SECRET THAT CHANGES EVERYTHING.

PRIVATE MOSCOW

A STAND-ALONE THRILLER

THE COAST-TO-COAST MURDERS

James Patterson
& J. D. Barker

Michael and Megan Fitzgerald are siblings who share a troubling past. Both adopted, and now grown, they trust each other before anyone else. They've had to.

When a young woman is found murdered in Michael's LA apartment, he is the chief suspect and quickly arrested. But then there's another killing that is strikingly similar. And another. And not just in LA – as the spree spreads across the country, the FBI become involved in a nationwide manhunt.

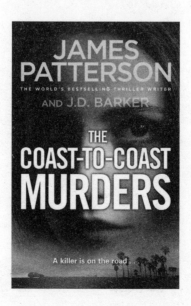

THE *SUNDAY TIMES* NON-FICTION BESTSELLER

THE KENNEDY CURSE

James Patterson
& Cythia Fagen

Across decades and generations, the Kennedys have been a
family of charismatic adventurers, raised to take risks and
excel. Their name is synonymous with American royalty.
Their commitment to public service is legendary. But, for all
the successes, the family has been blighted by assassinations,
fatal accidents, drug and alcohol abuse and sex scandals.

To this day, the Kennedys occupy a unique, contradictory place
in the world's imagination: at once familiar and unknowable;
charmed and cursed. *The Kennedy Curse* is a revealing,
fascinating account of America's most famous family,
as told by the world's most trusted storyteller.

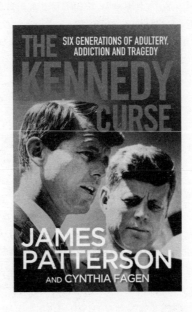

Also by James Patterson

ALEX CROSS NOVELS

Along Came a Spider • Kiss the Girls • Jack and Jill • Cat and Mouse • Pop Goes the Weasel • Roses are Red • Violets are Blue • Four Blind Mice • The Big Bad Wolf • London Bridges • Mary, Mary • Cross • Double Cross • Cross Country • Alex Cross's Trial (*with Richard DiLallo*) • I, Alex Cross • Cross Fire • Kill Alex Cross • Merry Christmas, Alex Cross • Alex Cross, Run • Cross My Heart • Hope to Die • Cross Justice • Cross the Line • The People vs. Alex Cross • Target: Alex Cross • Criss Cross • Deadly Cross

THE WOMEN'S MURDER CLUB SERIES

1st to Die • 2nd Chance (*with Andrew Gross*) • 3rd Degree (*with Andrew Gross*) • 4th of July (*with Maxine Paetro*) • The 5th Horseman (*with Maxine Paetro*) • The 6th Target (*with Maxine Paetro*) • 7th Heaven (*with Maxine Paetro*) • 8th Confession (*with Maxine Paetro*) • 9th Judgement (*with Maxine Paetro*) • 10th Anniversary (*with Maxine Paetro*) • 11th Hour (*with Maxine Paetro*) • 12th of Never (*with Maxine Paetro*) • Unlucky 13 (*with Maxine Paetro*) • 14th Deadly Sin (*with Maxine Paetro*) • 15th Affair (*with Maxine Paetro*) • 16th Seduction (*with Maxine Paetro*) • 17th Suspect (*with Maxine Paetro*) • 18th Abduction (*with Maxine Paetro*) • 19th Christmas (*with Maxine Paetro*) • 20th Victim (*with Maxine Paetro*)

PRIVATE NOVELS

Private (*with Maxine Paetro*) • Private London (*with Mark Pearson*) • Private Games (*with Mark Sullivan*) • Private: No. 1 Suspect (*with Maxine Paetro*) • Private Berlin (*with Mark Sullivan*) • Private Down Under (*with Michael White*) • Private L.A. (*with Mark Sullivan*) • Private India (*with Ashwin Sanghi*) • Private Vegas (*with Maxine Paetro*) • Private Sydney (*with Kathryn Fox*) • Private Paris (*with Mark Sullivan*) • The Games (*with Mark Sullivan*) • Private Delhi (*with Ashwin Sanghi*) • Private Princess (*with Rees Jones*) • Private Moscow (*with Adam Hamdy*)

NYPD RED SERIES

NYPD Red (*with Marshall Karp*) • NYPD Red 2 (*with Marshall Karp*) • NYPD Red 3 (*with Marshall Karp*) • NYPD Red 4 (*with Marshall Karp*) • NYPD Red 5 (*with Marshall Karp*) • NYPD Red 6 (*with Marshall Karp*)

DETECTIVE HARRIET BLUE SERIES

Never Never (*with Candice Fox*) • Fifty Fifty (*with Candice Fox*) • Liar Liar (*with Candice Fox*) • Hush Hush (*with Candice Fox*)

INSTINCT SERIES

Instinct (*with Howard Roughan, previously published as* Murder Games) • Killer Instinct (*with Howard Roughan*)

STAND-ALONE THRILLERS

The Thomas Berryman Number • Hide and Seek • Black Market • The Midnight Club • Sail (*with Howard Roughan*) • Swimsuit (*with Maxine Paetro*) • Don't Blink (*with Howard Roughan*) • Postcard Killers (*with Liza Marklund*) • Toys (*with Neil McMahon*) • Now You See Her (*with Michael Ledwidge*) • Kill Me If You Can (*with Marshall Karp*) • Guilty Wives (*with David Ellis*) • Zoo (*with Michael Ledwidge*) • Second Honeymoon (*with Howard Roughan*) • Mistress (*with David Ellis*) • Invisible (*with David Ellis*) • Truth or Die (*with Howard Roughan*) • Murder House (*with David Ellis*) • The Black Book (*with David Ellis*) • The Store (*with Richard DiLallo*) • Texas Ranger (*with Andrew Bourelle*) • The President is Missing (*with Bill Clinton*) • Revenge (*with Andrew Holmes*) • Juror No. 3 (*with Nancy Allen*) • The First Lady (*with Brendan DuBois*) • The Chef (*with Max DiLallo*) • Out of Sight (*with Brendan DuBois*) • Unsolved (*with David Ellis*) • The Inn (*with Candice Fox*) • Lost (*with James O. Born*) • Texas Outlaw (*with Andrew Bourelle*) • The Summer House (*with Brendan DuBois*) • 1st Case (*with Chris Tebbetts*) • Cajun Justice (*with Tucker Axum*) • The Midwife Murders (*with Richard DiLallo*) • The Coast-to-Coast Murders (*with J. D. Barker*) • Three Women Disappear (*with Shan Serafin*)

NON-FICTION

Torn Apart (*with Hal and Cory Friedman*) • The Murder of
King Tut (*with Martin Dugard*) • All-American Murder (*with
Alex Abramovich and Mike Harvkey*) • The Kennedy
Curse (*with Cynthia Fagen*) • The Last Days of John
Lennon (*with Casey Sherman and Dave Wedge*)

MURDER IS FOREVER TRUE CRIME

Murder, Interrupted (*with Alex Abramovich and Christopher
Charles*) • Home Sweet Murder (*with Andrew Bourelle and
Scott Slaven*) • Murder Beyond the Grave (*with Andrew
Bourelle and Christopher Charles*) • Murder Thy
Neighbour (*with Andrew Bourelle and Max DiLallo*) •
Murder of Innocence (*with Max DiLallo and Andrew
Bourelle*) • Till Murder Do Us Part (*with Andrew
Bourelle and Max DiLallo*)

COLLECTIONS

Triple Threat (*with Max DiLallo and Andrew Bourelle*) •
Kill or Be Killed (*with Maxine Paetro, Rees Jones, Shan
Serafin and Emily Raymond*) • The Moores are Missing
(*with Loren D. Estleman, Sam Hawken and Ed Chatterton*) •
The Family Lawyer (*with Robert Rotstein, Christopher
Charles and Rachel Howzell Hall*) • Murder in Paradise
(*with Doug Allyn, Connor Hyde and Duane Swierczynski*) •
The House Next Door (*with Susan DiLallo, Max DiLallo
and Brendan DuBois*) • 13-Minute Murder (*with Shan
Serafin, Christopher Farnsworth and Scott Slaven*) •
The River Murders (*with James O. Born*)

For more information about James Patterson's novels,
visit www.penguin.co.uk